THE SHIFTER'S MATE
OTHER WORLD SERIES BOOK THREE

RAMONA GRAY

THE SHIFTER'S MATE

OTHER WORLD SERIES BOOK THREE

Reese Warren knew she should never have gone out to investigate that glowing orb in her back yard. Curiosity killed the cat, as her mother always said. And while her curiosity may not have gotten her killed, it's certainly changed her life forever. Sucked into another world, she's held captive in a compound with dozens of other women and a warden who auctions them off like their animals.

When she's bought by a wolf shifter and his pack mates as a potential mate for their cruel alpha, Reese flat out refuses to accept a life of forced marriage and pushing out wolf babies. She just has to ignore her ridiculous attraction to the arrogant shifter, Kane, and find a way to escape him before he delivers her to his alpha.

Kane hates humans. Humans murdered his parents in cold blood, and his loyalty to his alpha is the only reason he's bringing them into their pack. But he didn't count on his immediate attraction to the crazy human who speaks of a world filled with impossibilities.

He will not disobey his alpha's orders so why does his

urge to claim Reese as his own mate increase with each passing day?

CHAPTER 1

All things considered, it hadn't been the worse three months of Reese Warren's life. That top honour still went to the months following her parents' deaths. But the last three months certainly were the weirdest.

As she paced restlessly back and forth in the room she had begun to think of as the 'waiting room', she wished for the hundredth time that she had never gone outside to investigate the round ball of light hovering in the back yard.

She almost hadn't. She had almost chalked it up to some weird surge of electricity from the massive thunder and lightning storm and gone to bed, but in the end her natural curiosity couldn't be contained.

She snorted bitterly. Her mother had always told her that curiosity killed the cat and although it hadn't killed her, it hadn't prepared her to be sucked into some alternate universe like a woman in a bad science fiction movie.

Not an alternate universe, Reese. An alternate world. God, pay attention would you?

She could almost hear Louisa's disapproving tone in her head. She sighed and sank to the floor beside the barred window. She missed the old woman, missed her more than she would admit. She was the only link to her world, to *her* earth. With her gone, she was terribly lonely.

It's your own fault, she scolded herself fiercely. *Louisa tried to warn you to keep your mouth shut about your earth, but you didn't listen, did you? You just had to try and convince them that electricity and cars, and airplanes and stores that served nothing but coffee, existed. Tried to convince them that a giant globe of light had sucked you in and threw you down into this strange world.*

The men who had captured her only hours after she had walked out of the woods, dirty and bruised, had laughed and called her "barto". She had found out later that barto was the word for crazy in this world.

Perhaps because she was still numb from the deaths of her parents, perhaps because she half-believed she was in some strange never-ending dream, she hadn't really freaked out when the men had chained her and taken her to a large, gated complex. She was left in a room full of other women. They were nice enough to her at first, at least until she started babbling about her own world, and after that they avoided her.

Only Louisa had gone near her and that was only because she was from the same world as Reese. She had taken Reese's arm in a firm grip and dragged her away as Reese was trying, very patiently she thought, to explain to a young woman named Rhea about cell phones and the internet.

It took Reese a few days to understand exactly what Louisa explained to her. Even now, three months later, she wasn't sure she still entirely believed that there was no way back home for her ever again.

She sighed and stared out the window. Louisa was taken to auction two weeks ago, and Reese missed her more than

2

she thought possible. She hoped the old woman was okay, hoped that someone kind had bought her and was treating her well. She sighed again. She would never see Louisa again and now, it was her turn to go to auction.

The door to the room opened and Reese watched with a numb disinterest as the man she secretly called the "warden" walked through. He was followed by three of the biggest men she had ever seen in her life. All three of them had dark hair and dark eyes and they were all pulling and tugging on their clothing with obvious discomfort.

Malana was standing near her, her eyes wide and her mouth a quivering "o", as she stared at the three men. Reese tugged on the young woman's arm.

"What's going on? Are we not being taken to the auction room?"

Malana must have been truly desperate for comfort because she immediately wrapped her arms around Reese's waist and clung to her like a frightened child. "God help us."

"Help us from what?" Reese asked. "What's going on?"

"It's – it's a private sale," Malana whispered.

"Well, that has to be better than being paraded around like a cow in front of a roomful of men, doesn't it?" Reese replied.

Malana gave her a frightened look. "You don't understand. Those – those men are not men."

Reese glanced at them. They looked like men to her. Big men, but still just men. "What do you mean?"

"They're shifters, Reese," Malana whispered.

"What do you mean shifters?" Reese frowned at the smaller woman.

Malana gave her a look of frustration. "Shifters! They shift into animals."

Reese blinked in surprise. "What kind of animals?"

"If I had to guess, these ones are wolves or bears," Malana said. "They're so big."

She stared wide-eyed at the men. "We're dead if they choose us."

As the warden stood quietly and the three men talked amongst themselves, Reese rubbed Malana's trembling back. "Why would you say that?"

Malana swallowed hard. "Shifters rarely have anything to do with humans. Many of them hunt us like – like we're deer."

Reese felt a trickle of fear run down her spine. She took a deep breath and shook it off. "Why would they pay money for us just to hunt us down and kill us? Don't be silly."

Malana gave her a look of stark fear. "If they not buying us to hunt then they're buying us for sex. I would rather be hunted."

Before Reese could reply the warden moved to the middle of the room. "Line up, ladies!"

Reese and the other women - there were more than fifteen of them crowded into the small room - lined up obediently. The three men walked back and forth in front of them.

Malana squeezed Reese's hand painfully when their gazes landed on them and Reese winced. She tried to free her hand but Malana refused to let go until the men continued past them.

After a few moments, the men had a whispered conversation with the warden. He nodded and walked to the line of women. He pulled a few of them forward. When he stopped in front of Reese and Malana, the young woman began to cry.

"Stop your blubbering, girl," he said. "They have no use for you."

He took Reese's shoulder and pulled her out of the line. "Stand there."

Reese and four other women stood silently as the warden herded the other women from the room. He shut the door and stared at the women.

"These men are going to look you over. Resist and you'll be beaten. Do you understand?"

The women nodded. A few of them were beginning to cry as two of the men stepped closer. Reese, her body trembling and her breathing shallow, straightened her back. If these men really were some kind of half-man, half-beast mutation, her job as a vet tech had taught her not to show fear around animals.

She watched with wide eyes as two of the men examined the women standing to her right. They had the women open their mouths so they could look at their teeth. The men held the women's faces, examining their eyes and probing at their ears like they really were cattle.

Her mouth dropped open and she took a step back when the men slipped their hands under the plain blue blouses that all of the women wore. When Reese first arrived, they had stripped her of all of her clothing except her underwear. She had been wearing the same blue blouse and brown skirt that the rest of the women wore since then. Although it was actually sort of freeing to not be wearing a bra, she wondered exactly what her heavy breasts would look like ten years from now. She was young enough that they were still perky but after years of no support, she guessed they'd be hanging around her goddamn knees.

She shook her head. What the hell was she doing? She was about to be touched and examined like a piece of meat and she was concerned about her breast perkiness? She snorted and forced her attention back to the other women. The men were squeezing their breasts before running their hands over their abdomens and then grabbing their asses through their long skirts. The smallest of the men even bent and lifted one woman's skirt, studying her thick calves and thighs with interest.

Reese realized that all four women were similar to her. Although she was the tallest and heaviest, all of the women had large breasts and wide hips. As the two men worked their way down the line, she felt the hot breath of the warden on the back of her neck.

"Behave yourself, woman," he snarled.

Reese tensed when she felt his hand stroke her back. "Keep that smart mouth of yours shut or the beatings you received before this will be nothing compared to the one you'll get," he warned.

Reese arched her back away from the despicable man's touch. She hated the warden, hated him with every fibre of her being. It was all she could do not to turn around and spit on him. Her temper had always gotten her in trouble, and it was no different in this world. Even the frequent beatings she had received were not yet enough to curb her wayward tongue.

The smallest of the men stopped in front of her. He smiled at her in a friendly way and was about to reach for her when the third man stepped forward. Unlike his companions, he had not bothered to examine any of the women. He had stood back, staring at them with a bored expression on his face while the women were touched and examined.

"Move back, Theran." His voice was low and hoarse, as if he didn't use it much.

The man in front of her stepped away immediately and Reese stared up at the man who took his place. She was just shy of six feet, but she still had to crane her neck to look at him. He was the biggest of the three men, and she judged his height to be somewhere around the seven-foot mark. His shoulders and chest were broad and thick with muscle. His lower body was clad in a pair of loose cotton pants, but she had no trouble seeing how thick and strong his thighs were.

Dark scruff covered his angular jaw, and she felt a strange twinge in her stomach when she stared at his full lips. She forced her gaze up to his and saw surprise in his dark eyes. The rest of the women had cowered and stared at the floor while they were being examined, but she would be damned if she stood meekly by while some strange man groped her.

He stared at her eyes and she wondered what he was thinking. They were her most striking feature. Technically they were considered blue, but in most light they looked very close to violet.

She stood still when his large hands cupped her face and his thumbs pressed at her mouth. She opened her mouth and did nothing when he examined her teeth before checking inside her ears and running his hands over her thick, dark hair.

His breath was warm on her face and she continued to stare at him as he ran his hands over her neck and shoulders. It wasn't until he reached for her breasts, that she jerked back and shoved him hard in the chest. He gave a grunt of surprise, his eyebrows drawing into a frown, but didn't stumble back. She might as well have tried shoving a large boulder.

She cried out when the warden's fist punched her hard in the middle of her back. Not expecting it, she pitched forward into the chest of the giant standing in front of her. She could feel his low growl vibrating in his chest, and his arms clamped around her hips when she started to struggle back.

"She's a wild one." The warden reached to cuff her across the head and Reese cringed. Before he could land the blow, the man holding her grabbed the warden's arm in one hard hand.

"Enough," he grunted.

The warden winced and nodded before stepping back and rubbing at his arm.

"Hold still, human," the giant rumbled.

Reese glared at him. It wasn't like she had much choice. His arm was still clamped around her hips and it was like a band of steel. Her back was throbbing where the warden had punched her, and she flinched when the man ran his hand down her back.

He frowned and moved his hand to her ass to squeeze it firmly. Reese hissed at him like an angry cat and slapped at his hand. He scowled and took her wrists in one large hand, holding them in a tight grip.

"Hold still," he repeated.

His free hand reached for one full breast and Reese twisted violently in his grasp. "If you touch me there, I'll kill you."

He stared silently at her for a moment, his hand resting on her round abdomen, before dropping his hand to her hip. He rubbed her hip then slipped his hand under her shirt and stroked the bare skin of her side. She was dismayed to feel a tingle of lust go through her.

Shit, she thought frantically as a strange look came over his face. Big men had always been her weakness, perhaps because she was so tall herself, and this was the biggest man she'd ever met. It didn't help that he was actually kind of handsome with his dark eyes and full lips.

He leaned in and buried his face in her neck, inhaling deeply. Goosebumps rose on her flesh and she whimpered when he suddenly licked her throat with his warm, wet tongue. She wasn't sure what was happening to her. Lust had roared to life within her and without realizing it, she leaned into his warm body.

This time when his hand reached for her breast, she made no attempt to struggle away. He cupped her bare breast, his thumb rubbing over her erect nipple, and she made another soft whimper of need.

She stumbled and nearly fell when he pulled away from her. She stared mutely at him, her pulse pounding and her blood roaring through her veins, as he snorted derisively and turned back to his companions.

"He'll like this one. She's easily aroused."

Reese's face flamed with embarrassment and she bent her head and stared at the floor. What the fuck had just happened?

The warden cleared his throat. "Are you sure you want this one? She's not obedient. I know your – your kind like your women submissive."

The man ignored him and stared at his companions. "Do you agree?"

The one named Theran shrugged. "We can't take just her. He wanted a choice, remember?"

The man snorted angrily. "So, we have to feed a bunch of humans because he could not be bothered to make the trip himself and pick out one."

The second man laughed. "They'll be useful in other ways. You know that as well as I do, Kane."

Kane sighed. "I never thought I would live to see the day we had humans in our pack."

The second man pulled at the collar of his shirt. "We cannot disobey our alpha's demands."

"I know that, Hanif. Do you believe me to be simple?" Kane growled.

"Of course not," Hanif said. He bowed his head in a show of submission to the bigger man.

"We will each pick one. He can choose from them. If he

doesn't find any of them pleasing, he can come back and choose his own mate," Kane said with finality.

"We'll take her," he pointed to Reese, "and two more that my brothers will choose."

The warden nodded as Kane stepped forward and took Reese's wrist in one large hand. She pulled futilely, and he growled at her. "Enough or I will drag you from this room by your hair. Do you understand?"

She glared at him before following him towards the door.

CHAPTER 2

Reese and the other two women didn't have to wait long to find out what type of shifters had bought them. They were barely twenty feet into the woods that surrounded the complex before Kane stripped off his shirt and pants and shifted into a giant, gray wolf.

"Come." Theran gave them a friendly smile and waved them forward. "We want to get in some traveling before we lose the light."

Reese hesitated and stared into the trees around her. She wondered how far she could get before they caught her. If she surprised them, she might be able to disappear into the thick trees before they –

There was a low growl and she turned to see Kane staring at her. His eyes were green now and they glowed balefully at her. She had a suspicion that he knew exactly what she was thinking. He barked once at Hanif and the man frowned at her.

"Do not try and run. We will give you your freedom if you behave yourself but if you try and escape us we will chain you to one of us. Do you understand?"

Reese nodded as Theran scooped up Kane's clothing. They walked another fifty feet into the forest before they stopped. There was a large leather bag at the base of a wide tree and Theran picked it up and stuffed Kane's clothing into it.

"Theran, I'm going to shift. Are you all right with that?" Hanif asked.

Theran nodded. "Aye. I will stay in my human form for a while longer."

Hanif shed his clothes. He handed them to Theran who stuffed them in the bag on top of Kane's as Hanif shifted. He was smaller than Kane and brown instead of gray, but his eyes glowed with the same green light.

The two wolves trotted ahead of them, sniffing and growling to each other. Theran nodded to the women again. "Come, we must keep moving. It is a long journey to our home."

Reese was surprised when the two other women joined her and each of them took her hand. She gave them a small smile and squeezed the hand of the smaller woman, who was already starting to cry.

"Don't cry," she said encouragingly. "We'll be okay."

"Listen to your friend," Theran said. "If you obey us, we will not harm you. We are not like human men when it comes to their mates. We treat our mates with respect, and we certainly do not hit them."

His gaze flickered to Reese. "What are your names?"

The blonde woman on Reese's left, cleared her throat. "My name is Adina."

The dark-haired woman on Reese's right was still crying and she spoke in a soft, wavering voice. "I'm Ghita."

"And you?" Theran prompted.

"Reese."

"Reese." Theran tested it on his tongue. "What an odd name."

He leaned closer. "You smell strange. Even for a human."

"What do you mean?" Reese asked.

"I have never smelled anyone like you before. Your scent is very unique," Theran said thoughtfully.

Reese shrugged as they moved deeper into the woods. She took a deep breath of the good, clean air. She'd been trapped in the complex for three months and she was thrilled with her sudden freedom from the horrid place. It was cold in the woods and the hard ground was biting through the thin soles of her shoes, but she couldn't stop the small grin that crossed her face. She would never have to see the warden again. Never again would that horrible man punch her or beat her with his flat wooden stick.

"Why did you buy us?" Adina asked.

She was a pretty girl. Like most blondes, her skin was pale and she had light brown eyes and a smattering of freckles across her nose. Like the dark-haired Ghita, she had a soft and meek manner to her and she kept her eyes on the ground at her feet.

"Our alpha, his name is Dagon, is looking for a mate. The three of you have been chosen as possible mates for him."

Reese frowned. "Why does he want a human for a mate?"

She wondered inwardly at her resilience to this new world. Until an hour ago, she had no idea that there were any creatures other than humans roaming this world. Now she was talking to a man who could change into a wolf whenever he felt like it.

Theran shrugged. "Many shifters are taking human women into their packs now."

"But why?" Reese asked.

"For many different reasons. Dagon believes that it is

better for us to interact with the humans. Sooner or later we will be forced to co-exist with them. He thinks it is best if we start now rather than wait."

His eyes slid away from her as he spoke and Reese knew he was lying to her. There was a cold knot of fear in her belly and she took a deep breath. "What happens to the two he doesn't choose?"

"There will be a place for you in the pack. Most likely another member will take you as their mate. You are all attractive enough. If no others find you pleasing, you will still be welcomed in the pack. You will be helpful to our women in cleaning and assisting them in raising their pups."

"And if I don't want to be a housekeeper and nanny?" Reese asked.

Theran laughed. "I would not worry too much if I were you. Kane is right. Dagon will most likely choose you to be his mate. He does enjoy the feisty ones."

He eyed Ghita and Adina. "Although his last mate was quite submissive like the two of you."

"What happened to his last mate?" Ghita asked.

"She died," Theran said.

"What if we refuse to be his mate?" Reese said.

Theran gave her a confused look. "Why would you refuse? As Dagon's mate you will be given the highest regard in the pack. All of your needs will be attended to. Nothing will be required of you other than mating with our alpha and bearing his pups."

"Great," Reese said airily. "A life of pushing out wolf babies. What more could a girl ask for?"

Kane growled loudly and angrily. Reese stared defiantly at him for a few moments until finally looking away from his hot gaze. The damn shifters were in for a surprise if they thought she would just open her legs and allow a man she'd never met to impregnate her.

Theran opened his mouth and Kane barked sharply at him. He flushed and smiled at the women. "Our time for talking is done. Move more quickly please."

"YOU'RE SERIOUSLY NOT GOING TO BUILD A FIRE?" REESE stared in disbelief at Hanif. The shifter shook his head.

"No. It can bring unwanted creatures our way and besides, it is not that cold."

"Not that cold?" Reese said disbelievingly. Ghita's teeth were chattering and all three of the women were shivering in the cold air.

"We don't have fur to keep us warm. Do you understand that?" Reese asked.

Theran was returning to the small clearing they had stopped in with his arms full of different plants. Hanif gave him a desperate look.

"Theran, the humans say they are cold."

"Cold?" Theran frowned. "It's not cold." He hesitated. "Is it?"

He dumped the plants in front of the three women. "Here, I have brought you some food."

Reese stared at them in confusion but Ghita and Adina crouched and picked through the plants.

"Plants? Do you not have any meat?"

There was soft snarling and Kane appeared out of the darkness. He was carrying three dead rabbits in his mouth and he dropped them to the ground before shifting. Reese averted her eyes from his naked body as he strode across the clearing and took his pants from the leather bag. He slipped them on but didn't bother with a shirt. He picked up one of the rabbits and she watched fascinated as the nails on his fingers lengthened into sharp points. He skinned the rabbit quickly and then held the bloody body of the rabbit toward her.

"Help yourself."

Her stomach lurched with nausea and a look of disgust crossed her face. He grinned, his white teeth flashing in the gloom. "That's right, humans prefer their meat cooked."

He bit into the body of the rabbit and Reese put her hand over her mouth and turned away. She sat on the ground beside the other women and tried to tune out the sound of the crunching as the three shifters ate their dead rabbits.

"Here." Adina handed her a plant with a blue root.

"What is this?"

"It's good. It's sweet tasting. Tear the leaves off and eat just the stem," Adina urged her.

She stripped off the leaves and bit hesitantly into the stalk. Adina was right about it being sweet tasting and she ate it quickly. The other women showed her how to eat each of the different plants and they quickly made fast work of the pile of plants.

"Sure you don't want some rabbit?" Kane called mockingly.

Reese ignored him and Theran frowned at the big man. "Kane, do not tease the humans. They're not like us, remember."

He turned to Hanif. "We'll have to tell Dagon that the humans will need cooked meat and pelts to keep them warm if they do not become one of our mates."

"You really didn't think this whole, 'bring human women into the pack' thing through, did you?" Reese said.

Kane growled at her and wiped the blood from his face. "Watch your tongue, human."

Hanif stared at her curiously. "Why do you not know how to eat the plants, Reese?"

Reese didn't reply and Ghita spoke up timidly. "Reese says she is not from our world."

Hanif frowned. "What do you mean?"

"Nothing," Reese said.

"Answer the question," Kane said.

Ghita giggled nervously. "Reese says she was born in a different world. She told us many tales about how a big glowing ball of light sucked her in and put her in this world. She says that in her world there are switches on the wall that turn on candles, and that people ride in iron machines that move much faster than horses."

Hanif's mouth dropped open and he gave Theran a cautious look. Theran returned the look and shook his head.

"Excellent," Kane said. "We've chosen a mad woman for our alpha's mate."

"You chose her," Hanif said.

"I'm not mad," Reese said.

"You kind of are," Adina replied. "Sorry, Reese."

Reese sighed and stared moodily into the darkness. They sat in silence for another half hour or so. The air was growing steadily colder and the three women huddled together for warmth. It was pointless, Reese thought. The two women were colder than she was and their thin clothing was doing nothing to keep them warm.

Hanif frowned at the way they were shivering. "Why are they so cold?"

Kane barked harsh laughter. "The humans cannot keep warmth in their limbs like we do, Hanif. Just another way they are weak and useless."

"What do we do? We cannot bring Dagon back frozen humans," Hanif said.

Kane shrugged. "It matters not to me if they live or die."

"Kane!" Theran glared at him. "Our alpha has given us a task to do and we cannot fail at it."

"They'll be fine," Kane said. "It will not dip below freezing tonight."

"Let us build a fire. Please," Adina pleaded.

Kane shook his head. "No. It is too dangerous."

"We will each curl around a human tonight." Theran suddenly decided. "Our bodies will keep them warm enough. I'll take that one." He pointed to Ghita and Reese was a little amused to see the soft blush that coloured Ghita's cheeks. Theran was handsome enough and he seemed kind.

"Fine," Hanif replied. "I'll take the fair-headed one."

They looked expectantly at Kane who shook his head. "No. I will not lower myself by allowing a human to sleep next to me."

Theran sighed angrily. "Kane, she will freeze to death."

"Who cares? She's mad. You and I both know Dagon will not pick her for his mate once he realizes she's not all there in the head. Besides, she won't freeze to death. She's bigger than the other two. Her extra meat will keep her warm," he said.

Reese's cheeks flamed with anger. She hated the arrogant shifter as much as she hated the warden, she decided. Maybe more. The warden might have beaten her, but he hadn't humiliated her.

Theran and Hanif were giving her cautious looks and she was struck with the sudden urge to smack Ghita in the head. If the woman had just kept her damn mouth shut, the other two might have been able to convince Kane to help keep her warm. Now, they were looking at her with dismay. She realized with sudden clarity that they probably would let her die rather than bring a mad woman back to their alpha.

Theran took Ghita's hand and led her a few feet away. "Lie down." He encouraged her as Hanif took Adina's hand and led her away.

Ghita lay down on the hard ground, tucking her knees up and wrapping her arms around her body. Theran stripped off his clothes and shifted to his wolf form. He lay down beside her. His body was so large that he could completely curl around her body.

Beside them, Hanif was doing the same with Adina and Reese looked on with jealousy as the two women burrowed into the soft fur of the giant wolves. They were nearly covered by the wolves' bodies and Theran and Hanif curled their tails over the women's bodies for added warmth.

Kane had already shifted and he stared at her for a moment before lying down with his back to her. He rested his head on the ground and sighed. Reese curled into a small ball on the ground as her entire body shivered. She tucked up her knees, tugging her skirt down around her feet to try and keep them warm. She buried her face in her arms. The cold air leeched into her body and she shook violently.

Sunshine, a warm beach in Hawaii, a really hot bath, she told herself grimly. Maybe if she thought about warm things, it would help convince her she wasn't going to freeze to death.

CHAPTER 3

"Human, are you alive?" Theran's deep voice woke her from her doze and she blinked up at him as the soft light of dawn filtered through the trees.

"Y-y-yes," she stammered. She tried to uncurl her body and groaned with pain. She tried again, willing her frozen limbs to move and breathing a sigh of relief when they obeyed her the second time.

She stumbled to her feet, wincing at the pins and needles that were coursing through them. She waved her arms weakly in the air in a bid to warm them.

"Hanif, her lips are blue," Theran said worriedly.

He hesitated and then wrapped her in his embrace. Reese could have wept with relief at the feel of his warm body. She clung to him, burying her cold face into his neck and trying to wrap every part of her body around his.

He rubbed her back roughly. She winced when he touched the spot where the warden punched her as he encouraged her to slide her hands under his shirt. He sucked in his breath at the feel of her cold fingers against the bare skin of his back.

"God, they really cannot hold their heat," he grunted to Hanif.

Reese shivered against him. She had barely slept last night, and she was tired and aching from lying on the cold ground. She slipped off her right shoe and glanced down at her toes, a little afraid she had frostbite. They looked normal to her and she breathed a sigh of relief before sliding her bare foot up Theran's pant leg.

He cursed, his arms tightening almost painfully around her. "Your feet are freezing, human!"

"I kn-kn-know!" She chattered grumpily.

After a few minutes, she switched feet and Theran grunted again. He allowed her to seek his warmth for another few minutes before Kane, still in his wolf form, barked at them.

"We must get moving," Theran said.

She nodded and forced herself to move away from his warmth. She would walk quickly. The exercise would help to warm her up.

"HERE, REESE. LOOK AT THIS." ADINA WAS STANDING NEXT to a large tree. Its branches were drooping with large green pods and Reese watched as Adina plucked one.

She peeled back the green skin and Reese stared curiously at the white flesh-like meat within it.

"What is that?"

"It's called a charka." Adina scooped out the meat and popped it into her mouth. "They taste good and they have lots of protein. Charkas are good to eat when you don't have any meat."

She plucked another one and handed it to Reese. Reese

peeled it carefully and hesitated before digging out the meat within it. She sniffed it curiously and then shrugged and put the entire thing in her mouth.

She smiled with delight. The charka had a distinct nut-like flavour and her belly rumbled. "God, it's so good."

Ghita laughed and pulled more of the green pods from the tree. She slipped them into the pockets of her skirt until they bulged as Reese and Adina did the same.

Kane barked impatiently at them and Reese rolled her eyes in exasperation. They had been walking for most of the morning and after staring at Ghita's flushed face, Theran had insisted they stop for a quick rest.

Both Kane and Hanif had argued but Reese had already dropped to the ground. Her back was throbbing where the warden had punched her, her feet and thighs were aching and burning and she was weary from lack of sleep. She had let herself rest for fifteen minutes before dragging her body up when Adina had called her name.

"Time to go." Theran smiled at Ghita and the woman flushed prettily. Hanif and Kane had not shifted from their wolf forms but Theran had remained human. He had spent most of the morning walking beside Ghita. Reese had an idea that if the alpha did not choose Ghita, she would quickly find herself in Theran's bed.

"Do you see that plant?" Adina pointed to a cluster of large blue plants, swaying in the cold breeze.

Reese nodded and Adina quickly pulled one as they were walking by them. She was pinching the stem closed deftly and she lifted the plant to her mouth. She let go of the stem and Reese watched as liquid flowed in a steady stream from the stem into Adina's mouth.

She handed the plant to Reese who took a drink from it. It was tasteless but cold and she nodded her thanks to Adina.

"These will provide you with moisture when there is no water to be found," Adina said. "But do not eat the leaves or the stem. They're poison and will kill you."

"Good to know," Reese murmured. She yawned hugely and rubbed at her eyes. God, she was tired.

Hanif suddenly shifted. He walked next to them, not embarrassed by his nakedness, and stared curiously at Reese. Adina, her cheeks red, was staring at his swinging cock and Reese took her own quick glance. Unsurprisingly, it was large and thick and she could only imagine the size of it when it was erect.

"Reese, how do you not know any of this? I would know the truth," he said.

"I've spent most of my life locked up at the auction house," she lied feebly.

Ghita shook her head immediately. "No, you haven't. You arrived shortly after I did and we were only there for a few months."

She smiled at Theran. "I told you. She is from another world."

He laughed. "That is impossible."

Ghita shrugged. "I was in the room when they brought her in. She was wearing the strangest clothing. She wore pants like a man and the material was very heavy and thick. Her shoes were pink and furry looking."

Reese sighed. She was wearing jeans and her favourite slippers when she was sucked into this world. She stared down at the flat shoes she was wearing now. They were too small, and just a morning of constant walking had given her a blister on her heel and worn away at the thin sole. She missed her slippers.

"Tell us more about this world," Hanif said.

Reese shook her head. She had learned the hard way not

to speak of her own world. The other women had avoided her and the warden had beaten her. She would not make the same mistake again.

"Tell us, Reese," Hanif repeated. "It will help pass the time."

"No. There is no other world. I'm crazy, that's all," Reese said.

Hanif frowned as Adina cleared her throat. "How much further to your home?"

"It is at least another seven days, if the weather is good," Theran replied.

"Probably longer," Hanif sighed. "You humans move much slower than I anticipated."

"Seven days?" Reese groaned. She would be dead before they made it to the shifters' home. She would die of exposure if she didn't figure out a way to stay warm at night. Of course, on the plus side her death would mean she wouldn't be forced to rut with some crazy-ass, alpha half-beast.

"You will like our home," Theran told Ghita. "It is in a valley with mountains and a lake on one side and woods surrounding the rest of it. It is very beautiful."

"How many members are in your pack?" Ghita asked.

"We are a fairly large pack. There are more than thirty of us. Most of us are male, which is a bit unusual. Generally, there are more females in a pack than males but we get along well enough."

"Why don't you have many females?" Adina asked.

Reese, lagging further behind, yawned again and stared at her feet. Every muscle in her body seemed to be burning with weariness and there was a bleariness to her thoughts. She looked up in time to see a look pass between Hanif and Theran.

"The lack of females is one of the reasons why Dagon has

decided to bring human women into the pack," Theran said. "If you make us good mates and bear us children, we will probably purchase more human females."

"Lovely," Reese muttered. "It's a breeding program."

A flash of colour caught her eye and she looked up, smiling a little at the sight of the large purple flower nodding in the wind. It was exceptionally pretty. She slowed to a stop, staring at it.

"But why don't you have many females?" Adina persisted.

Reese was only half-listening and she suddenly decided she didn't care much what the answer was anyway. The scent of the purple flower was drifting toward her and it smelled wonderful. She wanted to touch the flower and bury her nose within its fragrant petals. She was getting even sleepier and her lids started to close as she bent toward the flower.

There was a sharp barking and then she was hit by some-thing that felt roughly equivalent to a large truck. She flew backward and landed with a thud on the hard ground. She was unlucky enough to land on a rock. It dug directly into the already painful area on her back and for a moment the pain was so great she could only writhe silently on the ground. The large gray wolf was crouching over her and she paid no attention when he shifted to his human form. Tears streamed down her face and her hands scrabbled weakly at the ground as she gasped for air.

"Stay away from the flower, human," Kane snapped. "It will put you into a sleep that you will not wake from."

She barely heard his terse warning. Pain was radiating across her back in slow waves and she rolled to her side, her hand twisting behind her back to try and soothe the offending area.

"What is wrong with her?" Kane asked as the others gathered around her.

"You hit her hard, Kane," Theran said. "Perhaps you have broken something."

Kane shook her arm. "Human, did you break something?"

She took a deep, sobbing breath. "No, my – my back is sore."

"What's wrong with it?" He reached for her shirt and she pushed his hands away before sitting up. The pain was starting to recede and she moved her head cautiously.

"I'm all right now." She could feel wetness on her back and she wondered how badly she had scraped it.

Great, she thought sullenly. *If exposure doesn't kill me, an infection will.*

"Let me see your back," Kane said.

"It's fine," she replied as she staggered to her feet.

He snorted angrily and turned her around. She kicked at him and he growled and slapped her sharply on the ass. "Hold still, human."

He pulled up the back of her shirt and she heard the soft gasps of Adina and Ghita. She turned her head to look at them, her face paling at the looks on the others crowded around her. Even Kane, whose expression was normally unreadable, looked a little sick.

"What? Is it that bad?" She tried to crane her head to see for herself, but Kane pushed her head straight before brushing her dark hair over her shoulder. He bunched up the back of her shirt and gripped her neck with his large hand, holding her steady as he and Theran bent and studied her back.

"Is it bleeding badly?" Reese asked apprehensively.

"No," Adina said. "It's only scratched a little from the ground. But you have a terrible bruise on your back."

"Why did you not tell us you were injured?" Kane

demanded.

Reese stared blankly at him. It had not occurred to her to even mention it. The shifters had made it perfectly clear that they didn't care if she lived or died, and complaining about her sore back would not have gotten her anywhere.

Theran shook his head in disgust. "The humans are so barbaric. And they call us the animals."

"I did not realize he had hit her so hard," Kane replied. The bruise was an ugly large splotch of dark blue and purple across the middle of her back. He traced the center of the darkness with the tips of his fingers.

She cried out and arched her back. She tried to twist away from him and his hand tightened on the back of her neck.

"Hold still," he grunted as he touched the bruise again.

"Stop touching it, for fuck's sake!" She shouted at him. "Do you have any idea how much that fucking hurts?"

He blinked in surprise at her sudden anger, and she scowled at him and twisted in his grip again. This time he let her go and she stumbled before shoving the back of her shirt down and glaring at him.

He turned away, her eyes dropped to his very tight and very naked ass, and motioned to the others. "We keep moving. There is a freshwater pool a few miles further. We will stop there for the night."

He shifted into his wolf form and loped ahead.

REESE SANK TO HER KNEES AND EASED HER TREMBLING hands into the water. It was ice cold and she gasped before cupping her hands. She drank the water quickly and dipped her hands back into the pool. She was thirsty and she drank her fill before splashing water on her face.

Despite the cold air, she was grimy and sweaty from the day of walking. She briefly considered taking a dip in the pool. She decided that a hot shower was the thing she missed most about her own world. She snorted to herself, remembering how she had taken all those daily showers with their glorious hot water for granted. She eyed the water again before sighing. She had better not. The cold water would leech what little body heat she had left, right out of her.

Beside her, Adina was mashing water and mud and dark green leaves she had picked from the water's edge into a soupy mix on the ground.

"What are you doing, Adina?" Reese asked.

"I'm making a poultice for your back. It will help soothe the pain and aid in healing it faster. Take off your shirt."

Reese pulled off her shirt and drew her knees up to her chest. She rested her head on her knees as Adina applied the thick, cold paste to her back. She shivered and winced. "It's cold."

"Aye, but it will help ease the ache. Trust me, Reese."

"How do you know all of this?"

Adina shrugged as she finished spreading the paste on Reese's back and dipped her hands into the pool to clean them. "My mother taught me, as her mother taught her."

"Where is your mother now?"

"She died a few years back. A sickness went through our village and she succumbed to it."

"How did you end up at the auction house?" Reese asked.

"I was travelling with my brother to the village where my grandparents lived. We were ambushed by the traders and my brother offered me to them in exchange for his freedom."

Reese stared at her, stunned. "Are you kidding me?"

"No," Adina said.

"That's awful."

Adina shrugged and pointed to Ghita who was sitting further down. Theran was sitting next to her. He had taken a long, brown reed and was running it up and down her bare arm. Ghita giggled and clutched at his muscled arm.

"Ghita's father sold her to the auction house because he needed money to pay a gambling debt."

"What is wrong with the people in this world?" Reese breathed.

Adina watched Ghita and Theran for a few moments. "She has a crush on him."

"Yeah. The feeling seems to be mutual," Reese replied. "If this Dagon doesn't choose her, I'm certain Theran will take Ghita as his mate."

Adina glanced at her. "Did you notice how they did not answer my question about their women?"

Reese nodded but before she could reply, Kane appeared beside them. Like usual, he was in his wolf form and he ducked his head and drank from the pool before staring at them with his light green eyes.

Reese leaned forward further and hid her naked breasts against her thighs as Kane looked her up and down. He approached her slowly and a shiver went down her spine when he sniffed at the paste covering her back.

He made a soft woofing noise and Adina said, "It is a healing paste."

He chuffed and trotted away. Adina let out her breath in a shaky little sigh. "Theran and Hanif seem nice enough, but that big one – he scares the tar out of me. He obviously doesn't agree with his alpha bringing humans into the pack. Nor does he seem concerned with keeping us safe. What are the odds that one or all of us die before we even make it to their home?"

"I'd say pretty high," Reese answered reluctantly. She

squinted at Adina in the growing gloom. "Don't worry. It'll probably be me who dies. When the morning comes where you wake up and find my frozen, dead body, promise me you won't let the shifters eat me."

She smiled at Adina, trying to get her to laugh but Adina frowned at her. "Do not joke about that, Reese. It is only going to get colder and if we do not get to their home before the rains begin, you'll die for sure."

"Don't worry about me. I have a layer of blubber to keep me warm, remember?" Reese said.

Adina shook her head. "I will ask Hanif to curl up around the both of us tonight. He is big enough to at least partially curl around the two of us. The heat they throw off is unbelievable."

"Thank you, Adina," Reese said.

"You're welcome." Adina patted her back gingerly. "Reese I – I am sorry for how I treated you at the auction house."

Reese frowned. "You didn't treat me badly."

The blonde woman stared down at her lap. "No, but I avoided you and called you barto behind your back like the other women did."

Reese patted her hand. "Don't worry about it. Can I put my shirt back on now?"

Adina touched the paste on her back. "Aye, it's dry enough."

Reese slipped her shirt over her head as Hanif walked up to them. He had two large water skins in his hand and he uncorked them before dipping them into the pool and filling them up. He corked them tightly and handed one to each of the women. "For tomorrow."

"Thank you," Adina replied.

He nodded and glanced up at the sky. "It is not safe to

stay around the pool at night. We will camp further into the woods. Come."

They stood and followed him into the woods and when Adina took her hand, Reese squeezed it and smiled at her.

———

"No, I won't do it." Hanif shook his head and Adina gave him a soft, pleading look.

"Please, Hanif. Why not? You are big enough to keep both of us warm."

"I said no," Hanif repeated.

Adina sighed with frustration before glancing behind her at Reese. "She nearly froze to death last night."

"She was fine," Hanif said dismissively.

"She was pretty cold," Theran spoke up. "Why won't you let her lie with you? What's the big deal?"

"Because she is mad!" Hanif said. "What do you think Dagon will do to us when he discovers we've brought him a mad woman?"

Theran glanced at Kane who was lying on the ground with his head between his paws. His eyes were closed and he appeared to be sleeping.

"Kane picked her, not us."

"It does not matter! You know how he is," Hanif replied. "It would be better for us and the human if she dies before she reaches our home."

"Hanif!" Theran snapped. He gave Reese a weak smile. She stared back at him impassively.

"It's true," Hanif said. "Besides, if you feel so bad for the human, you lie with her."

Theran shook his head immediately, a nervous look crossing his face. "No."

Hanif scoffed. "You know I speak the truth. It is why you won't lie with her either."

Reese stood. "Tell you what, boys. If you're so worried about what the big bad wolf is going to do to you when you bring the crazy lady into the pack, I'll save you both some worry and bid you farewell right now. I'd rather die a quick painful death alone in the woods than slowly freeze to death with cowards like you."

The two shifters flushed and Reese grinned bitterly at them. "I'll assume your silence means you're agreeable to it."

"Reese, wait," Adina said.

"Good bye, Adina. Good bye, Ghita. Good luck with the wolf pack. I hope you both are very happy and have many sweet, furry wolf babies."

She started to stalk into the woods and halted when the growling started. She sighed and turned back. Kane had sat up and he was staring at her, his eyes gleaming and a low, continuous growl erupting from his chest.

She didn't have to understand wolf to know what the growling meant and she stared silently at him. She considered simply turning and fleeing into the woods. No doubt the big wolf would catch her and rip out her throat but that would be quicker than freezing to death.

He growled again and she plopped back down to the ground, wincing a little at the pain in her back. Apparently, she wasn't quite ready to die after all.

KANE STARED THROUGH HALF-CLOSED EYES AT THE LARGE human. Ten minutes after he had growled at her, she had stood up and she was now yanking and pulling at the lower branches of a large pine tree.

She pulled at a particularly stubborn one, trying to tear it from the thick trunk. She leaned back, putting her considerable weight into it, and it tore from the trunk with a thick, ripping noise. Not expecting it to tear free so quickly, she lost her balance and fell backward. She yelped and rolled to her side, her hand curving around to press gingerly against her back. She lay on the ground and panted as the blonde one – he didn't remember her name – crouched beside her. She spoke quietly to the big one, but his hearing was excellent.

"Reese, what are you doing?"

"Trying to survive the night," Reese said. "Help me up, would you?"

The blonde one helped her stand and then joined her in pulling down more branches. When they had torn down a healthy amount of them, they carried them into the small clearing they were camping in and Reese sat down on the ground.

He watched as she curled up on her side and began to pile the branches with their thick green needles over her lower body. Once the blonde one realized what she was doing, she urged Reese to lie down and she finished the job of covering her with the branches.

"Okay?" She asked.

"Just ducky. Remember, if I freeze to death in the night don't let those damn shifters eat my body," Reese replied dryly before tucking her head under the fragrant branches.

He had to bite back his bark of laughter as the blonde woman returned to Hanif. The timid human was already curled into Theran's body and he chuffed his disapproval when Theran licked her arm. Theran ignored him and licked the woman's face. She giggled and buried her face in the soft fur of his neck as he rested his tail over her lower body.

Kane turned his attention back to Reese. He would never

admit this to anyone, but he was fascinated by the human. Had been since the moment he had seen her odd-coloured eyes and smelled her strange scent. Hell, fascinated wasn't exactly the right word. He wanted desperately to mate with her. Since the moment he had licked her neck and had smelled her immediate and strong desire for him, he had wanted to take her.

He snorted inwardly. What the hell was wrong with him? He hated the humans. Humans had slaughtered his parents. They had hunted them down like dogs and murdered them. He had spent his entire life having as little to do with the humans as possible and now he wanted to fuck one.

Of course, for a human she was surprisingly intelligent and strong. The idea to cover herself with branches to keep warm was a good one. The fact that she was not complaining about her back had, he admitted grudgingly, impressed him. She was a large human, the largest female of her kind he'd ever seen. He wondered if that was part of the reason he was attracted to her. Despite what he had said about her weight earlier, he liked how she looked. She was bigger than the female shifters he usually mated with and although he mated roughly, he thought she could probably handle him despite her fragile human bones.

He thought about the bruise on her back and anger stirred within him. When he had lifted her shirt and seen the bruising spreading across her back like a malignant flower, he was struck with an almost undeniable urge to return to the auction house and tear out the man's throat.

Even now, just thinking about the bruise on her soft skin made him feel anxious and unsettled. He stood, circled a few times, and settled on the ground again. What was wrong with him? He had never felt any type of concern or a need to protect any of the females he had mated with before. Hell, he hadn't even mated with this one and he had no intention of doing so. That was asking for more trouble than it was worth. Even if she did have firm, full breasts that fit perfectly into his large hands, and lips that looked like they were meant to be wrapped around his thick cock.

He chuffed loudly. Although he preferred to stay in his wolf form, he was finding it almost a necessity around the human. He was having trouble controlling his erections and he didn't want the human seeing how she affected him.

He closed his eyes and tucked his tail around his nose. Dagon would most likely choose her as his mate anyway. Her body was made for bearing pups, and the alpha would quickly curb her stubborn and independent nature. His stomach lurched at the thought of exactly how Dagon would break her will.

He stood and stretched before sitting and staring moodily at the woman buried under the branches. It was none of his concern. His alpha wanted a mate and he was bringing him one. He was doing what Dagon asked of him and that was all that mattered.

He will not want her when he finds out she's mad. You could take her as your own mate.

He growled softly. He did not want a mate. He preferred rutting and mating with as many different females as he could. He had no interest in mating with one female for the rest of his life, no matter how temptingly soft her skin was.

The branches moved, and the woman made a soft groan as she shifted. The branches were trembling and he knew that despite the cover of the heavy needles, she would still be cold. He was tempted to go to her, curl up next to her and allow her to fold her body into his and take some of his warmth. Instead, he turned his back to her and lay down. His obsession with the human needed to stop.

CHAPTER 4

R eese tugged wearily at the tree branch. It was another full day of walking, another day of eating charkas and plants, another day of watching Ghita and Theran flirt while she stumbled tiredly after Adina, Hanif and Kane. The branches had helped a little, but she had still barely slept. She felt nearly frozen to the bone when she had crawled out from the branches this morning.

She sighed and tugged again at the branch. She had never been so goddamn tired in her life. The lack of sleep, the hours of walking and the small amount of food had combined to make her feel like she was dying.

You're overreacting. Keep it together, she told herself. The shifters' reactions to her perceived madness had her convinced she would most likely be killed by the other pack members. She needed to suck it up and figure out a way to escape.

And go where? You were nearly killed by a goddamn flower yesterday, remember? If you even manage to escape from the shifters, you'll be dead within a day.

The branch let go with a sudden snap and she fell on to

her considerable ass. She stood and rubbed at her butt before reaching for another branch. At least she hadn't fallen on her back. It still throbbed heavily and she touched it gingerly. She'd had Adina look at it earlier in the day and the blonde had assured her that it looked a little better, but it certainly didn't feel better.

She tore off the branch and stared down at the small pile at her feet. There wasn't nearly as many as she had gathered last night but they would have to do. If she didn't lie down soon she would simply collapse where she stood. She gathered the branches and carried them to the campsite. Adina was eating a handful of charkas and she held a few out.

"Here, eat these."

Reese shook her head. "I'm not hungry."

Adina frowned. "You've barely eaten today. Take these."

"I said I wasn't hungry," Reese said grumpily. "I want to sleep, Adina."

She lay down and nodded her thanks when Adina helped her spread the branches over her body. She tucked her head into her arms. She wrinkled her nose at her own smell and closed her eyes resignedly. There were gaps in the branches and she could feel the cold air seeping through her clothes, but she was too exhausted to care.

She realized abruptly that she probably wouldn't survive the night. Oddly enough, the thought didn't frighten her. Instead she felt a simple sort of relief. Death meant that she would no longer be cold and her legs and back would stop hurting. She closed her eyes and dozed.

She woke only an hour or so later. Already her limbs were stiff and numb with cold, and she lay listlessly under the branches. After a few moments it occurred to her that she could hear soft moaning and she wiggled out from under the branches, wondering what it was.

She scanned the darkness and jerked with surprise. Theran, naked and in his human form, was on his knees behind Ghita. Ghita was equally naked and on her hands and knees. She made soft moans and grunts as Theran fucked her.

Reese stared quietly for a moment before looking away. Her cheeks flushed when she realized that Kane, his green eyes glowing in the dark, was staring at her. She quickly turned over, the branches sliding from her body, and stared into the trees behind her. After a few minutes, she climbed to her feet and staggered her way toward the trees. Ghita's soft moans cut out but Reese didn't turn and before she had even gone a few feet, the girl's moans began again.

Her body shaking with cold and exhaustion, Reese lifted her skirt and pushed down her underwear before squatting next to a large tree. When she was finished, she staggered a few feet away before her trembling legs gave out and she collapsed on the hard ground at the base of a tree. She moaned and closed her eyes. She was so cold and weirdly weak. She would rest for a few minutes, catch her breath, and then make her way back to the camp. She didn't care what Hanif said or did, she would try and curl up with him and Adina. The worse that would happen is he would kill her.

WHEN REESE DIDN'T RETURN AFTER A FEW MINUTES, KANE stood and trotted across the camp. He paid no attention to the rutting couple and Theran didn't stop his thrusting as he passed by them.

He inhaled, found Reese's scent easily, and followed it into the woods. She was lying beneath a large tree and he shifted into his human form and knelt beside her. Her eyes were closed and her skin was pale. He shook her roughly.

"Get up, human."

She moaned but didn't open her eyes, and he felt an odd trickle of fear in his belly at how cold her skin was. He scooped her up and sat down, resting his back against the tree and placing her on his lap. He wrapped his powerful arms around her and pulled up her legs, tucking her skirt over her feet.

"So cold," she muttered.

"I know, girl," he whispered. He pushed her head into his thick neck and she burrowed weakly against him. He was warm despite his nakedness and the cold air. Even in her semi-conscious state she pressed against him, seeking out his warmth.

He tucked her bare arms against his chest and then slid his hands under her shirt. He rubbed her cold back, mindful of the bruise, and she moaned at the feel of his warm hands.

After ten minutes, he put his mouth to her ear. "Better?"

"Yes. Thank you," she sighed. Her breathing slowed and deepened, and he buried his face in her soft, dark hair. She smelled strongly like the pine branches she'd been lying under, but beneath that he could smell her own unique scent. He closed his eyes and breathed deeply as she slept against him.

Just before dawn he carried her back to the camp. Her formerly pale skin was flushed with warmth and she was no longer trembling. The others were sleeping soundly and he carefully tucked her back under the branches before shifting to his wolf form and moving away from her. He lay down and waited patiently for the sun to rise and the others to wake.

"YOU LOOK BETTER TODAY." ADINA SMILED AT REESE AS they trailed after Ghita and the shifters.

"I feel better. I actually got some sleep last night and it didn't seem as cold. Did you find it warmer?"

Adina shrugged. "Hanif is so warm, a blizzard could come through and I wouldn't notice."

Ahead of them, Theran slapped Ghita lightly on the ass and the girl giggled. Reese smiled a little. The truth of it was, she didn't really know what happened last night. She remembered waking up and listening to Theran and Ghita having sex. She remembered staggering into the woods to pee. After that, it was a blank. Well, not entirely a blank. She'd had a strange dream where Kane was rubbing her back with his warm hands and talking to her in that low, raspy voice of his.

She glanced at the large gray wolf. It had only been a dream. She had woken this morning under the pile of branches. The shifter was in his wolf form and ignoring her and the other women like he always did.

She thought about the way he had licked her. How it had felt when his hard hand had first squeezed her ass and then cupped her breast. A small shiver of desire went through her and she shook her head angrily. Apparently, a good night's sleep was enough to bring her libido back to life. Unfortunately, her libido was hot for the stupid shifter.

Ridiculous. He refused to even help keep her warm at night and she was imagining what it would be like to have sex with him. She should be thinking of ways to escape him, not sleep with him.

She was jolted from her thoughts by Adina's hand squeezing her arm. The terrain was steadily growing steeper, and she looked up to see a lake in front of them. The day was overcast and cool. Thunder had been rumbling in the distance for most of the afternoon and the lake water looked murky and cold. A small rocky mountain jutted out to the right of the lake and it was in this direction that Kane was leading them.

There was a worn path of dirt and rocks at the base of the mountain and Reese craned her head. About thirty feet above them the path narrowed and wound its way across the side of the mountain.

Adina clutched her hand. "They cannot expect us to cross that," she squeaked nervously.

Kane was already starting up the path and Reese sighed. "I believe they do."

"I cannot." Adina was backing up. Her pale face was even whiter than normal and tears were sliding down her cheeks. "I – I am afraid of heights."

Kane had stopped on the path and he turned and barked impatiently at them.

"Just give us a minute for Christ's sake!" Reese said.

She turned back to Adina and stroked the woman's arms and shoulders. "It's fine, Adina. The path is probably not nearly as narrow as it looks from down here. Nor is it that high really."

She gave the woman a reassuring smile. "We will walk slowly and you can hold my hand, all right?"

"Can we not go around the other side of the lake?" Adina whispered.

"No, we cannot." Theran joined them and he gave her an impatient look. "It would add nearly two days to our journey and the rains are close as it is. If we do not cross the mountain, we will not get home before the rains come."

Adina made a small whimper of fear and Reese gave her a brisk shake. Growing up, her mother was no-nonsense and loving but firm with Reese's fears and it was this tactic she employed now.

"Enough, Adina. We have no choice but to cross. Dry your face and let's go. I won't let you fall, all right?"

The blonde woman nodded and took Reese's hand. Reese smiled encouragingly at her and led her up the path.

———

"YOU'RE DOING SO WELL, ADINA," REESE PRAISED. "IT IS not much further now."

Adina didn't reply. Her face was completely devoid of colour and her hand was clenched around Reese's. She was staring straight ahead with resigned determination, and Reese made another soft sound of approval.

"I can see the other side of the lake and already the path is starting to move downward. You can feel that it is. I know you can."

She peeked over the side of the path. Below her the lake glimmered murkily, and she tugged Adina forward. The path was twisty and narrow, and the edge of the path was alarmingly soft and crumbly beneath their feet. She had kept Adina close to the rock face and instructed her not to look down.

Reese wasn't afraid of heights, but she would be just as happy as Adina to have her feet back on solid ground. The wind off the lake was ice cold and it kept whipping her long hair around her face. All of the women were freezing and the wolves' fur was rippling in the wind. Only Theran had remained in his human form and he turned and gave them an encouraging look.

"Catch up, humans. Quickly."

Reese urged Adina forward and Ghita gave them a scared smile as she clung to the back of Theran's shirt.

"You can do it, Adina," Reese said encouragingly. "Just another twenty feet or so and we'll be - "

There was a sharp bark ahead of them and Reese watched in horror as the edge of the path crumbled beneath Kane's large paws.

He gave a strangled yelp and started to slide over the edge. His paws scrabbled for purchase and Theran shouted his name before he disappeared over the side. Ghita screamed shrilly and the others watched as Kane, his body twisting and turning, plunged into the murky water of the lake.

His shaggy head broke the surface and he barked hoarsely before disappearing under the water again. Theran cursed and Hanif barked frantically as they stared over the edge.

"Theran!" Reese shouted. "Can he not swim?"

"No!" There was terror in Theran's voice. "None of us can!"

"Son of a bitch!" Reese pulled Adina forward and ripped her hand free of the woman's tight grasp.

"Adina! Hang on to Ghita!"

She stood at the edge of the path and peered downward. Although it was only twenty feet or so to the lake, it suddenly looked much higher. Her heart pounding wildly in her chest, Reese took a deep breath and dove off the side of the mountain.

She hit the water smoothly, her body slicing through the water. It was much colder than any lake she'd ever swam in before and she kicked for the surface. Her lungs screamed for oxygen and her body was shaking with cold.

She broke the surface and took a gasping breath before looking around frantically. Kane, his green eyes filled with bright panic, was thrashing weakly not ten feet from her. She started to swim toward him with long, powerful strokes.

He howled in fear and disappeared under the water.

"Shit!" She immediately dove back under, searching the murky water for him. He had shifted to his human form and he was limp and sinking fast. She pushed through the water and struggled to reach him before he disappeared in the depths of the lake.

She grabbed his forearm in a tight grip and swam for the surface. She broke through the water, hooked her arm around his upper chest and under his armpit and swam for the shore.

They were at least thirty feet away and she could feel her limbs growing numb and heavy. She ignored it grimly and kept swimming, focusing her gaze on the shore as her lungs throbbed and burned.

The others had scrambled down the path and along the shore. As her feet finally touched ground and she hauled the large shifter toward dry land, Theran and Hanif splashed through the shallow water toward them. They took Kane's limp body from her and she collapsed on her knees for a moment, sucking in deep, gasping breaths of the cold air.

By the time she joined them on the shore, wading painfully through the cold water, the two shifters were shouting and pacing back and forth over Kane's still body.

"He's dead!" Theran cried and abruptly shifted to his wolf form, his clothes tearing apart around him. He howled into the cold air and Ghita and Adina clapped their hands over their ears. Hanif shifted and joined him in his howling.

"Shut up! Both of you!" Reese shouted. She placed her ear to Kane's chest. His heart was beating but he wasn't breathing. She tipped his head up, opened his mouth, and pinched his nose shut before clamping her mouth down on his and blowing air into his lungs. She waited a couple of seconds and then did it again.

Theran and Hanif whimpered as she bent her head a third time and blew another lungful of air into Kane. His body jerked and she gave a sigh of relief as he coughed and water erupted from his mouth. She rolled him to his side and patted and rubbed his back as he coughed and choked up the lake water.

"You're okay, you're fine. Take a deep breath, Kane," she soothed.

He turned onto his back and stared up at her. She smiled and smoothed his wet hair back from his face. "You're okay, big fella. Just a little lake water in the lungs."

His eyes widened in sudden panic and he snarled. His teeth lengthened and hair grew on his face before he lashed out. His hand caught her on the jaw and she fell onto her back, crying out a little at the pain from the bruise. He staggered to his feet and shifted. He howled in fear, and Theran and Hanif gave answering howls before Kane turned and ran into the forest.

Adina dropped to her knees beside Reese. "Reese, are you okay?"

"Awesome," Reese croaked. "I'm living the dream."

"How – how did you know to do that?" Adina asked.

"Junior lifeguard at Seasons family camp, three summers in a row," she croaked again.

"Lifeguard?" Adina said uncertainly.

"Never mind. Help me up."

Adina helped her to her feet. Cold water was streaming from her body and Reese shivered violently as she and Adina followed Ghita and the wolves into the forest.

CHAPTER 5

Kane returned nearly half an hour later. He trotted into the camp and sat down next to Hanif and Theran. He pulled away when they tried to touch him and barked sharply at them. They murmured apologies as Kane's gaze fell on Reese.

She had stripped off her wet clothing and was wearing his shirt. It fell past her knees and she hugged her arms around herself as he stared at her.

"My clothes were wet," she said defensively.

He didn't reply and she glanced at her own clothes spread out on the ground. "You can have it back in the morning."

He chuffed at her as Hanif shifted and barked at Adina. She squeezed Reese's arm. "Are you going to get some branches?"

Reese shook her head. "No. I'm tired."

Adina frowned. "Reese, you'll - "

"Yeah, yeah, I'll freeze to death. I'm too tired to care."

Hanif barked again and Reese glanced at him. "Your blanket is calling for you. Go on, Adina."

Theran, helping Ghita to lie down on the ground, smiled

tentatively at her. "Come, human. I will help keep you warm."

Kane snarled viciously and Theran jerked before glancing at the large wolf. "Kane, she saved - "

Kane snarled again and Theran gave Reese an apologetic look. "I am sorry, Reese."

She shrugged. "Whatever, Theran."

He frowned as Reese turned her back to him and lay down on the ground. She curled into a ball, tugging Kane's shirt down to her ankles and resting her head on her arm. The trek over the mountain, the jump into the lake and dragging the large shifter through the water had pretty much done her in. The adrenaline had drained from her body and she was worn out physically and emotionally. Her hair was still wet and she pulled it away from the back of her neck with a grimace. She closed her eyes and sighed. She had saved that asshole Kane's life and now he was going to let her die.

She nearly screamed when Kane lay down beside her. She rolled over and got a mouthful of fur for her trouble. She wiggled back a little and stared up at him. He was curling his large body around hers and he made no objection when she buried her toes in the thick fur on his belly and crowded her body against his. His large tail crossed over her hips and thighs and she pressed her face into his fur-covered throat.

He was unbelievably, delightfully warm and she sighed happily as he rested his large chin on the top of her head. His hot breath felt amazing on her wet hair and cold neck, and she burrowed even deeper against him. She sighed again and closed her eyes.

IN THE EARLY LIGHT OF DAWN, KANE STUDIED THE SLEEPING woman in his arms. He had shifted back to his human form a few minutes ago. She had muttered quietly but not woken and he brushed her hair back from her face. She frowned in her sleep and buried her face into his throat. Her lips brushed against his skin and his cock hardened against her hip.

He slipped his hand under her shirt and ran it along her thigh and up to her hip. He squeezed it gently before rubbing her side. She sighed and stirred against him and he stroked her round stomach.

She stretched and moved her head back, blinking sleepily before putting her arm around his waist and pressing her body against his. He slid his hand out from under her shirt and stroked her arm as she stared curiously at him. It took her a few moments to realize he was in his human form and he smiled a little when he felt her fingers dig into his bare back.

"Hello, human," he said.

She didn't reply, her eyes widening when he reached up and traced the dark bruise on her cheek.

"I'm sorry for this. I did not mean to hurt you," he said gravely.

"It's," she cleared her throat, "it's fine."

"Were you warm enough last night?"

She nodded. "Yes, thank you."

"Thank you for saving my life, human."

"You're welcome."

A flush was rising in her cheeks and she moved her arm from around his waist. She tried to sit up and he put his arm across her waist and held her tightly against him.

"It's not time to get up yet," he said. He pushed on her shoulder, urging her to lie on her back and grunting with satisfaction when she did.

His arm cushioned her head and she stared mutely at him

as he trailed his fingers down her arm. He lowered his head and sniffed her neck.

"You smell good, human," he whispered.

"No, I don't. I haven't had a bath in ages," she said.

He grinned at her and she inhaled sharply. He lowered his head again and licked her neck with his warm tongue.

Reese moaned and clutched at Kane's back. She had no idea what was happening. The shifter hated her and she hated him. He was arrogant and mean, and he had spent the last three nights watching her nearly freeze to death. So why was she tilting her head back to give him better access to her neck? Why was she allowing him to push his hard thigh between her soft ones? Why was she –

She gasped when he nipped at her collar bone. He lifted his head and stared down at her and she swallowed thickly. His dark eyes had turned green and they glowed when she licked her lips nervously.

"Kane, what - "

He kissed her, his lips coaxing hers open and his tongue sliding in to touch hers delicately. She shuddered and returned his kiss. He cupped her face and his thumb stroked along her cheekbone as she sighed and put her arms around him.

She was marveling at how gentle he was for his size and strength, when he raised her arms above her head. She blinked at him in confusion and then jerked in surprise when he quickly pulled his shirt up and over her head.

She put her arms across her naked breasts and looked nervously to her left. Hanif was still curled around Adina and they both appeared to be sleeping but she resisted when Kane tugged at her arms.

He frowned. "Let me see your breasts, human."

She glared at him and tightened her arms over her chest. "No."

He leaned over her and inhaled. "You want me. I can smell it. Show me your breasts."

"Not with the others right here!" She hissed at him.

He shrugged. "We mate in front of each other."

"Humans don't," she snapped.

"They don't?"

"No! Well, most of them," she conceded. "Sometimes they have parties where they, you know, get it on with anyone who's interested and in front of whoever but I'm not that kind of girl."

"So you'll fuck me, just not in front of my pack mates?" He asked.

She blushed at his coarseness. "I don't – I mean, I hardly know you and you called me fat and let me nearly freeze to death. I'm not sure that I'll even sleep with you."

He grinned. "You will."

"Not with that arrogant attitude I won't," she muttered. "Give me back my shirt."

Instead of doing what she asked, he slipped his hand inside of her panties, cupped her pussy and pushed one finger deep inside of her before she could even think of closing her legs. She moaned quietly. Her hips arched against his hand before she got a hold of herself.

She kept one arm across her breasts and used the other hand to grab at his arm. She pulled on it, but it was like trying to move a rock.

"You'll definitely fuck me," he whispered approvingly. "Look how wet you are and all I've done is kiss you."

She blushed furiously and yanked at his arm. "Move your hand right now!"

"You're a demanding little thing aren't you, human?" He

51

thrust his finger back and forth while his thumb angled upward to brush against her clit.

She groaned and then clamped her hand over her mouth, staring wide-eyed at the sleeping Hanif and Adina. She realized a fraction of a second too late that her breasts were now bared to him before he dipped his head and sucked one cold nipple into his warm mouth. She moaned behind her hand and then threaded the hand through his short dark hair, holding tightly as he sucked and laved at her tightened nipple. He moved his mouth to her other nipple and she arched her back even as she was tugging on his hair.

"Kane, move your hand dammit!" She whispered again. His thumb rubbing against her clit was rapidly breaking down her resistance. If she didn't stop him now, he'd be fucking her on her hands and knees in front of everyone in a matter of minutes. And she'd be fine and goddamn dandy with it.

"I am moving my hand, human." He licked her nipple, pressed her clit until she moaned again, and then slid a second finger into her. She bit her lip as he stretched her tight opening.

"You're very small." He frowned down at her. "Have you mated before?"

His fingers probed deeper and she clamped her thighs together around his hand.

"Yes, I've mated before!"

"How many times?" He was still stroking her clit with his thumb and he leaned down and nuzzled her breast.

"That's none of your business," she gritted out as another deep wave of pleasure filled her belly.

"My cock is large," he whispered against her mouth, "but you will get used to it."

His comment aroused her curiosity and she glanced downward. Her mouth dropped open and he chuckled at the look on her face. She shut her mouth with a snap and tore her gaze from the biggest cock she'd ever seen.

"It's not that big," she lied.

"Think about how it will feel sliding into your wet pussy, human." He circled her clit again and she shuddered against him as she nearly climaxed.

"I like how responsive you are. It makes me even more eager to fuck you." He smiled at her.

Reese could feel her cheeks flushing. His honest way of speaking and the way he acted like she would just spread her legs and let him take her, was turning her on so much it was embarrassing.

"I've never been with a human before." He stared at her breasts and his eyes glowed before he smiled at her.

"Why not?" She asked.

He hesitated as something dark flickered deep in his eyes. His hand tightened almost painfully around her crotch. "Human females are too small and fragile. I'm rough when I mate. I would break their bones."

"That's not very comforting." She yanked again at his hand.

He laughed. "You are the biggest human female I've ever seen. Your body will be able to handle me."

When she didn't reply, he leaned down and kissed her nipple. "I will go slowly until you are used to me. Do not be frightened, human. You're even bigger than most of the female shifters I've mated with."

"You sure know how to sweet talk a girl," she said.

He gave her a curious look and halted the slow movements of his fingers within her. "What do you mean – sweet talk?"

She sighed. "It means – hell, I don't know – that you use your words to convince a girl to sleep with you."

He frowned. "Why do I need to do that? You obviously want to sleep with me. I can smell it on you, and your body is wet and ready to take my cock."

Reese felt like she had been thrown head-first down the rabbit hole. Never in her entire life had she imagined she would be lying in her underwear in the middle of a forest with a half-man, half-wolf who had his fingers stuck up her crotch while she tried to explain the art of sweet talking.

"Humans can't smell another human's desire," she said patiently. "And I've never met a human male who just sticks their hand into a woman's underwear without asking permission first. Human women don't like that type of behaviour."

He cocked his head at her. "You like it. You've almost come twice already, and I haven't even fucked you yet."

She flushed again before muttering, "Just once."

He grinned at her and she scowled at him. "You can't - "

"Enough talking, human," he said suddenly. He leaned over her and kissed her again, his tongue pushing into her mouth as pulled his fingers out of her and rubbed her clit.

She cried out into his mouth. Her entire body was shuddering and her orgasm was starting with small tingles and jolts of pleasure in her pelvis. She panted and moaned when he dipped his head and lightly bit her nipple. He tugged on it with his teeth and she clutched at his hard arms.

"Oh God, oh - "

Soft barking made her stiffen against him, and she turned her head to see Hanif twitching in his sleep as he growled and barked.

"Stop!" She slapped his arm and gave the large shifter a frantic look. "Please, stop! He's waking up."

Kane frowned. He could smell the human's desire fading. It was being replaced by embarrassment, and he sighed and

54

pulled his hand out from her panties. She sat up and struggled into his shirt as Hanif jerked and woke up with a loud bark.

Adina winced and sat up. "What? What's wrong?" She asked groggily.

Hanif stood and shook himself before shifting into his human form. Behind Kane's broad back, Theran and Ghita were stirring. Kane cupped Reese's throat and pulled her head down to whisper in her ear. "Tonight I will take you into the woods and fuck you in private, human."

"Awesome," she said sarcastically before tearing away from him and standing up. Her legs were shaking and her pelvis was throbbing. She wanted to pull Kane into the woods, throw him on the ground and fuck his brains out.

She stared silently at him and, as if he read her mind, he gave her a wolfish smile. "Do you think you can wait until tonight, human?"

She flushed and glanced at the others before leaning closer. "It doesn't work that way, wolf boy. I'm not sleeping with you tonight."

He grinned again. "Of course you are. Why would you not?"

She clenched her hands into fists and nearly shrieked with frustration. "Your arrogance is unbelievable. Stay away from me, Kane. Do you hear me?"

"I'll stay away until tonight but mark my words, human. You'll be on your hands and knees and crying out for my cock before the night is done."

He shifted before she could reply and she gave a loud grunt of anger and frustration as Adina approached her.

"Reese, are you all right?"

"Fine, just fucking fine." She stomped away.

CHAPTER 6

R eese sighed and sat down on the cold ground. The sun
was sinking below the mountains and the wind was
ice cold. Dark clouds were gathering in the sky and Theran
gave them a worried look.

"The rains are starting, Hanif."

"I know," he replied grimly. "Kane is looking for shelter."

"Why are they so worried about a little rain?" Reese
asked Adina.

"It's not just a little rain, Reese," Adina replied. "It rains
for days and falls hard and fast. If it's cold enough, it turns to
freezing rain. And lower areas like this one, often flood
within a matter of hours. The shifters can survive being
caught in it because their thick coats will protect them but
humans aren't so lucky. If we don't drown, we'll die of exposure within a day or two."

"Do not worry." Theran patted Ghita's back. "There are
many caves in the side of the mountain. Kane will find us one
that is suitable to keep you safe."

Reese breathed a sigh of relief. If they were all forced to
share a cave while it rained, then she wouldn't be tempted

into having sex with Kane tonight. Halfway through the day they had stopped for a rest. She had gone further into the woods to relieve herself and when she had stepped out from behind the large tree, Kane was waiting for her. He had shifted into his human form for the first time that day and she had averted her eyes from his half-hard cock as her cheeks reddened.

"Hello, human." He grinned at her and she gave him an impatient look.

"I have a name. It's Reese."

He stepped closer and snagged her around the waist, pulling her up against his hard body. "Hello, Reese."

His raspy voice saying her name sent shivers down her spine.

"What are you doing here?" She squeaked out when his hand slipped down to cup her ass.

"I want to touch you," he replied.

"You can't just touch me whenever you feel like it," she said crossly as his hand slid down to her thigh and lifted it around his hip.

"Why not?" He pressed his cock against her.

"Because I'm not your damn property. You have to ask permission." She ignored the way her heart was beating rapidly against her chest as he stuck his hand up her shirt and stroked her belly.

"I like how you look in my clothing," he whispered.

She sighed and grabbed his hand through her shirt. Her clothes hadn't even been close to dry this morning and she was forced to continue to wear his shirt.

"Kane, seriously. You can't just touch me like this."

"There is no one else around," he replied. "That was your objection before, was it not?"

"Well, yes, but - "

"Then why can I not touch you? You crave my touch. I know you do."

He leaned in and nuzzled her neck affectionately and she moaned. "I hardly know you. All you want from me is sex and - "

"Of course I want to mate with you. As you want to mate with me." He sucked on her earlobe and then probed her ear with his warm tongue.

She shuddered all over, and when he reached for her breast she didn't try to stop him. He cupped her breast, pulling and pinching her nipple as she tightened her leg around his hip.

He kissed her and she returned it eagerly, pressing herself against him as he pushed her back against the tree. She gave a gasp of pain, arching her back away from the hard bark and he frowned.

"I'm sorry. I forgot that your back is bruised." He rubbed her lower back soothingly before trailing kisses along her neck.

"Kane, why are you doing this?" She whispered.

He lifted his head. "Because I want to fuck you."

"But why do you want to?" She asked.

He shrugged. "I have never mated with a human before and I find you oddly appealing. A few of my pack mates have fucked a human before and they say it is pleasant enough. I will mate with you and find out for myself. I need to fuck you before we return to my home. Dagon will claim you for his own, and I will lose my chance to mate with you."

She glared at him. "So I'm a damn experiment for you?"

He stared at her in surprise. "You're angry."

"Of course I am," she sighed. "Kane, humans aren't like shifters. We don't just go around fucking each other. At least, I don't."

Now it was his turn to sigh. "Why do you keep arguing with me, human? You want me."

"Are you seriously trying to tell me that your kind just fuck whoever they want in their pack?"

"Of course not. Many of us fall in love and mate for life just like the humans do," he replied.

"But not you?"

He shook his head. "No, I have no wish to be mated for life to another."

"Of course you don't."

He frowned. "Are all humans this confusing? You want me. You submit so eagerly to my touch, and yet you keep saying we cannot mate."

"You're right," she said. "I'm totally giving you mixed signals. I'm sorry for that."

He smiled and leaned down to kiss her. She pushed at his broad chest. "No, Kane. I'm serious. Have you never had a woman say no to you before?"

He stepped away from her. "It has happened on occasion, but their scent clearly indicated they did not want me. Yours does not. Why are you denying yourself what you want?"

She sighed again. "I'm not going to have sex with you when I'm most likely going to be mated to your damn alpha."

"So you'll fuck my alpha but not me?" He could feel jealousy burning in his stomach and he frowned. What did he care if the human fucked Dagon once he was finished with her?

"I'd rather not fuck anyone I barely know," she snapped. "But I have a feeling that your alpha isn't going to give me a choice."

"Probably not," he agreed.

"What happened to his last mate?" She asked suddenly.

"We told you. She died."

"How?"

"What does it matter?" He said evasively. "She is dead and he needs a new mate."

"How many mates has he had?" She had a bad feeling in her stomach.

"Many," he admitted.

"How many?" The bad feeling was growing.

He sighed harshly. "Do you always ask this many questions, human?"

"Yes."

"Let me give you a word of advice." He gave her a serious look and pulled her against him before brushing his hand down her hair. "Learn to curb your tongue when you are around my alpha. He does not like his mate to question him."

"I'm not good at keeping my mouth shut, Kane. Besides, I thought you said your alpha liked his women with spirit."

He gave her a look of frustration. "Just do as I say, human."

"Why? What will your alpha do to me if I don't?" She asked.

He didn't reply but there was a dark look in his eyes that set off alarm bells in her head. "How many mates has your leader killed?"

He kissed her hard on the mouth and gripped her head before staring at her. "Just keep your tongue quiet around him, girl."

He turned and stalked away.

Now, she wrapped her arms around her body and stared silently at the shifters and the two women. She hadn't told Adina or Ghita about her conversation with Kane and she decided she would pull the two women aside and tell the both of them. They needed to know.

A cold drop of rain fell on her arm and she looked up at

the sky. They were thick with dark clouds and the wind was picking up. Theran stared nervously at the sky before glancing at Hanif.

"He needs to hurry."

Hanif nodded. "I know. Do not worry, brother. Kane will find - "

He stopped and inhaled. A look of fright crossed his face as Theran turned to the right and inhaled as well. His eyes widened. "Hanif, do you smell - "

"Aye!" Hanif beckoned to the women. "Come, quickly!"

Ghita scurried to Theran as Hanif strode to Adina and took her arm. "Let's go." He glared at Reese. "Come, human. Right now!"

"What's going on?" Reese frowned at the two obviously frightened shifters. "Why are you so - "

There was a low, thick grunt and a large thicket of bushes to the right of her shivered violently.

"Reese! Run!" Theran suddenly shouted. Before she could even think of moving, a hand reached out from the bushes and seized her by the arm.

She shrieked in alarm and beat at it with her fist as the bushes parted and a giant of a man strode out from them. All of the air escaped from her lungs in a whispery little moan as Reese stared up and up. She had thought Kane was big, but the beast standing before her was at least twelve feet tall. His body was thick with muscle and covered in dark, black hair. He grinned at her with black and rotting teeth and his hand tightened around her arm.

"Human," it muttered delightedly.

The two shifters snarled in fear and bared their teeth at him as they pushed the two women behind them. They were starting to shift and the beast growled at them before raising the large, wooden club he held in his right hand.

"She is ours. Let her go," Theran snapped.

The beast laughed, a thick, rich sound that made all the hair on Reese's body stand up. "You dare tell a tagen what to do?" It replied.

"Give her to us and no harm will come to you," Theran growled.

"Watch your tongue, shifter." The tagen glared at him. "I can kill you and your brother easily."

Reese cried out when there was a loud crack of thunder and the skies opened up. Rain, hard and cold, poured down from the sky and instantly soaked her to the bone. The wind had become a howling moan and it whipped her wet hair against her cheeks.

Hanif shifted to his wolf form and whined. Theran glanced quickly at him before turning back to the creature holding Reese captive.

"You would be wise to disappear back into the cave you crawled from. The rains are upon us and I have never heard of a tagen being able to swim." Theran had to shout to be heard above the wind.

The tagen glanced up at the sky before back to Reese. He grinned again at her and she shuddered and yanked at the hand holding her. The tagen laughed and pulled her closer.

"I will make you a deal, shifters. You have no need for three women. Give this one to me and I will let you and the other shifter live. You can take your two females and find higher ground before you drown."

Hanif whined again and Theran swallowed before darting a quick glance at Reese. Her eyes widened with horror and her mouth dropped open at the look in his eyes.

"Theran, no!" She whispered.

"Reese, I am sorry," he moaned as he took Ghita's and

Adina's arms and began to back up, dragging them with him. "Truly, I am."

"Theran, you can't do this!" Adina shouted. She punched the shifter in the chest and he winced but didn't let her go.

"Listen to the shifter, human," the tagen rumbled. He looked Adina up and down with his black eyes. "Unless you would like to take her place?"

Adina paled and Reese, adrenaline humming through her veins, turned on the tagen and began to kick and punch him recklessly. He grunted and then bent and hoisted her over his shoulder like a rag doll. She screamed again and continued to pound on his back as he turned and disappeared into the forest.

CHAPTER 7

K ane, his shaggy head bent against the wind and the rain, loped into the trees. He had found a cave, one that was big enough and set high enough into the mountain to protect them from any flooding. Even better, it was deep enough that he could take the human to the back of it and fuck her without the others seeing. He was obsessed with the idea of taking her and he didn't know why. He –

He gave a startled growl when Theran and the others burst around a grove of trees. Theran was in his human form but Hanif had shifted and he was whining under his breath. Kane barked sharply at them and they skidded to a halt. The women were panting harshly, their hair and clothes plastered to their bodies. Kane felt a trickle of fear when he realized Reese was not with them.

"Did you find shelter?" Theran gasped out.

Kane shifted, wincing a little at the feel of the cold rain on his naked skin, and nodded. "Aye. Where is the big human?"

Theran glanced uneasily at Hanif and the trickle of fear in Kane's belly grew bigger. "We must get to the shelter, Kane."

"Tell me where she is, Theran."

"Kane, I had no choice. Please believe me."

"Theran!" Kane warned.

"There was a tagen," Theran whispered.

Kane strode forward and grabbed Theran's arm. "Is she dead?"

"No, but I…"

He trailed off and gave Kane a miserable look.

"Where is she?" Kane shook him.

Adina's body was trembling violent and she stuttered though blue lips, "The tagen took her. Theran traded her to save his own miserable life."

Theran winced. "I had no choice, Kane! We could not have defeated him and you know that. The tagen offered us a deal. He would take the woman and let us live."

When Kane didn't reply, Theran gave him a pleading look. "I am sorry, Kane. But you know it's for the best anyway. Once Dagon found out she was mad, he would - "

He stopped and glanced at Adina and Ghita before returning his gaze to Kane. "There is nothing we can do for the human now. Come, we must get the remaining females to the shelter before they freeze to death."

Kane dropped Theran's arm and pointed into the trees. "Go to the base of the mountain. There is a large moss-covered boulder. To the right of it is a path that will lead you to the cave. It is about thirty feet up and to the left of the path. You will find it easily enough."

"Are you not coming with us?" Theran frowned at him.

Kane shook his head. "No. I'm going after the human."

Theran gaped at him. "Have you gone mad, Kane? The tagen will kill you, if you can even find them. The rain will have washed their scent from the ground."

"I found the tagen's home when I was searching for our

shelter," Kane replied briefly. He flexed and shifted before running toward the mountain.

"Kane! This is madness!" Theran shouted after him. The shifter didn't stop and Theran gave Hanif a stunned look before tugging on the women's arms. "Let's go."

THE TAGEN DROPPED REESE TO THE HARD FLOOR OF THE CAVE and she scrambled backward until her back hit the wall. She winced at the pain and staggered to her feet. As the tagen moved to the front of the cave and knelt by the smoldering fire, she glanced around cautiously.

The tagen had carried her through the trees and up the side of the mountain. Although it was steep and the rocks were slippery, he was surprisingly nimble for his size. His home was set high in the mountain and he had climbed steadily. He had scaled the mountain, holding confidently with one hand to the slippery rock as he carried her higher. Eventually they reached a path but it was so narrow and slick, the tagen was forced to turn and inch his body along the face of the mountain. Hanging upside down over the tagen's back, Reese had stared at the sheer drop off the mountain and quit fighting him. Instead, she had clutched the beast's broad naked back and closed her eyes. She was certain they would fall to their deaths, and she had breathed a sigh of relief when the tagen had finally reached his home.

The cave was a big one and although dry, it was cold enough for her to see her breath. Her wet body trembling, she pushed her hair from her face and stared at the tagen's home. There were natural indentations in the side of the rock that the tagen used for shelves. They were filled with a variety of items including bottles, leather bags and crude cups and plates made of wood. She swallowed thickly as she stared at the top shelf. A human skull sat beside what she suspected was a leg bone and she pressed herself against the wall again, ignoring the pain in her back.

A nest of fur pelts was near the back of the cave and she peered past it into the depths of the cave. There was a tunnel veering off to the right, and a large wooden bucket sat at the entrance of the tunnel to what she assumed was a second section of the cave. The tagen grunted and she swung her terrified gaze back to him. A rocky ledge, about five feet wide, jutted out from the entrance to the cave. It was protected from the rain by an overlay of rock above it and the tagen had built up the fire until it was crackling loudly. He added a few more handfuls of dry grass to it and blew on it before hanging a large iron pot filled with water over the fire.

He turned and entered the cave, kicking off the leather boots he wore before pushing down his pants. Reese inhaled sharply and reached down to pry a rock from the floor of the cave. She held it in her hand, the weight of it comforting her. She stared at the tagen as he moved deeper into the cave and picked up another pair of pants piled neatly at the end of the pelts. His penis dangled between his legs and she moaned to herself at the size of it. He pulled on his pants and turned around to smile at her.

"Are you hungry, human?"

She shook her head and he frowned. "I am making dinner. You will eat it. You need your strength."

"For what?" She whispered as he eyed the rock in her hand.

"To mate with me, of course." He started toward her and she raised the rock threateningly.

"I'm not mating with you," she said.

"Of course you are. If you do not, what need do I have for

you? I might as well throw you off the side of the mountain and be done with it."

He was only a few feet away from her and she gripped the rock in her hand. "Stay away from me."

He gave her a look of amusement. "Do you believe you can defeat me with a rock? You may be big for a human but I am a tagen. You will only hurt yourself if you try and deny me what I want."

"I'd rather die," she spat at him.

He shrugged. "Deny me and you will."

He held out his hand. "Drop the rock and give me your hand, human. I wish to see you naked."

She shook her head and then hurled the rock at his head. He roared in surprise as it bounced off his jaw and she darted toward the mouth of the cave. She would most likely slip and fall to her death trying to climb down the mountain, but it was better than the alternative.

She had barely made it to the entrance of the cave when she felt the tagen's hand grip her hair. He yanked viciously on it, pulling her to the ground. She screamed and kicked at him as he knelt beside her and pinned her down with one large hand on her abdomen.

"Stop fighting me, human!" He snapped as he reached for the hem of Kane's shirt. One of her flailing fists caught him in the face and he growled with anger before slapping her hard across the face. The force of the blow bounced her head off the rocky floor and her ears began to ring. Her body went limp and she stared dazedly at the beast.

"There, that's better," he muttered to himself. He was reaching for her shirt again when a loud growling filled the cave. He turned and stared in surprise at the large shifter standing at the entrance of the cave.

It was the largest shifter he'd ever seen but the tagen felt no fear as he stood and stared at the wolf. "Lost your way, dog? Do you believe I will offer you shelter from the rains?"

The shifter's gaze dropped to the woman at his feet and the tagen grinned. "She was given to me as a gift by your mongrel brothers."

The shifter snarled at him and the tagen's grin widened. "Is she yours then? I will not give her up easily. The rains have come and I need something to keep me occupied. The human will be a perfect bed warmer and when the rains are done and I have no more use for her, I'll consider letting her go."

He glanced down at Reese. "Although let's be truthful. She is a big one, but she most likely will not survive sharing my bed. The last human I took to my bed only lasted for a couple of days before succumbing to her injuries."

He stared beyond the wolf at the rain pouring down. "The rains will last at least two weeks this time. I feel it in my bones. Do you think she will last a week, dog?"

The shifter howled and the tagen winced as the sound echoed in the cave. "Turn around and go back to your brothers, shifter. I am in a good mood and will let you live."

The wolf bared his teeth at him and crouched. The tagen grinned fiercely and started forward. "It has been many months since I've enjoyed a meal of shifter. I will make your woman watch as I skin your fur for my bed and tear the meat from your bones for our dinner."

The wolf howled again and leaped at the tagen.

THE HOWLING WAS LOUD AND DEAFENING. REESE SAT UP. HER head was ringing and she touched the back of her skull gingerly. She wasn't surprised to see blood on the tips of her fingers. What was happening? Where –

There was more howling and she staggered to her feet, her eyes wide and frightened. She turned around to see Kane with his fur coated in blood, attacking the tagen. The tagen was bleeding from various bite wounds on his arms and torso. He roared with anger and delivered a heavy blow to the side of Kane's body as the wolf sunk its teeth into his meaty thigh.

Kane howled with pain and danced away as the tagen stared in disbelief at the chunk of flesh missing from his leg. "You'll pay for that, dog!"

Reese backed toward the mouth of the cave as the tagen picked up his large, wooden club and swung it at Kane. Reese screamed as the shifter ducked and then ran forward. He launched himself at the tagen, hitting him directly in the chest as he tried to sink his teeth into the tagen's throat.

The tagen bellowed angrily. He dropped the club and wrapped his hands around Kane's upper body. He twisted and slammed the shifter into the hard wall. Kane howled with pain but dug his thick back claws into the tagen's abdomen and snapped viciously at the beast's face.

The tagen screamed as blood poured from the deep gouges in his stomach. He slammed Kane against the wall repeatedly before wrapping his meaty hands around Kane's neck and squeezing. The shifter twisted and squirmed as his eyes bulged from his head and his tongue hung limply from his mouth.

"Stupid dog!" The tagen hissed. "You should not have - "

"Hey! Big boy! I've got something for you!"

The tagen turned to see Reese standing directly behind him. Her entire body was shaking wildly and he had just enough time to register the iron pot in her hands before she threw the boiling water within it, on to his face and chest.

He shrieked with pain and dropped the shifter, clawing madly at his face and chest as large red blisters rose up on his skin. He screamed again, the skin tearing beneath his fingers as he staggered toward Reese. She scrambled backward toward the mouth of the cave as the tagen lurched forward. He opened his eyes and she gasped at the pain and horror within their black depths.

"I'll kill you!" It roared and swiped at her. She ducked away from its reach as the beast drove her back further. She was on the ledge now and she risked a quick glance behind her. Her stomach dropped as she looked over the ledge into the darkness below. She was trapped and if she was lucky, the tagen would simply heave her off the side of the mountain and kill her quickly.

"Mine now, human," the tagen moaned. His face and chest were covered in angry, red blisters and his one eye was puffed shut by the blister that had risen on his eyelid.

He darted forward and Reese twisted to the right as sharp barking echoed through the cave. Kane slammed his body against the tagen's. The tagen gave a bellow of fear as it teetered at the edge of the ledge. His large arms pin-wheeled madly, and his eye rolled to Reese in shock and surprise as he plunged over the side of the ledge into the darkness below.

Reese realized with horror that Kane's momentum was carrying him over the ledge as well and she threw herself at the shifter. She landed on his back with a heavy thud, pinning his lower half to the ground as his front half dangled over the ledge. She dug her hands into his thick fur and scrambled backward, dragging the heavy shifter with her. When he was on solid ground she rolled to her back, staring upward at the rock above her as her heart thudded painfully in her chest and she gasped for breath.

Kane whined and then shifted. He leaned over her, staring down anxiously at her face. "Human, are you all right?"

"I – yes," she panted. "I'm fine."

His hand stroked her hair and she reached up and patted his cheek with a hand that trembled badly. He kissed her on the mouth and then stood. He pulled her to her feet and led her into the cave and the pile of pelts. He made her sit down before running his hands over her body, feeling for broken bones.

"I'm okay," she assured him. He took her hands and she winced. She had burned them on the iron pot and he frowned at the large blister on the palm of the right one. He stood and walked naked to the shelves. Blood was running down his side and Reese staggered to her feet and stood beside him.

"You're bleeding!" She stared in alarm at the large, deep gash on his ribs.

"It's fine." He dismissed it. "It'll heal in a few hours."

"Are you – what?" She gave him a look of confusion.

"It will heal quickly," he said as he searched through the shelves. One of them held an assortment of glass jars and bottles and he scanned them quickly before grunting with satisfaction. He pulled a glass jar filled with a thick yellow fluid and unscrewed the lid. He sniffed it once and then dipped his hand into the jar and pulled out some of the mixture. It had the consistency of honey and he took Reese's hands and applied the salve to the blistered palm. It took away the sting almost immediately and she stared at him questioningly.

"What is this?"

"A healing salve," he grunted. He examined the swelling on her face where the tagen had hit her and applied the salve to her cheek. "Are you hurt anywhere else?"

"The back of my head is bleeding a bit."

He turned her around and parted her thick wet hair. She winced when he touched the back of her head and he squeezed her arm reassuringly. "It is only a scrape. He applied a bit of salve to it and she didn't object when he grabbed the hem of his wet shirt and pulled it from her body.

She stood shivering in her underwear as he applied more salve to the bruise on her back and then tugged her underwear down her legs. She stepped out of them and he left them on the floor as he picked up a pelt from the pile on the floor and wrapped it around her.

"Sit down, human." He pushed her onto the pile of pelts and she sat cross-legged, shaking wildly as the adrenaline faded from her body. She watched numbly as Kane crossed to the shelves again and rooted among them. He returned with a leather water bag and a handful of dried meat.

"Drink." He held the bag to her mouth and she drank a few mouthfuls of the cold water before he pulled it away. "Here, eat this." He held a piece of the meat in front of her mouth and she pulled her head back.

"What is it?"

"Deer," he said impatiently. "Eat it. It will help."

She opened her mouth and took the piece of meat he offered. She chewed at it. It was tough but good and she swallowed it obediently before taking another drink of water from the bag that Kane held to her mouth.

"Eat some more." He held another piece of meat in front of her and she shook her head.

"No, please. I can't. Not right now, okay?" She pleaded.

Despite the heavy pelt, her lips were blue and she was shaking wildly. She stared at the opening of the cave and at the heavy rain that poured down, and felt hysteria bubbling up in her chest. She had come very close to dying and she gave a choked, gasping moan as Kane watched her carefully.

74

"I'm sorry," she moaned again.

Without speaking he pulled a few of the pelts out from under her and unwrapped the pelt from her body. She whimpered when the cold air hit her naked body, and he pushed her down until she was lying on her side in the bed of pelts. He climbed in beside her, piled the pelts on top of them and gathered her against him. He tucked his arm under her and pushed her head down on to his chest. She wrapped her cold body around his warm one and clung to him as he rubbed her lower back.

"You're all right, human. Go to sleep now," he whispered.

She shook her head. "I'll never be able to sleep."

He didn't reply. His large hand continued to rub her back and her side and he made a soft soothing noise in the back of his throat. The heat of his body and the pelts warmed her quickly, and the steady beat of his heart beneath her ear was comforting. Her eyelids were suddenly incredibly heavy and she closed them, drifting into sleep as Kane held her close.

CHAPTER 8

W hen Kane woke, he was alone in the bed. He sat up and stared wildly around the cave. Reese was nowhere to be seen and he scrambled out of the pelts.

"Human! Where are you?" He shouted.

"Right here." Reese came out of the tunnel from the back of the cave. She was wrapped in a pelt and carrying a wooden bucket in her hand. He watched as she walked to the edge of the rock ledge and emptied it over the side before holding the bucket in the rain to rinse it. She emptied it again and carried it back into the cave, setting it down at the entrance to the tunnel.

"I had to pee," she said as her face coloured with embarrassment.

He walked to the edge of ledge. He urinated off the side of it and she rolled her eyes. "Show off," she muttered as he turned around and grinned at her.

"What time do you think it is?" She squinted at the sky but with the rain and the dark clouds, it was impossible to tell what time of the day it was.

He shrugged. "Late."

She crouched beside the fire. It had gone out while they slept and she poked at it with a stick. "Do you know how to start a fire?" She was shivering with the cold and she bunched the pelt around her as she sifted through the ashes.

He shook his head. "No."

He was lying. He could start a fire, but he didn't want a fire to keep her warm. He wanted her to depend on him for warmth, to be forced to lie with him in that nest of pelts while he explored every inch of her naked body and brought her pleasure.

She sighed. "I don't either. Serves me right for getting kicked out of Girl Guides."

"Girl Guides?" He raised his eyebrow at her.

She shook her head. "Never mind."

She walked back into the cave and examined the shelves as Kane moved behind her.

"How do you feel, human?"

"Fine." She turned and smiled weakly at him. "Much better, in fact."

He picked up her hand and examined the blister on it. It was nearly healed and she smiled again. "I don't know what's in that healing salve but I could make a fortune selling it in my world."

He frowned at her and she blushed as she realized her mistake. "I mean - this world?"

He didn't reply and she hurried on. "Is your side okay?"

He nodded. "Aye. It's healed completely."

"How is that possible?" She asked.

He shrugged. "Shifters heal quickly."

"Oh." She glanced around nervously. "How long until the rains stop?"

"Days, maybe weeks."

"Do you think Adina and the others found shelter?"

He nodded. "Aye, I told them where the shelter was before I came after you."

"Thank you," she whispered. "Thank you for coming after me and – and risking your life to save mine. I really appreciate it."

He nodded and stepped closer. He was still naked and she was acutely aware of the way his cock was hardening. She glanced down at it, a trickle of nervousness running down her spine at the size of it, and licked her lips.

He groaned at the sight of her tongue and she cleared her throat. "So, um what do we do now?"

He brushed his thumb along her mouth and then probed at the seam of it. "Open your mouth, human."

She shook her head and he cupped the back of her neck, holding her head still as he pushed at her lips again with his thumb. "Open your mouth."

She moaned and parted her lips. He pushed his thumb into her mouth and rested it against her tongue. "Suck."

She sucked on his thumb and his eyes darkened at the way her lips pursed around him. He made her keep sucking for a few minutes, rubbing his thumb against her tongue before he pulled it free.

"Come with me." He took her hand and led her to the pelts.

"What – what are we doing?" She whispered.

"You're going to show your appreciation to me for saving your life." He smiled at her.

"I – what? I said thank you!" She replied indignantly.

"Aye, and a very sweet thank you it was," he replied as he pulled her onto the pile of pelts.

"Take this off." He tugged at the top of the pelt she had wrapped around her naked body.

"I'll be too cold," she replied.

"Not for long." He grinned at her and tugged again on it. "Take it off, human."

She swallowed and let the pelt drop to the floor, her eyes closing with embarrassment as he scanned her up and down.

"So lovely," he whispered. Her eyes popped open with surprise when she felt his hands on her shoulders.

He pushed lightly. "On your knees, human. Show me your gratefulness."

She sank to her knees in the soft pelts and stared wide-eyed at his cock. It had hardened fully and he was stroking it with one hand as his other hand cupped the back of her neck and pulled her toward the wide head of his cock.

"Go on, girl. Show me," he whispered.

Reese stared at his cock. Her pussy was so wet she could feel moisture dripping down her thighs and her nipples were hard as glass. He had barely touched her and she was close to coming.

Get up! Her mind screamed at her. *Get up and slap the arrogant shifter in the face. Just because he saved your life doesn't mean you have to give him a blowjob! Get off your knees for God's sake!*

That was very true, she decided. She didn't have to suck his cock. Of course, he had saved her life and she really was grateful to him. What was the harm in showing him how grateful? He would definitely like it and if her throbbing pussy was any indication she would like it as well.

Reese! What are you thinking? Don't even -

She leaned forward and took the head of his cock into her mouth, effectively silencing her inner voice, as he groaned and his hand tightened in her hair.

"Good girl," he said. "Look at me, human."

She lifted her gaze to his face as she took more of his cock into her mouth.

"That's my good girl." He smiled at her. "Keep those beautiful eyes on my face while you suck my cock."

He stroked her hair back from her face as she sucked hard on his cock. Her tongue ran along the thick vein on the underside and he moaned with pleasure. Her lips widened around his width as she struggled to take him deeper into her.

Reese stared up at Kane as he continued to stroke her hair. She wrapped her fingers around the base of his cock and squeezed as her mouth slid back and forth over his large cock. It was so big she could barely breathe, but the string of compliments spilling from his mouth and the way his eyes glittered as she sucked made her eager to continue. She circled her tongue around the head of his cock before sucking hard on it. He moaned and thrust his hips into her mouth, cupping the back of her head to keep it steady.

"Keep looking at me, human," he whispered. She stared up at him as she pumped the base of his cock with her hand, tightening her fingers around his erection as he thrust back and forth into her mouth.

"God, human. You are so good at this," he moaned. His cock was swelling in her mouth and she sucked eagerly. She wanted to taste him on her tongue. She wanted to know what it was like to feel him coming in her mouth, and she increased the pressure of her mouth and hand.

He groaned and then abruptly pulled away from her. She pitched forward on to her hands, gasping in surprise as he stepped around her and pulled apart her thighs. He knelt between them and she twisted her head around to stare at him.

"Kane, why did you – ohh!" She squealed with pleasure

when his large hand cupped her pussy and his fingers rubbed her clit. She squirmed on his hand, pressing herself down on to it as he stroked her clit.

"Oh! Oh my God!" She shouted before climaxing hard all over his hand. Her legs weak and her body trembling wildly, she started to collapse on the soft pelts. Kane grabbed her hips and hauled her upward.

"On your hands and knees, girl," he growled.

She moaned when she felt his cock pressing between her legs. Suddenly nervous, she looked behind her. "Kane, you said you would be gentle."

He nodded and rubbed her ass reassuringly. "I will be. Just relax, human."

"Do you promise?" She whispered as his cock probed at her opening.

"I promise," he said. He rubbed her ass again. "Spread your legs for me, human."

She swallowed and spread her legs. He moaned appreciatively and held her hips as he eased the head of his cock into her tight opening. She made a soft cry of nervousness, and he leaned over her and licked between her shoulder blades as his hand reached beneath her and cupped her breast. He pulled on her nipple and she arched her back and pushed her ass against him. His cock slid further into her and she cried out with pleasure as he stretched her tight walls.

He groaned and his fingers dug into her hips as he paused and waited. "Are you all right, girl?"

"Yes," she moaned. "Please, Kane."

Slowly he pushed into her, stretching and easing her open. Her pussy fit around his cock like a smooth, warm glove and he groaned again when she pushed back against him.

"It feels so good, Kane," she whispered.

He stroked her ass in reply and she wiggled against him. He inhaled harshly and pushed fully into her. She stiffened and cried out with shock.

"Have I hurt you?" He rasped out.

She shook her head. "No, it feels good. I swear it, Kane."

He moved tentatively in her and she arched her back again and reached back to hold his wrist. He plunged in and out of her, his cock moving in long, languid strokes, as she moaned and panted with pleasure.

She was so tight, so wet, that Kane could feel his cock swelling after only a few minutes. He thrust faster, his hand tightening on her breast as she met him stroke for stroke. When he was close to coming, he released her breast and reached between her legs. He pressed his fingers between her wet lips and stroked her swollen clit. She screamed, the sound echoing in the cave, and came wildly. He cried out when her pussy tightened with excruciating pleasure around his cock. Grunting, he plunged in and out until he came hard, sending his warm seed deep within her.

She collapsed on the pelts and he dropped down beside her, breathing harshly as she panted and shook next to him. He stroked her back, it was damp with sweat, and then helped her climb beneath the pelts. She curled on her side and he spooned her. She relaxed against him and he turned her head and kissed her on the mouth, sliding his tongue between her lips to stroke hers. She returned his kiss, her hand squeezing his.

"Go to sleep, human," he whispered.

She nodded and closed her eyes. It didn't take long for her to drift into sleep and he eased away from her warm body. He typically shifted to his wolf form for sleeping and she would be warm enough with the pelts.

She frowned in her sleep and scooted her body backward, seeking his heat. He hesitated and then slipped back under the furs and molded his body to hers again. He would stay in his human form for a while longer. It was pleasant enough to feel her soft, naked skin against his. He cupped her breast, rested his face against the back of her neck and closed his eyes.

CHAPTER 9

Reese sighed and stared out the entrance of the cave. The rain poured steadily down. As she listened to the thunder and watched the lightning flash across the sky in bright sheets of light, she finally understood what Adina was talking about. She doubted that even the shifters would have survived the torrential rains.

She had woken this morning to find herself alone in the nest of pelts. Kane had shifted back to his wolf form and was sitting near the edge of the cave. She had given him a nervous hello and he had barked in reply but had not shifted to his human form. She had helped herself to some of the dried meat and drank some more water while Kane had stared silently out the cave entrance. That was hours ago and she was about ready to throw herself off the ledge of the cave from sheer boredom. She had asked Kane to shift but he had chuffed in disagreement before closing his eyes and dozing.

It was cold in the cave and she had tried unsuccessfully to start the fire before giving up in disgust. She had paced back and forth, waving her arms and stomping her feet but even that had done little to warm her. Finally, she had crawled back into the nest of pelts and piled them high until she could no longer feel the chill of the cave or see the sleeping body of Kane.

Now, she stared up at the ceiling of the cave and sighed restlessly. If she had to go the next two weeks like this, she would go mad. If Kane didn't start to be better company she would risk the rains and try and find the other shelter.

Don't be daft, girl. You'll die trying to get down from this hole in the mountain.

Completely true but she had always been a social and chatty person. Kane completely ignoring her was driving her crazy. She was more bothered by his silence than she wanted to admit. She didn't think she could take two weeks of it.

Be honest. You're not just a little bit hurt that he's already lost interest in having sex with you? Is it his lack of talking or his lack of fucking that's bothering you?

She tamped the voice down grimly and twisted under the pelts. What did she care if Kane didn't want to fuck her again? He had told her before that she was an experiment. He wanted to fuck a human, he did, and that was that. What did she think would happen? Her chubby body and totally awkward approach to sex would be a turn on for him? She sighed and twisted to her other side. She had slept with exactly three men before the shifter and only one of them had made her come. Hell, Kane was only the second guy she had given a blowjob to and while he had seemed to enjoy it at the time, his lack of interest now was a surprisingly hard blow to her ego.

He said you were good at it, remember?

She snorted in disgust. She might not have much experience but she was fairly certain that most men would say anything to keep a woman sucking their dick, regardless of how talented she was at it. She blew her breath out angrily, wishing for the first time that she had more experience with seducing the opposite sex.

She sat up abruptly and stared across the cave at Kane. He was still in his wolf form and sleeping. His long tail was curled around his body and his large head was resting on his front paws. She thought back to how it had felt when he had touched her clit. The roughness and surety of his fingers had sent her rocketing into a near-instant climax and she was shocked by it. It normally took her forever to climax even with her own hand, but there was something about the large shifter that kept her seemingly on the edge of arousal all the time.

Her pulse sped up and her core began to ache with a sweet, maddening throb as she relived the way he had pushed her to her knees and guided her mouth to his cock. Her reaction to Kane's caveman behaviour was a complete mystery to her.

Still, she couldn't deny that she did like it. Her nipples hardened beneath the pelt as she remembered the way Kane had knelt behind her and the way her pussy had so eagerly accepted his thick, hard shaft. Her breathing was growing shallow and the ache between her thighs grew until she considered finding her own relief from it. The shifter was sleeping, he wouldn't –

She swallowed nervously when Kane lifted his head and inhaled before looking at her. His eyes gleamed in the dim light and he stood and stretched before shifting to his human form. Without speaking, he crossed the cave and climbed under the pelts beside her.

His hand cupped her breast through the pelt that was wrapped around her and he made a snort of displeasure before pushing the pelt to her waist. He reached for her naked breast and she pushed his hand away nervously.

"What are you doing?"

"You want me," he replied. He dipped his head and sucked on her neck, increasing the pressure until there was a dark, red mark on her neck.

"Stop that," she whispered. "I – I don't want you."

He laughed. "This again, human? Stop lying to yourself. I can smell your need. It fills the entire cave."

She blushed as his hand cupped her breast and squeezed. "Lie back, human."

"Kane, I - "

"Lie back." He pushed her onto her back and yanked the pelt from her body. He tossed it to the side before pushing the pelts on top of her down to her knees. He studied her naked body and she cleared her throat.

"I'm not having sex with you, Kane."

"Why not?"

"You've spent the entire day ignoring me, and I'm not going to just spread my legs and let you fuck me because you think you can smell my – my desire for you. It's not for you. I was thinking of someone else," she said.

He grinned at her. "You're funny, human."

He pinched her nipple and his grin widened at her soft gasp before he took her hand and guided it to his semi-erect cock.

"Rub it," he demanded.

She glared at him even as her fingers were tightening around him. He groaned his approval when she stroked him hard and he bent his head to kiss her. He probed at her warm mouth with his tongue until she was moaning.

"Tell me you want to mate with me, human." He rubbed his thumb across her bottom lip.

"I want to mate with you," she whispered.

She was hypnotized by the look of dark need in his eyes

and when his hand dropped to her pussy, she widened her legs immediately. He stroked her clit for a few minutes before dipping one finger into her, gauging her wetness and her need.

"Do you want me to fuck you?" He whispered before sucking on her neck again.

She nodded, her hand tightening around his cock, as he trailed kisses down to her breasts. He sucked on one hard nipple and her back arched helplessly.

"Say it, human." He gave her a wolfish grin.

"I – I want you to fuck me," she moaned.

"Good girl," he murmured.

He laid on his back and urged her to climb on top of him. She hesitated. It might be dim in the cave but she had a feeling his eyesight was much better than hers, even in his human form. He would see all of her wobbly parts and the stretch marks on her belly.

"No, Kane. I want you on top of me," she protested weakly as he gripped her by her arms and moved her until she was straddling his pelvis.

He shook his head. "Not this time, human."

He reached up and cupped both of her heavy breasts, lifting and kneading them until she was rocking her pelvis against him in response. He rubbed her nipples and she moaned, the sound echoing in the cave.

"Do you like that?" He rubbed her nipples again and she nodded frantically, arching her back so that more of her breasts filled his hands.

"I like how easily I can turn you on," he said candidly as he stroked and rubbed her breasts. "I've never mated with someone as responsive as you. Are you like this with every male you mate with?"

She could feel a blush rising in her cheeks and she looked

away in embarrassment. His hard fingers gripped her chin and forced her to look at him. "Are you, human?"

She shook her head. "No." She hesitated and then said, "I don't normally come when I'm um, mating, with someone."

"Why not?"

"I don't know. Just nervous I guess and the other males – men – I've slept with said I need more time to uh, warm up."

He frowned at her in confusion. "Warm up?"

"You know, get ready for sex, um, mating." She blushed again.

"Did they not sweet talk you?" He raised his eyebrow at her and she was helpless to stop the giggles from escaping.

"Yes, they sweet talked me."

He sat up abruptly and curved one large arm around her ample waist. He lifted her with little effort and she squealed with surprise when he impaled her on his large cock. He released her waist and she sunk down onto his cock fully, gravity doing all of the work as she stared wide-eyed at him.

As she stretched around his thick length, he cupped her face and stared at her. "You have very pretty eyes, human. I have never seen eyes this colour before. I like them."

"Thank you," she whispered distractedly. Her pussy was still adjusting to Kane's cock and she wiggled a bit, making him inhale sharply.

"You're pretty," he said abruptly. "Your skin is soft and your hair smells good."

She blinked at him as he stroked her belly before looking down to where their bodies were connected. She wanted him to move and she rocked against him in an inviting way, but he continued to talk. "Your breasts are nice and heavy, and I like how big your nipples get when I suck on them. Your pussy is very tight. I like the way it clings to me."

"Kane, what – what are you doing?" She asked.

He stared at her. "I'm sweet talking you."

She gaped at him in surprise and then giggled. Her entire body shook and he groaned when she inadvertently tightened around him. He cocked his head at her. "What's so funny, human? Did you not say a human female likes to be sweet talked?"

"I – yes," she snickered. "But the sweet talking usually happens before you put your dick in her."

"Oh."

He leaned back on his elbows and grinned at her. "Enough sweet talking. Go on, human. Fuck me."

"What?" She stared nervously at him.

He arched his eyebrow at her again. "Fuck me."

She licked her lips and feeling awkward and unsure, raised herself up and down slightly. His breath hissed out between his teeth and he made a low growling noise.

"Do you – does that feel good?" She asked.

He nodded. "Keep going."

She rose up and down on his cock, keeping her movements slow and easy. She had always balked at being on top with other men, always worried about her weight and about how much she jiggled. When Kane's eyes dropped to her breasts, she crossed her arms over them nervously.

He frowned and pulled her arms away before reclining on his elbows again. "Don't cover your breasts, human. I want to see them."

"All right." She moved slowly again, bracing herself on her knees, and watched as Kane's eyes began to lighten.

"Harder," he suddenly demanded.

"I – I don't want to hurt you," she muttered.

He snorted with amusement. "You're not going to break it, human."

"I'm too heavy." She gave him a look of embarrassment and he rolled his eyes.

"No, you're not," he replied impatiently. He reached out and lazily tweaked one hard nipple. She gasped and jerked against him and he grinned at her.

"Fuck me," he said again.

She bit her bottom lip and braced her hands against his chest before rocking against his cock. He groaned his approval and she stared into his eyes as she moved harder and faster.

"Good girl," he whispered. He moved his hand to her clit and rubbed. She made a soft squeak of surprise and jerked against him. He groaned with need, and circled and pressed against her clit. The pleasure was flowing through her now and she lost the last of her self-consciousness. Arching her back and moaning, she rode him hard, bouncing on his cock enthusiastically as her pulse pounded in her ears.

Kane was staring at her jiggling breasts but instead of feeling self-conscious another strong thread of pleasure flooded through her. She cupped her breasts and pulled on her nipples. She smiled when his eyes turned green and glowed brightly.

"I like that, human. Do it again," he demanded.

"Reese," she whispered.

He paused and then said, "Reese."

Hearing her name in his low and husky voice sent tingles of pleasure down her spine, and she cupped her breasts again and pinched her nipples. She gasped and his nostrils flared before he sat up, pushed her hands away and took one nipple into his mouth. He sucked at it and she threaded her fingers through his hair and gripped him firmly before staring up at the ceiling of the cave.

As she rocked and thrust against him, he planted rough

nips and bites on her chest and neck. She gasped sharply at a particularly hard one and he gave her a worried look.

"I'm sorry, human. Have I hurt you?"

She shook her head. "No."

He dipped his head to place a gentle kiss on her collarbone. She moaned and he gathered her closer to him until her breasts were pressed against his chest, and thrust into her. She cried out with pleasure and clung to him as he plunged in and out of her.

When he slipped his hand between their bodies and pinched her clit, her entire body stiffened and she shrieked his name as she came wildly around his cock. He groaned and arched into her. His cock swelled as she tightened around him before he climaxed deep inside of her.

She collapsed against him, panting harshly. He rolled her onto her side before covering her with the pelts. He started to ease out from under them and she grabbed his arm.

"Please don't shift, Kane," she whispered. "Stay here with me."

He nodded and relaxed beside her. She curled her body into his and he stroked her back as she rested her head on his chest.

CHAPTER 10

A few hours later, Kane watched as Reese slid out from under the pelts. She gave him a clear look of disappointment before picking up the wooden bucket and disappearing further into the tunnel at the back of the cave.

He rested his head on his paws and stared moodily out the entrance of the cave at the rain that was pouring down. He wanted the human again. He had thought that fucking the human once would be enough to quench his desire, and it disturbed him that his need for her still pulsed through him even after he had taken her twice.

He didn't want to lust after the human. Forgetting that generally speaking, he hated humans, Dagon would most likely take her as his mate. If, that was, she was able to keep her mouth closed around him. Her madness wasn't readily apparent, but it was there, lurking under the surface. Dagon was smart. He would sense her madness quickly if she did not learn to hide it better.

Perhaps it would be better if she didn't hide the madness. Dagon will not choose her and then you'd be free to take her as your own. You could –

He stood and shook himself before circling and lying down again. He had no desire to be mated to a female of his own kind, let alone the large human.

Reese returned from the tunnel and emptied the bucket off the ledge before rinsing it and setting it down. One section of the ledge wasn't covered by rock and she walked toward it and held out her hand out, flinching a little at the feel of the cold rain. Without looking at him, she walked back into the cave and began to rummage through the shelves. In a jar she found a few bars of white material and she lifted one out and sniffed it cautiously.

"Is this – is this soap?"

She carried it to the ledge and held it out in the rain before rubbing it between her fingers. She gave a soft squeal of delight. "It is!"

She glanced back at him, obviously indecisive about something before turning away. He watched curiously as she took a deep breath and then dropped the heavy pelt wrapped around her. At the sight of her large, firm ass and smooth back, lust swept through him and he sat up and watched her intently with glowing, green eyes. Reese took another deep breath, hesitated a moment longer and then stepped out into the rain.

"Oh, oh, oh! Fuck, that's cold!" She cried out as her skin tightened and broke out into goose bumps. The rain soaked her hair and skin immediately and dripping and shivering with the cold, she stepped back out of the rain and rubbed the soap over her hair. She washed her hair quickly and then stepped into the downpour as he watched with amusement.

"Fuck!" She cried again. She panted harshly as she bent and ran her fingers through her long hair, rinsing the soap from the dark strands. Soapy water pooled at her feet and she straightened before beginning to wash her body quickly. As he watched her lips turn blue he wondered if she was regretting her decision. She ran the soap over her throat and chest, and he wondered why she briefly winced.

"Fuck, fuck, fuck," she stuttered through trembling lips as she ran the soap over her arm. He walked up behind her and she screamed when his large arms circled around her and he pressed his chest against her naked back.

"What are you doing, human?"

"Sh-showering," she said through chattering teeth. "I smell."

He laughed. "You don't."

"I do," she insisted as he took the soap from her numb fingers. "Give that back."

"Be quiet," he instructed. He washed her other arm and then lathered the soap between his hands before handing it to her. "Hold this."

She took it, her entire body shaking and trembling with cold, and he quickly washed her breasts and abdomen before washing her back and ass. He knelt and cleaned her legs before standing and taking the soap from her. He lathered his hands again and pushed at her thighs.

"Open your legs, human."

She parted her thighs and he slipped his hand between them, cupping her sex before beginning to rub his hand over it. He washed her quickly and then cupped water from the rain in his hand and rinsed her sex clean.

He pulled her back from the ledge and wrapped a pelt around her shivering body. He stared at her pale skin before squeezing the water from her hair. "Better?"

She nodded. Her lips were blue and she was trembling violently but she smiled gamely at him. "Are you going to shower?"

"Do I smell?"

She blushed. "Actually, yeah. A little."

He grinned and stepped out into the rain. She watched as he quickly soaped his naked body before rinsing clean and stepping back into the cave. Even his skin was covered in goose bumps and she handed him a pelt from the bed.

He dried his body and dropped the pelt to the floor of the cave before taking her by the arm and leading her to the nest of furs. She dropped the damp pelt and crawled between the dry ones. She breathed an audible sigh of relief when he crawled in beside her. She wrapped herself around him like a vine and he grunted when she rested her cold feet on his calves.

"Is being clean worth this, human?" He asked gruffly.

She nodded. "Y-yes."

He studied her carefully in the dim light. "Your lips are blue. How do you humans survive in the winter? You're so fragile."

"We normally have clothes and fire to keep us warm," she replied.

He felt a moment of guilt and briefly considered building up the fire before he bent his head and kissed her cold mouth. She sighed and returned his kiss, opening her mouth so he could slide his tongue between her cold lips.

He cupped her breast. Her nipple was a hard pearl against his palm and she moaned before arching her back. He dipped his head to kiss her chest and paused, his hand tightening on her breast.

"What's wrong?" She murmured.

"I hurt you."

Anger and a bit of shame flooded through him. His sharp teeth had left her skin bruised. He traced the bruising and bite marks on her chest and throat. "Why did you not tell me I was hurting you?"

She shrugged. "It didn't hurt at the time."

He scowled and slipped out from the pelts, returning with the jar of salve. He rubbed the thick salve on to her chest before turning her and rubbing more salve into the healing bruise on her back. When he was done he set the jar down and pulled her into his embrace. He rubbed her lower back as she stared up at him.

He didn't care what she said, humans were fragile and he would have to be more careful the next time he took her. Her soft skin could not handle his roughness. A frown crossed his face as he pictured the way she would look when Dagon was done mating with her. His alpha wouldn't care about her fragility. He would take her as roughly as he took his shifter mates, and he would feel no remorse about bruising or hurting her. His arms tightened around her and she squirmed in his grip.

"Kane? Why are you angry?" She asked.

He shook his head. "I'm not. Go to sleep."

"I just woke up. I'm not tired," she replied.

He scowled at her. "Go to sleep, human. You need your rest."

"I'm not tired," she repeated stubbornly.

She ignored his sigh of annoyance and stared up at the ceiling of the cave. After a few moments, she said, "Do you have any siblings?"

"No."

"Is that unusual? You guys live in packs, right? Wouldn't you normally have big families?" She asked hesitantly.

"My parents died when I was a boy," he said gruffly.

"I'm sorry," she replied sincerely. "I know what it's like to lose your mom and dad. My parents died less than a year ago."

He didn't reply and she cleared her throat nervously. "Who raised you after your parents died?"

"I have other family in the pack. My father's siblings. They all kept an eye on me."

"It must have been lonely for you."

He hesitated. "I have a cousin – Radek. He is like a brother to me."

"That's good," she replied. "You must miss your parents though. I miss mine terribly. I wasn't super close to my dad. I made a lot of choices he didn't approve of but I was really close with my mom. Still, I miss them both equally. Isn't that strange?"

"How did they die?" He asked suddenly.

"In a car accident," she replied without thinking.

He frowned at her. "A car?"

She gave him a nervous look and shook her head. "Never mind. They just – there was an accident and they died."

"How did your parents die?" She hurried on.

"The humans hunted them down and slaughtered them like dogs," he said shortly. He expected that would quiet her tongue and he grunted with surprise when she sat up and stared at him.

"Oh my God! That's terrible. I'm so sorry. No wonder you hate us." She patted his broad shoulder timidly. "Do – do most humans hunt shifters?"

The pelts had slid to her waist but she either didn't notice or didn't remember her nakedness, and he eyed her naked breasts quickly before shaking his head. "No. Back then, we had hardly anything to do with humans. It's only in the last ten years or so that we've started to openly interact with them. Not that shifters haven't been fucking humans for years, they have, but until recent years they would never have brought them into their packs."

"Why did the humans kill your parents?"

"They thought my parents were taking their cattle."

"Were they?" She asked bluntly.

"No. We enjoy hunting. There's no enjoyment in hunting dumb, defenseless cows."

"I'm surprised they were able to – to kill your parents. You're so large and, well, scary."

"There were many humans hunting them," he said briefly. He gave her a considering look. "Do I scare you, human?"

She shook her head. "No. I don't scare easily though, never have. My dad said it was because I didn't have a lick of sense, but my mom always said I was just tough as nails."

A rueful smile crossed her lips. "If she could see me now, she'd probably take that back."

"What do you mean?" He asked.

She shrugged. "I'm afraid."

He felt an odd tingle of dismay go through him. "You said you weren't scared of me."

"I'm not afraid of you, Kane."

She abruptly fell silent and stared moodily out the entrance of the cave before raising her knees and resting her arms on them.

"What are you afraid of?"

He blinked in surprise at the sound of his voice. Why had he asked that? Why would he care what the human was afraid of?

He waited patiently for her answer and scowled when she said, "It doesn't matter. You're right, Kane. I should get some more sleep."

Before she could lie down he had sat up and gripped her arm. "Tell me what you're afraid of, human."

"I have a name!" She said. "How would you like it if I just referred to you as shifter?"

He shrugged. "I don't care what you call me."

He was lying. He liked how his name sounded coming from her mouth. He especially liked how she moaned his name when he was inside of her. His groin stirred. He took another quick peek at her breasts before squeezing her arm.

"What are you afraid of?"

She made a grunt of frustration and he stared, a little amused, at the frown lines that appeared between her brows. He wanted to touch them with his fingers, to try and smooth them away but he resisted as she yanked again at his grip.

"Tell me," he ordered.

"Oh for God's sake!" She snapped. "I'm afraid of freezing to death. I'm afraid that somehow I'll end up back at that awful slave house with that sadistic warden. I was nearly killed by a flower for fuck's sake so now I'm afraid of flowers. I'm afraid of – of tagens and starving to death because I don't know what's edible and what's poisonous in this world. I'm afraid of being mated to your damn alpha and having him kill me like he did his last mate, and I'm so fucking tired of being afraid all the time!"

She stopped, breathing heavily and staring wide-eyed at him as her body trembled wildly. He put his arm around her. "I will not let any harm come to you, human."

She snorted derisively. "You and I both know that I'm going to die in this world, Kane. And it will be a horrible and painful death."

He flinched a little as she tried to shrug free of his grip. His arm tightened around her and she sighed. "I really, really miss coffee and indoor plumbing, and just getting in my car and driving somewhere. Oh, and bubble baths. God, I'd sell my soul for a bubble bath right now."

She was shivering violently from the cold and he made her lie back with him in the pelts. He drew the covers up around them and tugged her against his warm chest. She resisted but he cupped the back of her neck and pulled her against him. She rested her head against his chest as he stroked her bare back.

"What's a bubble bath?"

She laughed and a thread of relief went through him at the sound of it.

"It's – well – you sit in a tub of warm water and you pour this liquid in that turns to bubbles when the water hits it."

He was silent for a moment. "What is coffee?"

"It's a type of bean that you grind up and add to hot water to flavour the water. It gives you energy."

"And a car?"

She sighed. "It's a machine that moves really quickly. It runs on a flammable liquid called gasoline. You drive the car and it can go long distances in a very short amount of time."

Reese glanced up at Kane. He was giving her a careful look that she recognized well. He thought she was mad, just like everyone else in this world. She really needed to stop talking about her own world.

"How big are these cars?" He asked. His tone was one that suggested he would humour the crazy person for a little while longer, and she shook her head in defeat.

"Never mind, Kane. There is no such thing as coffee or cars or bubble baths. I'm – I'm just being crazy again."

She turned away from him and curled up on to her side. She was feeling lonely and incredibly sorry for herself and she was dismayed to realize she was close to tears. She blinked rapidly but the tears slipped down her cheeks anyway. Kane had curled up behind her and he cupped her head and turned her face toward his.

"Are you crying, human?"

"No," she sobbed.

He rubbed the moisture from her cheeks and showed it to her. "Why are you crying?"

"Because – because I'm homesick, and because you think I'm crazy."

"Please stop crying."

"Sure, I'll get right on that." She pulled her head away and buried it in her arms. He watched as she shook with the force of her sobs and he touched her back.

"Stop crying, human."

She lifted her head long enough to glare at him. "Don't female shifters ever cry?"

She buried her head back in her arms before he could reply.

Kane stared helplessly at her back. Females of his kind did cry, some of them annoyingly so, but seeing the large human cry was upsetting him for some strange reason. It was because he had never seen her crying before, he decided abruptly. She was tough, one just had to look at the bruise on her back and the multiple times she had come close to dying without breaking into hysterical sobbing, to know that.

Of course, crying now simply because he thought her to be mad was strange but he didn't have time to dwell on it. He just wanted her to stop her crying. It was making him feel helpless and weak and he didn't like that.

He thought about demanding she stop crying again and perhaps giving her a slap to the ass. He shook his head. He was a fool. He may have limited experience with crying women - hell zero experience, really - but he had observed how his pack brothers had handled their crying females. He had rolled his eyes with derision at the time and vowed never to act so foolishly but now, desperate to stop her sobbing, he was willing to try it.

He scooted closer and rubbed her back. "Don't cry,

human. You – you hide your madness well. It's only because you talk so much that others know of your madness. You talk too much. You should hold your tongue and then you will appear normal."

She turned to look at him, her eyes wide and her mouth slightly ajar, and he smiled at her. "Do you feel better now, human? Will you stop your crying?"

To his utter dismay she burst into even louder sobs and wiggled away from his warmth.

"Human, what - "

"Shut up, Kane. Okay? Just – just leave me alone. I know you want to shift anyway, so just go ahead and do it. Since you find my talking so annoying, I promise I'll do my best to keep my damn mouth shut."

"That isn't what I meant, human," he protested. "I meant - "

"I know exactly what you meant." She glared at him and then shoved him hard in the chest. "Get out of the bed. I want to be alone and you're happier in your wolf form, anyway. Leave me alone!"

He blinked in surprise and confusion but slid out from under the pelts. She turned her back and yanked the heavy furs over her head, hiding herself completely from his view. Shaking his head, he shifted to his wolf form and lay down a few feet away from her. He stared silently at her for a few minutes before closing his eyes.

CHAPTER 11

K ane stared at the human through half-closed eyes. It was nearly two days and she hadn't spoken a single word to him. He had shifted to his human form yesterday afternoon. He hoped that it would draw her out, but she hadn't even looked at him. She spent most of her time sitting at the entrance of the cave and staring at the rain, or lying in the furs with her back turned to him.

He chuffed and sat up when she walked by him, but she ignored him before climbing back into the pelts. He barked his annoyance, the sound echoing in the cave. She turned her back and pulled the furs over her head.

He growled and stood before circling and collapsing back on the floor of the cave. He hated to admit it but he missed the sound of her voice. He had grown used to both her talking and the way she looked at him. The scent of her desire for him had disappeared completely and it bothered him. He still wanted her, more now than ever, and it was driving him crazy that she no longer wanted him. He chuffed again and stared at the rain. It was still pouring down and tonight was the coldest night yet. Even he was feeling the chill.

Reese listened to the large shifter chuffing and wrapped her arms around her shivering body. It was freezing in the cave and as night approached, it would only get colder. She considered inviting Kane to join her in the bed and then snorted to herself. She would rather freeze than take the shifter back into her bed.

She sighed and pulled the furs more tightly around her. She knew exactly how childish she was acting and although she was embarrassed by it, she couldn't seem to stop. Kane's words had hurt her feelings and she didn't have a clue why. There was nothing happening between them other than his need to experiment with having sex with a human, so why did it bother her that he thought she talked too much? Hell, she did talk too much. Always had and always would.

She sighed again and closed her eyes. The cold and relentless rain, homesickness, fear, and her anger at Kane had combined to leave her feeling tired and weak. She was sleeping too much and using it as a way to hide from her problems, but what did it matter? She was just going to die in this miserable world anyway.

WHEN SHE WOKE, SHE HAD NO IDEA HOW LONG SHE HAD BEEN sleeping or what had woken her. She listened to the rain falling steadily and realized that despite the cold she was warm. She was too warm in fact, and she felt a thread of fear when she tried to move her legs and they didn't budge. She pushed the furs back and squinted into the darkness as a loud whimper resonated through the cave.

"Kane?" She stared in confusion at the large shifter. He was in his wolf form and sleeping across her lower body, his large head resting on her pelt-covered hip. As she watched, he twitched violently and made another loud whimper. His tail was sweeping back and forth, and he curled his upper lip and growled before it trailed off into a whimpering cry.

"Kane? Wake up." She pushed on his broad shoulder hesitantly. He didn't move and she stroked his fur roughly. "Wake up, Kane. You're dreaming."

He barked and she winced before pushing at him. "Wake up, you big lug!"

His entire body was trembling and he made a whining cry as he twitched and shook on the pelts. A low, continuous whimper was erupting from his throat and she swallowed thickly, her fingers tightening in his fur.

"Kane? Come on, honey. Wake up."

He made a sudden lurching shudder and then he was standing over her, the fur on his neck raised and his eyes glowing brightly. He stared at her in fear and confusion as his hot breath washed over her face. She reached up and stroked the side of his face, digging her fingers into his warm fur.

"You're all right. It was just a nightmare."

He whined and then shifted abruptly. He crouched over her and she stared at the goose bumps on his skin before silently pushing back the pelts. He crawled under them without hesitating and burrowed his body against hers. He pushed his face into her neck and she rubbed his broad back tentatively.

"What were you dreaming about?" She whispered.

"My mother." His voice was muffled against her throat and he squeezed himself even closer to her. "I was in the field and watching the humans take her head and skin her fur from her body."

"Oh God." She tugged on his hair until his head was tilted back and he was staring up at her. "Tell me you weren't actually there."

He shook his head. "I wasn't."

She breathed a sigh of relief. "Thank God."

He was still trembling and she could see pain and sorrow in his dark eyes. She smoothed her hand across his forehead and gave him what she hoped was a reassuring smile. "You're okay, honey. It's just a bad dream."

"I've missed your voice," he whispered.

She blinked in surprise. "Kane, I - "

"Go to sleep," he said gruffly. He started to turn away from her and she clung to him with a surprisingly strong grip.

"Why were you lying on top of me?" She asked.

"It's cold. I was afraid you wouldn't be warm enough."

"That was nice of you," she whispered. She was acutely aware of his nakedness, of the way his hard body felt pressed against her soft one. She had missed his warmth and his kisses and if she was honest with herself, his cock.

He stared silently at her before whispering, "Are you cold?"

"Yes," she lied. "Will you make me warm, Kane?"

He sniffed the air. Her desire had returned and he was almost giddy with relief and excitement and need. "Aye, if you want me to."

"I do," she murmured.

He pressed his mouth against hers and she kissed him, sliding her tongue into his mouth as he gripped her ass and pulled her against his rapidly-hardening cock.

"Your skin is so soft," he muttered against her mouth.

She stroked his back, liking the way the large muscles rippled under her fingers. She gasped when he cupped her breast and pulled on the nipple.

"Oh God," she moaned.

"Say my name again," he suddenly demanded.

He had just enough time to see the gleam of amusement

in her eyes before she bent her head and licked his throat. "Why should I, shifter?"

He growled, his hips arching helplessly against hers when she nipped him with her teeth. She licked the spot and then bit him again, this time hard enough that he jerked against her.

"Say it," he growled warningly.

"What? You don't like being called shifter?" She kissed his chest and then traced his collarbone with her tongue. He cupped the back of her neck, breathing harshly and moaning a little when she lifted her head and sucked on his earlobe.

"I want to hear you say my name, human. I like it," he confessed hoarsely.

"Hmm, that's too bad for you. Isn't it, shifter?" She teased before kissing his shoulder with warm, wet kisses.

He snorted with frustration before flipping her on to her back. He pushed her thighs apart and settled his large body between them, rubbing his cock against her wetness. She moaned and arched her pelvis upwards as he kissed her hard on the mouth, nearly shoving his tongue between her lips. When they finally broke apart, she was moaning and trembling against him, and he smiled with satisfaction at the look of need in her eyes.

"Say my name," he whispered into her ear as he placed the head of his cock at her tight entrance.

She shook her head in refusal and wrapped her thighs around his hips. He took her wrists and held her arms above her head, pinning them to the furs as he stared at her naked breasts. He bent his head and teased her nipples with his mouth and tongue, moving from one to the other until she was moaning and twisting beneath him.

"Please!" She begged.

He pushed the head of his cock into her wet warmth and stopped as she moaned and arched her back.

"Don't stop!" She gasped out.

"I want you to say my name," he repeated. He hesitated and then lowered his face to hers. His warm breath washed over her. "Please, Reese."

"Kane," she moaned it immediately and a large shiver of lust went through him. He thrust into her and waited with gritted teeth as she stretched around him.

Kane stared down at Reese. Her eyes were closed and she was biting at her bottom lip compulsively. Her nipples were hard against his chest and when he released her wrists, she immediately wrapped her arms around him. Her fingers dug into his back and she pushed her hips against his.

It felt a little odd being on top of her with his body nestled between her legs and all of her limbs clinging to him. Female shifters preferred to be on their hands and knees or riding him, and he never took them in this position. He was surprised to discover how much he liked it, and how turned on he was by the feel of her soft body nestled under his.

She was large and strong for a female but tucked under his body like this with her legs parted around his hips and unable to close, made her powerless and he was once again surprised by how much he liked it. Lust coursed through him and he thrust in and out of her, taking her more roughly than he intended.

She cried out and her fingernails raked across his back. He stopped and gave her an anxious look. "Do you like this? Am I hurting you?"

She shook her head immediately. "No, I like it. Don't stop, Kane."

He hesitated a moment longer. "Are you sure?"

Her eyes popped open and she gave him a look of frustration mixed with need. "Yes, dammit! Kane, you're driving me crazy!"

She slapped him sharply on the back and he grinned down at her. "I like how needy you are for my cock, human."

She glared at him. "For the love of God, shifter! Now who's talking too much?"

She suddenly squeezed her inner muscles around him, grinning like a satisfied cat when he moaned and thrust into her in response. He bent his head and took one swollen nipple into his mouth, teasing it with his tongue and lips as she twisted and squirmed on his thick shaft.

"I like this position," he suddenly announced. "I like how you look underneath me, and that you can't stop me from fucking you."

"Sweet Jesus," she muttered grouchily. "I'm glad you like it. Now, could you shut the hell up and actually start fucking me?"

"I can do that," he agreed. He thrust in and out of her as she clung to him and met each of his strokes. "You feel so good, Reese."

She made a little moan, her pussy tightening around him when he said her name. He released his breath in a harsh rush before putting his mouth to her ear. "You're mine, Reese. Tell me that you're mine."

"I'm yours," she gasped out, her hips thrusting frantically against him. "I'm yours."

"You will mate with no one else but me. Do you understand? You will not mate with a human or a shifter, and not Dagon." He punctuated each point with a hard thrust of his pelvis, and she cried out with pleasure.

"Say it, Reese." He wrapped her long hair around his hand and pulled on it, exposing her pale throat. He licked her soft skin and she shuddered beneath him.

"No one else, Kane. Only you," she moaned.

"You belong to me, Reese," he whispered into her ear as he squeezed and kneaded her large breasts.

"I belong to you," she repeated.

"That's right, you do." He hooked her legs over his arms, pushing them up and out until she was completely open to him. Propping himself on his hands, he plunged in and out of her, his eyes glowing and a low, hoarse howl starting in his chest.

Reese, her body pinned under his and her hands digging into his shoulders, cried out and stiffened beneath him. His cock was flooded with the hot wetness of her orgasm. Her pussy squeezed madly around him and the howl burst from his throat as he thrust one final time and climaxed explosively inside of her.

Weak as a kitten, he collapsed against her soft body. She muttered a curse and pushed at his broad shoulders. "Kane, I can't breathe."

Panting, he rolled off of her and on to his back. He had just had the best orgasm of his life and it was with a human. He stared stunned at the ceiling of the cave. Reese bent over him, staring worriedly at his face.

"Kane, are you all right?"

"What do you mean?" He asked hoarsely.

"You have a funny look on your face. Did you hurt yourself? You were um, thrusting pretty hard at the end there," she said.

A small grin crossed his face. "No, human. I did not hurt myself."

"Just checking." She smiled cheerfully at him.

"Did I hurt you?" He suddenly asked anxiously and she shook her head immediately.

"No, of course not."

"Are you positive?" His gaze fell on the faint marks on her chest. "You did not tell me the last time I hurt you."

"I'm fine." She relaxed on the pelts, curling up on her side with her back to him. He turned and spooned her. He pressed his body against hers and cupped her breast possessively as he buried his face between her shoulder blades. She twitched with surprise.

"What?" His voice was muffled against her back.

"Nothing," Reese said quickly. She didn't know why he wasn't shifting to his wolf form like he normally did but she wasn't going to ask. He had told her she belonged to him and that she wasn't allowed to mate with Dagon. For the first time since she had found out what the shifters had bought them for, a trickle of hope went through her. Perhaps she wouldn't have to be the alpha's mate after all. Perhaps Kane would take her as his mate. She could think of worse things than warming Kane's bed every night.

He won't. He said he had no interest in mating with someone for life, remember?

She sighed and, her mind whirling, listened to the sounds of Kane's soft snoring.

CHAPTER 12

"Kane?"

"Aye, human?"

"Did you mean what you said earlier?" Reese, her body wrapped in a pelt, joined him at the entrance to the cave.

He stared out into the darkness and the rain without answering and she touched his shoulder hesitantly. "Kane? Did you mean it? About me not mating with anyone else? About belonging to you?"

He sighed heavily. "No."

She stiffened and took a step back from him. "Why did you say it then?"

"I do not know."

"Oh."

"I cannot go against my alpha's orders. If he wants you as his mate, nothing can be done about it. You will be mated to him."

She didn't reply and he took a quick glance at her. He worried that she would be crying again but she was dry-eyed with a strange look of pity mixed with disgust on her face.

"I'm sorry, human."

She shrugged and turned away from him. "Don't worry about it, shifter. I'll figure it out myself."

He caught her bare arm. "What do you mean?"

"I mean, I'll figure out a way to get out of being Dagon's mate. He might not choose me anyway, right? And if he does, I'll just talk his ear off." She grinned bitterly. "Neither you or your pack mates seem to think he'll want me if I'm mad."

An odd trickle of fear went through him and he spun her around more roughly than he intended. She winced and he loosened his grip on her arms. "If he chooses you, do not show him your madness. Do you hear me, human? You keep it hidden from him."

She frowned. "Why should I? I don't want to be his mate. If that means riding the crazy train all the way to the station, then I will."

"Stop talking so foolishly!" His fear was growing and he pulled her closer. "If he chooses you, keep your tongue in your mouth and do whatever he asks of you. Do you understand?"

She actually laughed. "Do you really think I'm capable of that?"

He shook her. "This is not a joke, human! He will kill you! If he thinks you're mad, he will take your head. He will show you no mercy."

"Some leader you have there," she said.

"Please, Reese. Do this for me. Would you rather be dead than mated to Dagon?" He nearly shouted.

"You're hurting me," she said mildly.

He looked down and whined. His fingers were disappearing into the soft flesh of her arms and he released her abruptly. He made another soft whine at the red marks that appeared.

"I'm sorry, Reese. I did not mean to hurt you."

"I know," she replied. She turned and walked back to the pelts.

"Will you do what I ask of you?" He called after her.

She just shrugged and climbed into the bed of furs. He howled with anger and shifted abruptly. She watched as he paced back and forth in his wolf form, and clamped her hands over her ears when he sat at the mouth of the cave and howled repeatedly into the cold night air.

"IF YOU'RE GOING TO LIE ON THE BED WITH ME THEN SHIFT into your human form." Reese's voice came floating out of the darkness and Kane jerked in surprise. He shifted to his human form and knelt on the furs.

"I thought you were sleeping."

"Nope."

"I don't want you to be cold," he said as he crawled under the pelts beside her.

She laughed. "Liar. You want to fuck me again."

"Reese - "

"It's fine. I want to fuck you too." She reached for his cock, stroking it with her soft fingers and he groaned as he immediately hardened.

"I thought you were angry with me," he said hesitantly.

She shrugged. "I'm not."

"Reese, shifters are not like humans. They live in packs and there is a very clear hierarchy within it. Dagon is the alpha and I cannot disobey him. It does not mean that I don't uh, care for you or - "

"I *know*," she snapped. "Jesus, shifter. I'm willing to fuck you. You don't have to sweet talk me or pretend to have feelings for me. I'm a big girl and I know what this is."

"What is this?" He asked.

"Oh for God's sake. It's a way to keep warm, a way to pass the time, a way to have a little fun before I'm murdered by your damn alpha. What does it matter?" She said testily.

"A way to pass the time?" He was surprised at how much her words stung.

She rolled her eyes. "Are you kidding me, shifter? You told me yourself that I was an experiment, remember? So let's experiment."

She started to squirm down under the pelts and he frowned at her. "Reese, I don't think - "

"Stop thinking, shifter." Her voice was muffled and he pushed back the pelts.

"Just wait a minute. We should talk about - "

Her hot, wet mouth slid over the head of his cock and he groaned. Her hand squeezed the base of his cock and pumped it as she suckled hard on the head. Her soft and slippery tongue traced the sensitive ridge and he gripped her head. He twisted his fingers in her hair and held tight as she slid her mouth up and down.

He moaned and panted and thrust his hips at her as the cave was filled with the sounds of his loud groans and her sucking. She cupped his heavy balls in her hand, stroking them before tracing the skin on his inner thighs.

"Reese, please," he whispered when she trailed a path of hot wet kisses across his flat abdomen before dipping her tongue into his navel.

"Please what, shifter?" She grinned at him before nipping each of his hip bones.

"I want to be inside of you," he moaned.

She smiled and moved to her hands and knees, spreading

her legs and reaching back to trail her finger down his chest. "Go on, big boy."

He frowned before he pushed her onto her back and cupped one large breast. He pulled on her nipple before dipping his head and sucking it into his mouth. She moaned her approval and arched her back, running her hand through his short hair. He kissed his way down her body and licked the soft skin of her stomach before placing a kiss on the curls between her legs. He moved until he was lying between her legs and slid his hands under her ass. He lifted her up slightly before staring up at her. She was studying the ceiling with her hands cupping and kneading her breasts, and he frowned again.

"Reese? Look at me."

She glanced quickly at him, giving him a brief smile before returning her gaze to the ceiling. "Make me feel good, shifter."

"Kane." He needed to hear her say his name.

"Make me feel good, *Kane*," she said with a touch of impatience in her voice. Her hand came down and pushed on the back of his head and he kissed the wet lips of her pussy. She moaned and spread her thighs wide.

"Keep going," she demanded.

He licked her with his warm tongue, sliding it between her lips to find her clit. He touched it delicately with the tip of his tongue and she groaned and thrust her pelvis at him. He kneaded her ass as he licked and sucked at her clit. It was swelling in his mouth and he sucked harder as he slid one thick finger into her.

She cried out, her hands tightening in his hair, and twisted and squirmed beneath his mouth. He placed one arm across her stomach and pinned her down as he licked her clit with flat strokes of his tongue.

"Oh, oh, oh!" She moaned helplessly before she stiffened and gave a hoarse scream. Wetness flooded his face and he licked her sweetness as she shuddered and writhed beneath him. When she had collapsed against the furs, he slid his body up and kissed her breasts and then her throat.

She pushed weakly at his shoulders. "Here, I'll get on my hands and knees for you. I know you prefer it."

He shook his head. "It's fine." He rubbed his cock back and forth against her dripping wet pussy.

She pushed again at him. "I don't mind. Let me up and I'll - "

He pushed into her and she gave a soft gasp of surprise as her thighs clamped uselessly around his narrow hips. It sent a lightning bolt of desire through him and he thrust deeper until he was completely enveloped in her wet tightness.

"I want you like this, Reese," he whispered.

"All right."

She stared up at the ceiling of the cave as she stroked his broad back with her warm hands. "Fuck me, shifter."

He hesitated and stroked her face with the tips of his fingers. "Reese, are you okay?"

She squeezed her inner muscles around him, making him moan. "Never better."

"Look at me," he suddenly demanded.

She gave him another one of those quick darting glances before kissing him hard on the mouth. "Go on. Don't make me beg, shifter."

"Kane. Say it. I want you to say my name." He refused to move and she gave a soft grunt of frustration.

"Fine! Fuck me, Kane!" She squeezed him again before wrapping her long legs around his waist and hooking her feet together in the small of his back. "Do I suddenly need to show you what to do?"

He growled angrily and plunged in and out of her. Her pussy clung wetly to him and he wanted to come almost immediately. He held it off grimly, determined to make her come again before he did.

She was making soft moans of encouragement and he stared down at her sweet face. She was looking at the ceiling again and he sighed. "Reese, look at me."

She closed her eyes instead and bit down on her bottom lip. He ignored the unfamiliar ripple of hurt that went through him and leaned over her. "Please, Reese. I want you to look at me."

She made a harsh noise of frustration and glared up at him. "What?"

"You're so beautiful," he whispered and her gaze softened.

"Thank you, shifter."

"Kane," he muttered. "Please, Reese."

She didn't reply but she continued to stare at him and she touched his face with her fingers. He turned his head and kissed the palm of her hand as he moved slowly within her.

"Keep looking at me," he whispered.

She stared unblinkingly at him and he studied the lovely, strange shade of her eyes. Even in the darkness he could see them clearly and he leaned down and kissed her on the mouth. "Your eyes are so pretty."

She didn't reply and he gave her an anxious look as he continued to slide in and out of her. "Reese?"

She lifted her head and kissed him. "Harder."

She unlocked her legs from around his waist and braced her feet on the furs. "Make me come, shifter. Right now."

He plunged in and out of her, staring into her eyes as she began to pant and toss her head. Her pussy was warm and deliciously tight, and he could feel himself starting to lose control.

"You're mine, Reese," he said. "You belong - "

Her hand clamped down over his mouth and she shook her head at him. "Don't say that to me."

"Reese, I - "

She shook her head again and then she was thrusting her hips at him, squeezing and releasing him in a rough unexpected rhythm that pulled his orgasm from him in a giant, roaring rush of pleasure. He shouted her name and she cried out beneath him as her body shook and shuddered with her own release.

He stayed inside of her as his cock softened, resting his body against hers and kissing her repeatedly on the mouth. She returned his kisses for a moment and then pushed on him.

"You're too heavy, shifter."

He moved to her side. She turned her back to him and pulled up the pelts as he touched her back hesitantly. "Reese?"

"Go ahead and shift," she said. "I'm warm enough."

"You will grow too cold," he said immediately.

"I won't."

"You will," he argued.

He turned her over easily, despite the way she flattened herself into the pelts to prevent it, and pulled her against his hard chest. He cupped the back of her head and pushed it into the curve of his neck before taking her leg and hooking it around his hip. Every part of their bodies were touching and he rubbed her back.

"Put your arm around me, Reese," he murmured.

She slid her arm around his waist. "You're holding me too tightly."

He relaxed his grip and stroked her back and side for a few minutes. "Reese, will you tell me - "

"I'm really tired," she interrupted him. "I'd like to just go to sleep, okay?"

"Okay," he sighed.

She hesitated and then lifted her head and kissed him on the jaw. "Good night."

"Good night, Reese."

CHAPTER 13

"Tell me about your world."

She sat up in the furs and stared out the entrance of the cave. "God, will it ever stop raining?"

He sat up next to her. "It's been raining for over a week. It will end soon."

"I'm so tired of the rain," she sighed. "If I don't see the sun soon, I really will go mad."

Kane gave the human a worried look. She had a pinched, strained look on her face and her skin was very pale. She had lost weight in the last week. He had a feeling she only ate because he forced her to. He touched her naked back.

"Will you tell me about your world?"

She shook her head. "There is no 'my' world. I'm from this one."

He continued to rub her back. A change had come over the human. From the moment he had told her that he would do nothing to stop Dagon from taking her as his mate, a switch seemed to have been flipped inside of her. She was still mating with him. In fact, her appetite for him seemed insatiable. He understood her need. As deep as her need ran for him, his need ran deeper. She was an open and generous lover and eager to please him in bed but when they weren't having sex, she cut herself off from him. Hell, even when they were in bed there was a distance to her that he couldn't seem to bridge.

He snorted to himself. It was ironic that he was now anxious to know more about her, to hear her soft voice and her warm laugh, and she had no interest in anything other than fucking. He studied her solemn face carefully and then squeezed the back of her neck.

"Please, Reese. I would hear about your world."

She reached between his legs and stroked his cock before giving him a pale smile. "Wouldn't you rather have my mouth on your cock?"

"Do not distract me," he said.

She sighed and folded her hands into her lap. "Fine. I'm with the big bad wolf. Why not tell a fairy tale, right?"

He frowned. "Fairy tale?"

She smiled a little. "A story that parents tell their children when they tuck them into bed."

"Why?"

She shrugged. "I don't know. To make them happy, I guess. Or to help them fall asleep." She glanced up at him. "What do you want to know about my world?"

"Do you have any siblings?"

"No. I was an only child."

"Did you have a mate in your world?"

"No."

He frowned. "Who took care of you?"

"What do you mean?"

"Who kept you warm? Who kept you fed and protected you?"

"I took care of myself. Well, my parents took care of me when I was younger but I moved out when I was nineteen."

"How old are you?" He asked.

"I'm twenty-five." She gave him a curious look. "How old are you?"

"Twenty-eight."

She stared thoughtfully at him. "You act older. I suppose you have to grow up fast in this world."

"I still don't understand how you took care of yourself." He gave her an earnest look. "You don't know how to hunt or even start a fire."

She laughed. "In my world you don't need to hunt or have fire-making skills to survive. My world is much more – advanced, I guess you'd say. Our homes have running water and electricity and heat. We can just flick a switch on the wall and lights come on, or turn a tap and water comes out of them."

He frowned. "How is this possible?"

She shrugged. "It just is. It would take too long to explain how it works and I'd just end up confusing you more."

"Where did you go when you left your parents' home?" He asked.

"I rented a house with a few girlfriends. I was working the night shift at a convenience store and going to school during the day to become a vet tech."

"Vet tech?" He frowned at her.

"Veterinarian technician. It's a person who helps animals. If they're sick we make them feel better."

"You worked with animals?" He gave her a curious look. "Like cows and horses?"

She shook her head. "Small animals – like dogs and cats."

"Cats." He snorted disdainfully. "I hate cats."

A grin crossed her face. "Big surprise. Anyway, I finished

school and got a job and my own place. I wasn't rich but I had enough money to enjoy life."

"Why did you not take a mate?"

"Most men don't find me attractive. I'm tall and fat and I'm too opinionated. There may not be shifters in my world but there are plenty of human men like you. They might not admit it as readily as you do, but they want their women quiet and obedient and to look like a supermodel."

"Supermodel?"

"A very pretty woman who gets paid to sell clothing, or cars, or toothpaste or whatever to other people." She shrugged.

"You're very pretty, Reese."

"Thanks."

"I mean it," he persisted, "and I like listening to you talk."

She burst out laughing. "Sure you do."

He flushed. "I'm speaking the truth."

She snickered. "Of course you are.

He cupped her face. "Reese, when I say to curb your tongue I mean around Dagon. I do not want to get you to hurt."

She pulled her head free. "I know." She looked away from him. "I've told you about my world, now tell me about your fearless leader."

He shook his head. "No. I do not wish to speak of him."

She gave him an irritated look. "If you expect me to survive being mated to him, don't you think I should know a little something about him?"

Kane rubbed his face. "Dagon is older than me by a few years. His father was the leader of our pack before him. He died four years ago."

"So the leadership falls from father to son?" She asked.

"No. Dagon had to fight for the alpha position."

"What do you mean?"

"An alpha can be challenged by another member of the pack or even by an outsider. The alpha must accept this challenge or the other pack members will consider him weak. When Dagon was my age he challenged his father for leadership of our pack."

"What? Why?" Reese frowned.

Kane shrugged. "Dagon wanted to be alpha. His father was older and Dagon believed no longer capable of leading us."

"What happened then?"

"His father accepted the challenge. They fought and Dagon won." He stared blankly at the rain. "The old man was tougher than he looked. Dagon was so cocky and sure of his victory that he was very nearly defeated."

He sighed heavily. It was nearly a whimper and Reese hesitated before rubbing his naked back. "Did you like Dagon's father?"

"Aye. He was a good man. When my parents died, he took me under his wing a bit. I had my uncles and they raised me, but Maven was always good to me. I miss him."

"I'm sorry." She was still rubbing his back and a small thrill went through him. She didn't go out of her way to touch him and he took comfort in her soft touch.

"How did he die?" She asked tentatively.

He gave her an odd look. "Dagon killed him."

"What?" Her mouth dropped open and her hand stilled on his back. "He – he killed his own father?"

He nodded. "Aye. If an alpha is challenged, it is to the death."

Her face was very pale and he put his arm around her. "Reese, are you all right?"

"What kind of man kills his own father?" She whispered. "Do you – does that happen all the time?"

"No. Until Dagon, no son had ever challenged his father's right to rule. Normally, another member of the pack would challenge the alpha. If that pack member won, then the son may choose to challenge him. If they wanted to rule, that is."

"What happens if an alpha dies from just, like, natural causes?" Reese asked. Her face was still very pale and her lips were trembling wildly.

"Other pack members make it known if they want to be the alpha and challenges are set up until there is only one remaining shifter. He becomes alpha."

"So much death," she whispered.

He shook his head again. "Not necessarily. Many years ago, a challenge always resulted in death. It was considered an insult to the alpha if the challenger did not kill him."

"That's so fucked up," she muttered.

He rubbed her shoulder. "The thinking has changed over the last decade or so. More and more often, a challenger lets the alpha live. It is not considered so disrespectful now to do so."

He gave her an encouraging look. "We are not as brutal and harsh as it appears. Our packs are very close and we protect and take care of one another. You will see."

She was staring at him with a new look of horror in her eyes. He squeezed her against him. "Reese? What is wrong?"

"He – he had the chance to let his father live and he didn't?" She whispered.

He groaned and could have hit himself for being so stupid. He was anxious to show Reese that they were not as barbaric as she thought and now she was more horrified than ever. And why wouldn't she be? She had just found out that her potential mate had murdered his own father.

"Reese, I - "

"How many of his mates has he killed?"

He could hear the panic in her voice and he tried to pull her into his lap. She resisted, pushing at his chest with her hands and scooting backward until she was pressed up against the cold wall of the cave.

"How many, shifter?"

"He has had four mates," he said.

"Oh my God," she whispered.

"We do not know for sure that he killed them," he said anxiously. "Two of them we know he did not."

"How do you know that?"

"They killed themselves," he replied.

"So, they committed suicide rather than be his mate?"

He gave her an uncomfortable look. "They did not bear him any pups and they became despondent over it."

She laughed bitterly. "He's been your alpha for only four years and he's killed as many mates. This just gets better and better."

"Reese, I - "

"How did the other two die?" She interrupted.

"They, well, they looked like accidents. One of them drowned and Dagon said the other was attacked and killed by a tagen when they were out hunting together."

She stared down at her lap. "I'm going to die."

He slid over and cupped her arms, shaking her a bit roughly. "Do not say that, Reese. You're not going to die. Just - "

"Just what? Keep my mouth shut and part my legs whenever he tells me to? Just hope that I can bear him children and that he doesn't get tired of me and I end up dead? Jesus Christ, shifter! Do you have any idea what you're saying?" She shouted.

He winced and pulled her into his arms. She struggled violently, kicking and punching at him but he held on grimly until she finally collapsed against him.

"I'm sorry, Reese. I'm so sorry," he whispered. He cupped her face and stared down at her. He had expected she would be crying but she was dry-eyed and calm.

"You could let me go," she said. "When the rains stop, we can just go our separate ways. You can tell Theran and Hanif that the tagen killed me before you got here. Please, Kane."

"You'll die in the forest. You won't survive a week and you know it."

She shrugged. "I would rather die in the forest than be mated to your alpha."

"He may not choose you." He rubbed his thumb along her cheekbone. "He may choose one of the other females."

"Oh great. So, I should hope that poor Ghita or Adina are chosen instead of me?" She gave him a look of anger. "You think it makes me feel better to know that he might murder one of them instead?"

He didn't reply and she gave him a pleading look. "Please, Kane. Let all of us go. The three of us have a better chance of survival in the woods. Ghita and Adina will keep me safe."

He snorted. "They will not. They will abandon you the first chance they get."

"No, they won't. Besides, what do you care if I live or die? You don't even know me and you hate humans. When I die it's just one less stupid human in your world."

He pulled her even closer and stroked her hair. "You are not going to die, Reese."

"I am," she sighed morosely. "Why won't you just accept that?"

"Why don't you fight harder for your life?" He was suddenly angry and she gasped when his arms tightened painfully around her.

"I'm trying!" She retorted.

"No you're not!" He shouted. "You act as though you're already dead, as though my alpha will take one look at you and kill you where you stand. He may not choose you as his mate. If he does not then you will have a very – very pleasant life in our pack."

She tried to struggle free from his arms, but he refused to release her. "A pleasant life? As a maid and a nanny to the wolf babies in your pack? No thanks, shifter."

He sighed with frustration. "Another in my pack will choose you as his mate." His stomach tightened and he could feel jealousy threading through him at the thought of Reese in another's bed.

She scoffed angrily. "If your pack mates are like you, I'll pass on finding a mate among them."

He blinked at her. "What do you mean, human?"

"Jesus." She shook her head. "You really have no idea, do you?"

When he stared blankly at her, she laughed bitterly. "Never mind. I'll continue to be your fuck buddy until we get to your home and then you can hand me over to your damn alpha."

"Reese - "

"Forget it, shifter." She slumped against him. "I'm beating a dead horse here."

He frowned. "Why would you beat a dead horse?"

She barked harsh laughter. "It's just a saying."

Confused and feeling helpless, he hugged her. "You aren't going to die, Reese. I will keep you safe."

"Yeah, thanks," she replied in defeat. She squirmed free and huddled under the furs. "I'm tired. Good night, shifter."

He curled up against her back and rested his large hand on her hip. He placed a soft kiss against her bare back. "Good night, Reese."

CHAPTER 14

When she woke, it was lighter in the cave. Kane was sleeping beside her and she sat up and studied his face before tracing the line of his jaw. He frowned and then relaxed. She pressed her lips together and sighed. She wasn't in love with the shifter, at least she didn't think she was, but over the last two weeks she had started to care for him. It was impossible not to – for her, anyway. She had never been the kind of girl who could just sleep with someone without at least feeling some kind of connection and this was no different. Even knowing that he didn't care for her and that he would hand her over to his alpha without a second thought, didn't seem to make a difference. She cursed herself for being a fool. There was no point in having any type of feelings for the shifter. He felt nothing for her but lust.

Are you sure about that, Reese? Her inner voice piped up. *He's different now. It doesn't feel like just fucking when you're in his arms. If all he was interested in was sex, why does he keep asking about your world? Why does he keep asking you so many questions about your life?*

She rolled her eyes. He thought she was crazy and his

questions were just plain old curiosity. Nothing more. She was a fool if she thought he was starting to care for her. They were obviously compatible sexually but that didn't mean he wanted more. He wanted somewhere to stick his dick and she was happy to oblige.

She stared out the entrance of the cave. She needed to come up with a plan for escaping the three shifters. She would speak with Ghita and Adina, share the information about Dagon, and let them decide for themselves if they wanted to come with her. She hoped they would. She was pretty sure that Adina would but Ghita was attracted to Theran. It would be harder to convince her to –

She suddenly gasped and threw back the pelts. The rain had stopped. She stood and ran naked to the edge of the cave, staring with delight at the sky above her. It was still mostly clouded over but in the distance she could see glimpses of blue sky.

"Oh, please," she whispered. She had never been so desperate to see the sun and she clenched her hands into tight fists and tried to will the clouds to part. They stayed stubbornly still but she continued to stare at the small patch of blue in the distance.

When Kane's warm arms slid around her, she jerked in surprise and glanced up at him. "It's stopped raining."

He nodded, resting his hands against her stomach and rubbing. She ignored the immediate flare of desire in her belly and continued to stare at the sky. "We should try and find the others."

He shook his head and pulled her back against his hard body. "Not yet. It may rain again. We will wait until the sky is clear."

He dipped his head and placed a warm kiss against her neck. "You need to eat, Reese."

"I'm not hungry." She scanned the sky anxiously, searching for more blue.

He grunted his disapproval. "You grow too thin, human. You're not eating enough."

She laughed. "Hardly, shifter."

"Kane," he said grumpily. "I have a name."

She giggled, the first sound of genuine amusement he had heard from her in days, and an answering smile crossed his face before he nuzzled her throat affectionately.

"What?"

"Nothing." She giggled again. "It's just ironic that," she paused, "never mind." She patted his hand and then pushed him away before leaning against the wall of the cave and staring outside.

"Go and have something to eat, Kane. I'll eat later."

He shook his head. "No. You will eat with me."

She sighed irritably. "I told you I'm not hungry."

He pulled her away from the wall before bending and hoisting her over his shoulder like a sack of potatoes. She squealed in surprise before slapping him on the bare ass.

"Put me down, you Neanderthal!"

He cupped her bare ass and squeezed. "No. You will eat and then you - "

He roared with surprise when she bit him on the back and he dropped her to the pelts with a hard thud. She rubbed her ass and grinned up at him as he felt the faint indents from her teeth in his back.

"You bit me."

"You're not the only one who knows how to bite," she replied saucily.

He grinned at her. "Someone deserves a spanking."

She scrambled to her feet, her eyes lit up and her face flushed. "You'll have to catch me first."

He made a low growling noise and she felt a rush of desire and excitement when his eyes turned green and glowed brightly at her. "The cave is small. I will catch you easily."

She inched to her right. "We'll see about that."

He growled again and she stuck her tongue out at him. His cock was hardening rapidly and she gave it a quick glance, her cheeks flushing, before she looked away.

He grinned again, a predatory grin, and her heart thudded against her chest. The rain stopping, the glimpse of blue sky, had lifted her spirits for the first time in days and she couldn't stop her cheeky grin at him. "What are you waiting for? Is the big bad wolf afraid of a little girl like me?"

He lunged forward so quickly that she felt his fingertips brush against her arm as she shrieked and skittered away. He stalked her as she circled around him and he winked at her. "Give up now, Reese, and I'll go gentle on you."

She stuck her tongue out again in reply and he made another hoarse growl. "I can think of a much better use for your tongue."

His cock was so hard it was aching and he stared at her breasts as she glanced behind her. Her nipples were rock hard and he closed his eyes and inhaled. He could smell her desire for him and it flamed his higher, turning his need for her into an uncontrollable burn.

Her eyes glanced to the left before she made a break for the right. Her ruse didn't fool him and he dodged to the right and caught her around the waist as she sprinted for the back of the cave. She shrieked and laughed, smacking him on the chest and shoulders as he lifted her and carried her back to the pelts.

"Mine now, human." He gave her another predatory grin that turned to surprise when she threw her weight against him and knocked him to the pelts. Quick as a flash, she tried to scramble free and laughed again when he grabbed her by the ankle and dragged her back toward him.

He flipped her onto her back and she squirmed and twisted and laughed when he started to tickle her. He tickled her mercilessly for a few minutes until she was panting and pleading with him.

"Stop, Kane! Stop! I can't breathe!" She laughed as he tickled her ribs.

He grinned down at her and brushed her hair back from her face. She returned his smile, her face flushed and her breasts heaving. He leaned over her and kissed her thoroughly on the mouth. She moaned and wrapped her arms around his neck, kissing him back enthusiastically.

When he pulled away and flipped her to her stomach, she squeaked in surprise and tried to wiggle free. He pressed his hand into the middle of her back, holding her down, and she pouted up at him.

"Let me go, shifter."

He shook his head. "No. I told you – you deserve a spanking."

Her nostrils flared and a fresh wave of her desire washed over him. His cock responded and he groaned before staring at the pale globes of her ass. After a moment, she cleared her throat.

"I thought you were going to spank me."

He shook his head. "No. I cannot. I will never hurt you, Reese."

He stroked her ass, his fingers caressing and touching the firm flesh and she moaned and arched her back. He rubbed her ass until she was twisting beneath him and then slid his hand between her legs. She was soaking wet and he growled in approval before sitting back and stretching out his legs.

"Ride me, Reese," he demanded.

She climbed into his lap, spreading her legs and resting her knees on either side of his hips. He guided his cock into her wet opening, both of them sighing with need when he entered her.

"Ohhhh." She groaned as he pulled her legs around his waist. She clung to his broad shoulders as he put his hands on her hips and lifted her up and down.

"That feels so good, shifter," she moaned as his thick cock slid in and out of her.

"Kane," he demanded.

He pulled her closer, wrapping his arm around her waist and thrusting back and forth as he cupped her head with his other hand. He kissed her mouth, relishing the taste of her sweetness as she slipped her tongue into his mouth and licked at his tongue.

"Say it." He pulled back and looked at her, rubbing his thumb along her cheekbone. "Say my name."

"Kane," she murmured.

"Good girl." He pushed his thumb into her mouth. His eyes darkened when she sucked at it and he continued to plunge in and out of her. She sucked on his thumb but when her eyes closed, he growled deep in his throat.

"No, don't close your eyes. Look at me, Reese."

She opened her eyes obediently and he stroked his thumb in and out of her mouth as his cock slid in and out of her warm, wet pussy. He pulled his thumb free and ran it across her swollen, bottom lip.

"Tell me you belong to me," he demanded.

She shook her head and he gave a grunt of frustration before sliding his hands around her back and cupping her shoulders. He thrust in and out of her and she made a soft moan of submission, her head falling back as she clung to him.

"You're mine, Reese," he muttered into her ear.

"I'm not!" She gasped out as her fingers dug into his back. "Stop saying that, shifter."

"You are. Say it!"

"No!" She reached between them and rubbed frantically at her clit. "I'm not yours. I'm not, I'm…"

She trailed off as her body began to tremble wildly.

"You're mine!" He nearly snarled. His lust and his need to claim her was out of control. His eyes glowing and his fangs lengthening, he bent his head and sank his teeth into the soft meat of her shoulder.

She gave a startled cry as her blood filled his mouth and then her entire body was shaking around his, her pussy clamping down on to his cock as she came wildly. He tore his mouth away and pointed his head to the ceiling. He howled as his hips thrust against her and he came deep inside of her.

Reese clapped her hands over her ears as Kane howled again.

"Kane, stop!" She shouted. He fell backward onto the pelts, his chest heaving and his face pale. He stared at the bite on her shoulder and at the blood trickling down her chest, and she touched his chest tentatively.

"Kane, are you all right?"

"What have I done?" He whispered. He gave her a look of stark despair and she patted his chest.

"It's okay."

He shook his head and eased her off of him before jumping to his feet. He nearly ran to the shelves in the wall and she flinched when he knocked a few of the bottles from their perches. They shattered on the stone as he grabbed the jar of salve and hurried back to her.

He used one of the pelts to wipe away the blood and then smoothed on a heavy layer of salve. She winced and he made a soft sound of hurt in the back of his throat. "I'm so sorry, Reese."

"It's fine. It was an accident." She gave him a warm smile and his stomach churned.

She relaxed against the pelts and he quickly laid down beside her and pulled her into his arms. He stroked her hair and then her back.

"I'm fine, Kane. The salve will heal it and it'll be back to normal in no time."

That was where she was wrong, he thought miserably. The salve would heal it but she would be marked forever. He shuddered and she squeezed his arm reassuringly as he stared blankly at the ceiling of the cave. The bite he had given her was a claiming bite. It was meant to mark, to show other shifters that she belonged to him. His stomach churned again and a low whine slipped out before he could stop it. Shifters only bit a partner when they intended to claim them as their mate. Not once had he even considered claiming a woman and now he had just claimed Reese, the potential mate of his alpha. If Dagon chose Reese as his mate, the moment he saw the mark - when he realized that Reese had been claimed by another...

He shuddered again as he had a vision of Dagon taking Reese's head in a fit of anger. He had put Reese in terrible danger and he had no idea what to do. He realized Reese was speaking to him and he forced himself to look at her.

She was staring up at him, concern etched across her face, and she patted his cheek almost timidly.

"What did you say?" He asked hoarsely.

"I asked if I was going to turn into a shifter," she said.

He stared blankly at her for a moment. "Why would you think that?"

"Because you bit me. In my world if a werewolf bites a human they turn into a werewolf."

"What is a werewolf?" He frowned at her and she shook her head.

"Never mind. Am I going to become a shifter now? Is that why you're so worried?"

"No." He pushed her head down to his chest and stroked her hair again. "You are not going to become a shifter, Reese. I am worried because I – I feel bad for biting you."

She squeezed his waist. "I told you, I'm fine. Just maybe next time try and keep your teeth to yourself. Okay, big fella?"

"Okay," he whispered. He stared at the ceiling of the cave again as Reese sighed and closed her eyes.

CHAPTER 15

"Just a few more steps," Kane said reassuringly. "We're almost there."

Reese nodded shortly. She was using all of her concentration to cling to the slippery rock and she lowered her foot and pressed it into the indent in the rock before moving her other leg.

It was three days later. The sun had finally appeared the day before yesterday but despite her impatience to leave the cave, Kane had refused. Now, as Kane's strong hands circled her waist and lifted her down to the ground, she finally realized why. It had been two full days of sunshine but the air was still cold and the ground was wet beneath her feet. She stared around in silence at the trees that had fallen and the branches that littered the ground.

"Come. We must find the others, quickly." Kane was giving her an impatient look as he held his hand out to her.

She glanced behind her and Kane stepped forward and took her hand. "Reese, let's go."

She stared at him solemnly. "Kane, please."

He shook his head immediately. "I will not, Reese."

"This is my only chance. You know that," she said.

"You will die in the forest," he responded harshly. "Do not ask me to set you free knowing your fate."

She sighed and allowed him to lead her into the trees. She glanced behind her, staring a little wistfully at the side of the mountain. She was happy to see the sun again but a large part of her mourned the loss of her time with Kane. Once they found the others and he brought her to his alpha, she would never be with him again.

He had taken her this morning before they had climbed down the mountain. He had held her close, licking the mark on her shoulder repeatedly as he had slid in and out of her in a slow, gentle motion. The salve had healed the wound from his bite quickly but she was left with a scar. She slipped her hand under Kane's shirt and ran her fingers over the raised skin.

"We must move faster, Reese." Kane tugged on her hand and she gave him an irritated look.

"Give it a rest, shifter. I haven't seen the sun in days and I'm going to enjoy it." She lifted her head to the sunlight filtering through the trees and took a deep breath. Kane was uncharacteristically slow and tender in his lovemaking this morning. He had whispered in her ear that she belonged to him and she hadn't argued, just clung to him and closed her eyes.

She wasn't his. She knew that and so did he but it still brought a sweet warmth to her insides. She wanted to be his, wanted it desperately in fact, and she blinked back the tears. Kane had made it perfectly clear that he would never disobey his alpha. She needed to forget about a life with him and concentrate on finding a way to escape the shifters. Kane tugged on her hand again and with a soft sigh, she followed him through the trees.

"KANE!"

They were walking for only ten minutes when Theran appeared. He growled happily and hugged the shifter. He pounded him on his back and stared up at him. "I was certain you were dead."

Kane shook his head. "The tagen was easy to defeat."

Reese snorted and Theran grinned at her. "Hello, human."

"Hello, Theran. Where are the others?"

"Not far. They are waiting for us. We had not lost hope that you were still alive, and so I came searching for you."

Kane gripped Reese's hand and they followed Theran. The shifter was moving quickly as he kept up a steady stream of chatter and Reese smiled a little. Despite the fact that Theran had given her to the tagen, she was still happy to see him.

"We nearly starved to death," Theran said as they passed a large bush dotted with yellow berries. "Hanif and I were forced to go out in the rains to gather plants for the humans. We got lucky and stumbled on a stag that was stuck in the mud. It was nearly dead anyway, but we put it out of its misery and dragged it back to the cave. Ghita and Adina skinned it and cooked some of the meat, and Hanif and I tried it cooked. You know, it wasn't half bad. I mean, I wouldn't eat it cooked all the time but - "

"You had fire?" Reese interrupted.

Theran gave her a strange look. "Aye. We built one to keep the humans warm. It was safe enough to build one in the cave that Kane found."

"You know how to build a fire?" Reese asked.

"Of course we do. All shifters can build a fire. We are not simple. I told you before, we did not build a fire when we were traveling because it was too dangerous. But once the rains came, no creature would willingly go out in them." Theran glanced at Kane. "Did the tagen addle her brains?"

Kane didn't reply and he had the decency to blush when Reese gave him a dirty look. "Is there a particular reason you let me nearly freeze to death?"

"You weren't going to freeze to death," Kane protested. "I kept you warm enough."

Theran sniffed at Reese. "That you did. She is covered in your scent, Kane. Dagon will not be pleased that you have fucked one of his potential mates."

"You're one to talk," Kane snorted. "Do you think we didn't notice you fucking the human each night before the rains came? Besides, who said I fucked the human? I merely kept her warm during the rains."

He gave Reese a hard look and she rolled her eyes before looking away. It was obvious the shifter wanted to keep their fucking a secret. She had no idea why Kane didn't want Theran to know they had sex, but he hadn't needed to warn her to keep her mouth shut. She didn't particularly want the others knowing they had slept together either.

Theran shrugged. "The odds of Dagon choosing Ghita are slim, you know that. She is too shy for him. Once he has chosen Reese or Adina, I will take Ghita as my mate."

"A human as a mate?" Kane blinked at him. "Truly, Theran?"

"Aye. She's sweet and would make a good mother for my pups."

"You barely know the girl," Kane protested. "You should wait and be sure that - "

"I'm not waiting. If I do not claim her quickly, another in the pack will try and claim her. Not all of us have the hatred for humans that you and Radek do."

"I don't hate them," Kane said quickly before giving Reese another darting glance.

Theran laughed. "Since when? You've hated humans your entire life. No one blames you for it, of course, but you will have to learn to at least tolerate them."

He glanced at Kane. "Do you not remember the time you and Radek snuck out as teenagers and raided the human's farm? If Maven had not gone after you, you would have killed - "

"Hold your tongue, Theran!" Kane said sharply. "Or I will rip it from your mouth."

Theran blinked at him in surprise. "What has gotten into you, Kane?"

"Nothing," he snapped. "I am tired and ready to be home and in my own bed."

Theran nodded. "Well, it is not much further now. A few more days and we'll be home."

Reese's stomach clenched. She had only a little time to convince Adina and Ghita that they needed to escape. Although from the sounds of it, Ghita would not be willing to leave Theran. She would have to - "

"Reese!"

Hanif, Adina and Ghita were just ahead of them. Adina's happy shout brought a smile to her face and she pulled her hand free of Kane's and ran to the blonde woman. They embraced as Hanif pounded Kane on the back and Ghita wrapped her arms around Theran's waist.

"I am so glad you're okay." Adina smiled at her and Reese gave her an impulsive kiss on the cheek.

"I'm happy to see you, Adina."

Kane pulled his pants from a leather bag that Hanif handed to him and slipped into them as Hanif gave the bag to Reese. She rummaged through it and found her skirt. It was dirty but dry and she pulled it up her legs and over her hips but didn't bother to change from Kane's shirt to her own. Despite the cool air, she knew he would be warm enough without it. Besides, she was a little surprised that he wasn't shifting to his wolf form.

Adina studied her closely. "Are you all right, Reese? Did the tagen – did he hurt you?"

Reese shook her head. "No, Kane saved me before he could do anything."

"Good." Adina squeezed her arm affectionately as Hanif shifted to his wolf form. "I really am glad you're not harmed. I was - "

She stopped when Kane took Reese's arm and pulled her back to his side. "We must keep moving, humans."

Reese frowned at him and tried to shake free of his grip. "I want to walk with Adina."

"No, you will stay by my side." He took her wrist in a firm grip and pulled her forward. She sighed and trailed after him.

"It is odd that Kane hasn't changed to his wolf form at all today," Adina said in a soft mutter. They had stopped for the night and after eating a meal of charkas and plants, the two women were huddled together in the growing darkness. Ghita was sitting on Theran's lap and she kissed his thick neck as he stroked her thigh through her skirt.

Kane and Hanif were talking in low voices and Reese put her arm around Adina's shoulders and rubbed the woman's arm briskly. The air was cold and they were already shivering madly. She was kicking herself for not thinking to bring one of the heavy pelts from the tagen's den.

"Don't you think?" Adina raised her eyebrow at her.

"It is," Reese agreed briefly.

She knew why Kane hadn't shifted to his wolf form. He hadn't wanted her to speak to Adina and the easiest way to stop her was by keeping her with him the entire day. This was the first time he had left her side since they had met up with the others, and she gave him a quick glance before squeezing Adina's shoulder.

"We need to speak, Adina," she said in a soft mutter. "Dagon is dangerous and we cannot stay with the shifters. He has already - "

"Reese!" Kane was suddenly standing in front of them and he held his hand out toward her. "It is time to sleep."

"I'm speaking with Adina, just give me a minute." She gave him a defiant look and he scowled at her before reaching down and lifting her to her feet.

"No. You need to sleep. We have a long day of travel tomorrow."

He pulled her away from Adina as Hanif shifted and barked. Adina, frowning a little, moved to Hanif and curled into his body as Theran kissed Ghita before removing his clothes and shifting. He laid on the ground and Ghita laid down beside him before throwing her arms around his fur covered body and burying her face into his neck. He chuffed and spread his tail over her lower body before closing his eyes.

Reese waited for Kane to shift. When he didn't, she frowned at him. "Are you not going to shift?"

He shook his head. "No. I can keep you warm enough in my human form. Lie down."

He stretched out in the grass and patted the spot beside him.

She glanced dubiously at his naked upper body. "It's cold

and you'll be warmer and more comfortable in your wolf form. You should shift."

"I'll be fine. Lie down with me, Reese," he said impatiently.

"This is ridiculous." She glared at him. "Why aren't you -"

She gave a soft squeal when he sat up and grabbed her around the hips. He hauled her downward and she landed with a hard thud on his half-naked body. He shifted to his side and wrapped his arms around her before pushing her head against his chest.

"Go to sleep, Reese."

"This can't be comfortable for you," she argued as she squirmed against his body. The sun had shone all day today and she was thankful that the ground was no longer wet but it was cold. She touched Kane's bare back. The skin was toasty warm but after a few hours of lying on the cold ground, he would be freezing.

"Be quiet and go to sleep, Reese," he muttered into her ear.

She was quiet for nearly fifteen minutes, listening to the soft even breathing of the others as they slipped into sleep before tapping Kane on the back.

"Why aren't you shifting?" She refused to go to sleep until he gave her an answer. "You're going to freeze to death in the night and then I'll freeze to death!"

He grunted in frustration before reaching down and slapping her lightly on the ass. "I am just as warm in my human form."

"I doubt that," she retorted. "I want to know why you're not shifting."

A low growl escaped his lips and he wrapped his hand in her long hair and tugged her head back. "If I am in my wolf form, I cannot do this," he kissed her as her arms tightened around him, "nor can I do this."

He slipped his hand under her shirt and cupped her bare breast, kneading it as she bit back her moan of pleasure.

"I'm not fucking you in front of your friends, shifter," she muttered in a low whisper as she glanced at the others.

"I know that," he breathed into her ear. "Now go to sleep."

He stroked her nipple with his thumb and ground his erection against her soft center when her pelvis arched against him.

"Stop doing that!"

He squeezed her breast once more before moving his hand higher. She rested her head against his chest as he repeatedly traced the scar from his bite with the pads of his fingers. He had been doing that almost obsessively since it healed, and she pressed her hand against his.

"It's fine," she whispered.

"Do not show the others the scar," he whispered abruptly.

"Will you get in trouble?"

"Aye," he said. "Promise me, you will keep it hidden."

"I will, shifter."

"Kane." He scowled at her.

She stared at him before stroking his cheek. "Go to sleep, Kane."

REESE FINISHED PEEING AND STOOD, PULLING UP HER PANTIES and dropping her skirt before moving back toward the camp. She was tired, her back hurt and she had a bad feeling that she was about to get her period. She sighed inwardly. Not that she wanted to be knocked up with a wolf baby but there was a small part of her that had wondered what would happen if she was. Dagon wouldn't want her if she was carrying Kane's baby, and perhaps Kane would take her as his mate if she was pregnant with his child.

She snorted to herself. Wishing to be pregnant just to avoid being mated to a murderous wolf wasn't exactly the best reason for bringing a child into the world. Besides, did she really want to have a baby in a world that she knew very little about? She felt a wave of homesickness for her own earth and she leaned against a tree and blinked back the tears. She would never find her way home again and she needed to stop pretending that she might. It didn't do any good. She stretched before rubbing her aching abdomen. Her menstrual cycle was always long and painful and she was dreading the long day of walking tomorrow. They had spent all day trudging through the never-ending forest and once again, Kane had stayed in his human form and left her no opportunity to speak to Adina. If what Hanif had said earlier was correct, they would reach the shifter's home before the end of tomorrow. It would be too late for her to warn Adina and Ghita. Perhaps she could wake Adina after the shifters fell asleep and –

She stiffened when she heard the branch crack. She was suddenly aware of just how far from the camp she was and as her heart began a jittery beat in her chest, she looked around frantically for a weapon of some kind.

A shadow loomed to her left and she whipped around, sagging against the tree with relief when Kane appeared next to her.

"You scared the hell out of me, shifter!" She snapped at him.

He didn't reply and as the moonlight caught the hard features of his face, adrenaline rushed through her veins again. The look on his face was one of pure lust and her body reacted immediately. Her nipples hardened, the ache in her abdomen faded away, and her pussy began to throb and pulse. She hated to admit it but after days of doing nothing but fucking the large shifter, she was nearly frantic with need for him. It was almost two days since he had taken her and she licked her lips as he drew closer.

"Kane, I - "

He pushed her up against the tree and covered her mouth with his. As his tongue slid into her mouth, she wrapped her arms around him and returned his kiss with eager abandonment. His hands slipped under her shirt and he cupped her large breasts, rubbing and caressing them as she rocked her pelvis against him.

He reached between them and unbuttoned his pants, pulling out his erect cock and rubbing it against the soft fabric of her skirt. She reached down and stroked him. His back arched and he shoved her skirt up around her waist before yanking her panties down her legs. She kicked them off impatiently as he lifted her and braced her against the tree. His hand slid between her legs and a feral grin of satisfaction crossed his features when he discovered how wet she was. Without a word, he pulled her thighs apart, hoisted her a bit higher and sunk his cock deep into her warmth.

She moaned and he pushed in and out of her as he clamped his large hand over her mouth. He buried his face in her neck, licking and sucking at her soft skin as he surged back and forth. She moaned again and he quickened his pace. She wrapped her legs around his waist and clutched at his shoulders as he slammed in and out of her. Her entire body was on fire with pleasure and she screamed into his palm when he slid his other hand between their bodies and pulled on her clit, bringing her to a hard and immensely satisfying climax. He groaned her name and bucked his hips against her as the familiar warmth flooded through her.

Panting harshly, he continued to hold her against the tree as he pulled her shirt to the side and licked the scar on her shoulder. He kissed it before raising his head and staring at her. "Are you all right, Reese?"

She nodded and he eased out of her before setting her down on the ground. He helped her into her panties, pulling them up around her hips, and straightened her skirt as she smoothed down her hair.

"We need to get back," he said as he buttoned his pants. "Before the others come looking for us."

"Right," she whispered. He squeezed her hand and kissed her mouth before leading her back to the camp.

CHAPTER 16

"Reese? What's wrong?"

It was early the next morning and Adina crouched next to Reese. Reese had rummaged through the leather bag and pulled out her shirt, and Adina watched as she tore it into long flat strips before folding them neatly. She paused with her face drawn down in a moue of pain before pressing her hand against her stomach.

"Are you sick?" Adina asked.

Reese shook her head. "No, not really. It's just that time of the month. Bad cramps, you know?"

"You're very pale." Adina placed her hand on Reese's forehead.

"I'll be fine." Reese gave her a faint smile. "Excuse me for a moment."

Carrying one of the folded strips of fabric, Reese disappeared into the trees. Adina waited patiently for her to return and put her arm around Reese's shoulder when she reappeared a few minutes later. "I will look for tappin root as we walk today. Ground up and boiled in water, it makes a tea that will help ease your cramps. All right?"

"Sure. Thanks, Adina." Reese glanced around nervously. Oddly enough, Kane had gone hunting for the shifter's breakfast this morning instead of sending Theran or Hanif and she was alone with Adina.

She grabbed Adina's arm as the woman began to walk away. "Adina, wait. I need to speak with you."

"What's wrong?"

"This alpha of theirs, this Dagon, he's dangerous. He's had four mates in the past four years and all of them have died. And it was under very suspicious - "

"I know, Reese," Adina interrupted.

Reese blinked at her in surprise. "You know?"

"Aye. Hanif and Theran told us all about Dagon while we were in the cave and waiting for the rains to end."

"Then you know we can't go with them to their home," Reese said. "We have to escape, Adina. We need to get away from the shifters today."

Adina didn't reply and Reese gave her a hard look. "Adina? We can't stay."

"We have no choice, Reese."

"Of course we do," Reese whispered. "We can come up with a plan to distract the shifters and escape into the forest."

Adina shook her head. "You know that's not possible. Even if we did manage to get away from them, they would find us quickly. We cannot hide our scent from them."

"So what? We just march with them to their home and wait to see which one of us Dagon chooses? If he chooses you, Adina, he might kill you like he killed his other mates."

"He didn't kill them. They were accidents," Adina replied.

"Do you really believe that?" Reese asked.

Adina hesitated. "It doesn't matter, Reese. We have no way of escaping our fate."

She glanced at Ghita. "Hanif says Dagon will probably not choose Ghita. She is too timid for him." She turned her gaze back to Reese. "And you are too mad. Which means that I will most likely become his mate."

"Which is all the more reason for escaping the shifters!" Reese forced herself to lower her voice as Hanif gave them a curious look. "You can't just give up like this, Adina."

The blonde woman gave her a look of anger. "Let's pretend that we could escape the shifters and that we could somehow cover our scent so they could not track us. What then? We are deep in the forest, Reese, and there are creatures that live among the trees who would have a far worse fate for us than the shifters. We would not last more than a few days. At least with the shifters we will have protection, warmth, and food. If the alpha chooses me I will do my best to please him. The women in my family are fertile. I am confident I will bear him pups."

"Adina - "

"Enough, Reese!" The woman said harshly. "If you really are from another world, then you must trust that I know what I speak of and do not attempt to escape the shifters. It is not just tagens you need to fear in these woods."

Reese bit the inside of her cheek and stared woodenly at the ground as Adina's features softened. She patted her shoulder. "I'm sorry. I don't want to upset you but it's time you faced the truth. The shifters are our best chance of survival."

Reese nodded and continued to stare at the ground. Her back was aching and the cramping in her stomach was making her feel nauseous. She tucked the folded pieces of fabric into the pocket of her skirt as Adina patted her back again.

"Are you all right?"

"Yes."

She wasn't. She was in pain and nearly paralyzed with worry and homesickness but she forced herself to smile at Adina. "I'll be better when we get to their home and I can lie down for a bit."

Adina gave her a worried look. "It is a full day of walking."

"I know. I'll be - "

"What are you talking about?" Kane had returned and he dropped the rabbits he was carrying and stalked toward Adina and Reese. "What are you whispering so secretively about?"

"Nothing." Adina gave him a nervous smile and then took a step back when Kane scowled at her. "Reese isn't feeling well and I was just encouraging her."

"What is wrong?" Kane asked with a note of alarm in his voice. He stepped closer and grabbed Reese's arm. "What is - "

He paused with an odd look on his face before he leaned in and inhaled. A small smile crossed his face and Reese scowled at him. "My pain makes you happy, shifter?"

"Of course not, Reese." He rubbed her arm. "I'm sorry you are not - "

He stopped abruptly, glancing behind him at Hanif and Theran. They were giving him odd looks and his hand tightened around Reese's arm before he glared at her.

"Stop your whining, human. We will be walking quickly and you will keep up."

"Yes, sir!" Reese gave him a sarcastic salute before turning and walking away. She stiffened and bent over a little with her hand pressing against her stomach, and Adina hurried after her. The woman rubbed her back and spoke into her ear as Kane stalked back to the dead rabbits.

He skinned his rabbit quickly and bit into its still-warm flesh. Beside him, Hanif and Theran were doing the same and he forced himself to eat large bites of the dead rabbit. Truthfully, his stomach was rolling with a mixture of happiness and worry. He didn't like that Reese was in pain, hated it in fact. He wanted to go to her and hold her until the small lines of pain around her mouth and eyes were gone. He felt a surge of anger at Hanif and Theran. If they weren't here he could be soothing his mate the way he was supposed to. He scowled angrily at them as they crunched happily on their own rabbits.

They didn't notice and he took a deep breath. He didn't like that Reese was hurting but it was better for her. Dagon was oddly squeamish about certain things, and even if he did choose Reese as his mate he would not go near her until her cycle was finished. It would give him more time to come up with a plan to keep Reese from Dagon. Once he saw the claiming mark on her shoulder, she was as good as dead. His hands clenched around the body of the rabbit at the thought of Dagon hurting Reese, and Theran gave him an odd look.

"What is wrong, Kane?"

"Nothing," he gritted out. He wiped the blood from his face and stared morosely at the rabbit in his hand.

"What is wrong with the big human?" Hanif asked as he sucked at the leg bone of his rabbit.

"The moon is full for her," he replied briefly.

"Great," Theran muttered. "You know how Dagon is. He won't go near her."

Hanif shrugged. "Truthfully, we'll be lucky if he chooses any of them. They all look terrible."

Kane studied the three humans. Hanif was right. Although Reese looked the worse, all of the humans were pale and tired-looking with dark circles under their eyes. The long days of walking and sleeping on the cold ground, the lack of food, and the rains had taken their toll on them.

"When he sees how weak they are we'll be lucky if he

doesn't just order them killed," Hanif said conversationally. "I'll never understand why Dagon believes that bringing humans into the pack is a good thing. They are not strong enough."

"They will be fine once they have more food and a few nights rest in an actual bed," Theran replied. "Even I am ready for my own bed and a warm fire."

"What will you do if Dagon chooses Ghita?" Hanif suddenly asked.

"He won't," Theran said anxiously. "You know he won't."

"But if he does? Marna was timid like her, remember?" Hanif persisted.

"He won't choose her," Theran repeated. "But if he does, I will challenge him for the alpha position."

Kane stared at Theran in shock as Hanif's mouth dropped open. He shook himself before clutching Theran's shoulder. "Do not speak so foolishly, Theran."

"I am not," he replied calmly.

"You cannot defeat Dagon. You know that. You would risk your life for a human?" Hanif asked.

"I would. I love her."

"You do not," Hanif snorted. "It hasn't even been a month that you have known her. You are just smitten with her, nothing else. If Dagon does choose her, you need to keep your mouth shut and accept it."

Theran, a small, strange smile on his face, shook his head. "I will not, Hanif. If he chooses Ghita I will challenge him and win."

"Kane, tell him what an idiot he's being," Hanif demanded.

"Hanif is right," Kane said. "You cannot challenge our alpha. If you love the human, then you should take her and leave."

Theran stared at him. "You would have me disobey our alpha's orders? Leave the pack? I cannot do that, Kane."

"You could start your own pack," Kane replied.

Theran shook his head. "I love Ghita but I will not leave my family, nor will I disobey Dagon. Besides, how long do you think a single shifter and his human mate would survive in the forest? We would have to move to a village and live amongst the humans. I won't do that."

Kane nodded. He understood what Theran was saying. As much as he feared for Reese, as much as he had grown to care about her, he couldn't imagine not being with his pack. To never see Radek or Raina again, and to live among humans who had no understanding of what a true family was. The very thought made his skin crawl. Not to mention he would be disobeying his alpha. Despite his dislike for Dagon, going against the alpha's orders made him feel physically ill.

Kane dropped his half-eaten rabbit into the dirt as Theran sighed. "Dagon will not choose Ghita. He realized his mistake with Marna. He prefers the fiery ones like Reese."

"Only because he enjoys breaking their spirits," Kane said bitterly.

As Theran and Hanif gave him curious looks, he stood and glared at the three humans. "Humans! We are leaving!"

———

"IT IS NOT MUCH FURTHER NOW, REESE," THERAN SAID encouragingly. He was walking with her and the other women and he patted her shoulder a little timidly.

Reese nodded grimly and forced herself to stagger on. Her stomach felt like one big cramp and her back was aching so badly she could barely walk. She was so tired she wanted to collapse. Despite her fear of meeting Dagon, she was actually looking forward to arriving at their home. At least then she could lie down in one of their damn caves and sleep.

"What I wouldn't give for some fucking Midol," she muttered to herself.

"Midol?" Adina asked. "What is that?"

"Nothing," she muttered again.

Adina gave her a sympathetic look and rubbed her lower back. "I found some tappin root, Reese. As soon as we are at the shifters' home I will ask them if I can boil some water and make you tea. It will help, I promise."

"Thanks, Adina," Reese replied wearily. "I'm sure I'll be - "

She stumbled over an exposed root and fell painfully to her knees. She rested for a moment with her hair hanging in her face as Adina crouched beside her.

"Here, let me help you - "

"Move." Kane was suddenly in front of them and Adina scurried out of the way as he scooped up Reese.

"Put me down, shifter. I can walk," she said tiredly, even as her head was dropping to his chest.

"Be quiet, Reese," he murmured.

She nodded and closed her eyes. She was cold and Kane's body heat felt wonderful against her skin. The steady beat of his heart beneath her ear and his warmth and the gentle sway as he walked soon lulled her into sleep.

"WAKE UP, REESE."

Kane's low voice murmured in her ear and she blinked blearily before raising her head. Her mouth dropped open in surprise. They were in a large clearing in the woods. In the middle of the clearing there was a huge campfire circled with stones, and she could see multiple cabins scattered throughout the trees. Most of them were small but there was a larger one that was set apart from the others. As Kane set her on her feet and steadied her, she studied her surroundings in the growing dark.

To the right of the cabins, a large mountain rose in the distance and she stared up at Kane. "You – you have houses."

"Were you expecting that we sleep among the trees?" Hanif snorted.

"Caves," she said wearily.

Hanif laughed as the other shifters in their pack emerged from the cabins. Kane moved away from her and the three women huddled together nervously as more and more shifters appeared. Most of them were big, strong-looking men although it appeared that Kane was one of the larger ones. There were a few women amongst them and they stared at the humans with a mixture of apprehension and curiosity as there was a loud squeal of delight.

Reese watched as a smaller female, she couldn't have been more than fifteen, launched herself at Kane. He caught her and hugged her as she pressed kisses on his cheeks and forehead.

"You are back! I was so worried when the rains came and you were not home yet!" She shouted before kissing him again.

"I told you I would return, did I not, Raina?" Kane set her down on the ground. She wrapped her arms around his waist.

"Did you find a suitable human mate for Dagon?" She asked.

"We have brought back three," he replied.

"Three!" She peered around Kane's large body. "She's a big one." She pointed at Reese and Kane frowned at her.

"Watch your tongue please, Raina."

"Sorry," she said cheerfully. "I was only being truthful. Which one do you think Dagon will choose?" She studied the women again. "None of them look very strong."

"They are tired and hungry. It's been a long journey for them," Kane replied. "Where is your brother?"

He searched the crowd of shifters as they gathered closer.

"Off hunting in the woods," Raina answered. "He'll be back soon. He'll be glad to see you, cousin. He's missed you more than I have and I missed you a lot."

"I've missed you both." Kane ruffled her hair affectionately before stiffening.

The door to the main cabin had opened and Reese watched as the shifter emerged. Her breath caught in her throat. The shifter was massive, bigger than even Kane, and he was dressed in a pair of pants and nothing else. He strode toward them and Reese wrapped her arm around Adina as the blonde woman began to tremble.

"Welcome home." He had a low, deep voice, dark hair and bright green eyes and Reese swallowed thickly when his gaze landed on her. She released her breath in a soft rush when his gaze left her and he smiled at Kane and the others.

"How was your journey?"

"Long," Theran replied. "We are glad to be home."

Dagon grinned at him. "I imagine you are. I see you were successful in your task."

"We were," Theran replied. "We have brought back three females for you to choose from."

"Good." Dagon studied the women again before pointing his finger at Adina. "Step forward, human."

With a nervous look at Reese, Adina stood in front of the alpha. He looked her up and down before sniffing at her.

"She smells of you, Hanif. Were you fucking my potential

mate?" Dagon's voice was soft but Reese could hear the anger in it."

"No, Dagon," Hanif said quickly. "The humans cannot hold their heat and we were forced to sleep with them at night to keep them warm. We each took a human."

"Did you?" Dagon glanced behind him at Kane. "Even Kane?"

"Aye," Kane said shortly.

Dagon raised his eyebrows at him. "I am surprised you did not simply let her freeze to death. It is not in your nature to be nurturing. Especially to a human."

"I did not want to fail my alpha's command," Kane replied.

A grin crept across Dagon's face. "You were wise to set aside your hatred for the humans, Kane."

He turned back to Adina and his smile faded. "She looks terrible. She is pale and trembling and she smells of weariness."

He glanced at Reese and Ghita. "Were these three the best you could find?"

"Aye," Theran replied. "They were the biggest and the strongest, Dagon."

"They don't look strong to me," Dagon retorted.

"It has been a long journey for them," Hanif said a bit desperately. "Once they have gotten some sleep and food in their bellies, they will be better. They are tired and cold right now."

Dagon snorted. "I did not think about their inability to stay warm. I suppose it isn't a big deal. I will keep the one I choose warm enough and as for the other two – if they are not taken as mates by another in the pack, they will just have to adapt to the cold."

"We can get them warmer clothes, extra pelts for their beds," Kane said.

Dagon stared at him. "Your sudden affection for humans is surprising to me, Kane."

"It is not affection," Kane replied. "We paid money for them. I would think you would want to keep them alive."

"True," Dagon mused. He reached out and touched Adina's hair before cupping her breast. She stiffened but didn't move away as he squeezed it. "This one has nice breasts."

He dropped his hand and moved toward Ghita and Reese. Ghita made a soft moan of fear and Dagon frowned at her. "Do not be so frightened, human. I am not a monster."

He studied them both, his eyes lingering on Reese's hips and her large breasts, before he stepped closer. "This one is too fat but she would probably survive giving birth to my pups."

He reached out to touch her before a look of distaste crossed his face. He sniffed at her and Reese blinked in surprise when he took a hurried step back and put his hand over his nose. "When did her cycle start?"

"This morning," Kane replied.

Dagon made a soft sound of disgust before moving away from all of them. "Well, I'm not making my decision today. They all look and smell terrible. I'll give them a week or two and then make my decision."

A nasty grin crossed his face. "In the meantime, the humans will stay with the three of you. You can continue to care for my potential mates and keep them warm."

His grin widened as he stared at Kane. "No doubt this is a troubling task for you, Kane, but I trust you will not disappoint me."

"Of course not." Kane forced himself to look both angry

and disgusted as Dagon laughed. Truthfully he was thrilled that Dagon had forced Reese upon him but if he allowed even a hint of his happiness to show, Dagon would be immediately suspicious. He knew of Kane's hatred for the humans and it was a testament to his cruel nature that he demanded Kane continue to care for Reese.

Dagon clapped Hanif on the back. "Go. Take the humans to your cabins. Warm them up, let them rest and fill their bellies with food. I will let you know when I'm ready to make my decision."

Reese didn't protest when Kane took her arm and hurried her across the clearing. His cabin was tucked back in the trees. She grimaced and tried to hold back her groan of pain as Kane nearly dragged her into the cabin and shut the door.

His grip on her arm loosened and he rubbed it as he gave her an anxious look. "Are you all right, Reese?"

"Fine, shifter." She rubbed her stomach and stared around the cabin. It was small, just one big room really, with a good size fireplace. Two armchairs were in front of the fireplace and a large wooden bed was pushed up against one wall. On the other side, four cupboards ran across the top of the wall and a small, wooden table and two chairs made up the kitchen.

"This is nice." She gave him a tentative smile as he hurried to the fireplace and quickly started a fire.

She snorted and rolled her eyes as he gave her a guilty look. "Come sit by the fire."

Before she could reply, there was a knock on the door and Raina stuck her head into the cabin. "Hi!"

"Hello." Reese gave her a tired smile as the girl bounced into the cabin and slammed the door shut.

"I'm Raina."

"Reese."

"What a pretty name." Raina grinned at her.

"Raina, she needs to rest." Kane frowned at the young girl. "You can visit with her later. Come sit by the fire, Reese."

"I have to use the bathroom." She grimaced as another cramp struck, and she rubbed at her belly as Raina gave her a sympathetic look.

"The moon is full for you. Is it very bad? You're very pale."

"I'll be fine." She pulled a strip of fabric from her pocket. "I'll be right back."

She headed for the door and frowned at Kane when he followed her. "I don't need your help, shifter."

Kane hesitated and then smiled at Raina. "Show her to the bathroom. Would you, Raina?"

"Aye, I will," Raina said cheerfully.

She opened the door and Reese followed her into the trees behind Kane's cabin. "Is there like a particular tree you use or something?" She asked.

"Tree?" Raina gave her an odd look before pointing to a small wooden outhouse. "Here's the bathroom. You have to share it with Radek and me," she gestured to the cabin to the right of Kane's, "but Deena and Borek have their own."

"Deena and Borek?" Reese asked as she hurried toward the outhouse.

"They live in the cabin to the left. Deena is a bit odd, but Borek is nice." Raina smiled at her. "I'll just wait for you here, all right?"

"Thank you."

Reese opened the door to the outhouse and could have wept with relief. She hadn't used an outhouse since she went camping as a child, but knowing she would no longer having to squat and pee on the ground was making her ridiculously happy.

Darkness had fallen by the time she finished. She didn't object when Raina took her hand and led her carefully through the trees toward the cabin.

"Can you see in the dark at all?" Raina asked curiously.

Reese nodded. "Yes, but probably not as well as you can."

"Probably not," Raina agreed.

Raina opened the door to the already-deliciously warm cabin and followed Reese to the bed. Kane was gone but Reese was too tired to wonder where he was. She collapsed on top of the thin blanket. The bed was surprisingly soft and comfortable and she buried her face in her arms as Raina sat down next to her.

"Human?"

"Yes?"

"Are you going to sleep?"

"Yes."

"Oh." There was disappointment in Raina's voice and Reese lifted her head and smiled at her.

"I'm sorry. I'm very tired. I would like it if you came by tomorrow and visited with me though. All right?"

"I can do that." Raina smiled happily at her. "Good bye, human."

"Bye, Raina."

CHAPTER 17

"Wake up, Reese." Kane's warm hand shook her shoulder.

She muttered and buried her face deeper into her arms. "Go away, shifter. I'm tired."

"I know," he replied, "but I have a surprise for you."

She cracked one eye open. "What are you talking about?"

"I have a surprise for you," he repeated. "Sit up."

She forced her weary body into a sitting position. "How long have I been sleeping?"

"Only an hour or so. Look." He cupped her face and turned her head toward the kitchen. A large metal tub was sitting on the floor and it was filled with steaming water.

"Is that – oh my God, is that a bathtub?" She said stupidly.

He nodded. "Yes. I warmed some water for you. I thought you would like to have a bath."

She slid off the bed and nearly ran toward the tub, holding her stomach gingerly. "I definitely want a bath."

Kane rubbed her back. "Climb into the tub, Reese." He

pointed to a small wooden bowl sitting on the floor next to the tub. It was filled with a white gel and there was a cloth resting on the edge of the bowl.

"That's soap."

"Thank you." She gave him a sweet smile and he hesitated before leaning down and kissing her.

"I will return in a bit."

"Sure." She was dipping her hand into the water and he slipped out of the cabin, smiling happily to himself.

Reese quickly stripped off her clothes and climbed into the tub. The water was almost too hot, but she sat down anyway and sighed with delight. The tub was surprisingly large and by scooting downward she could submerge her entire body in the steaming water. She dipped her head back to wet her long dark hair, and then closed her eyes and allowed the water to ease some of the ache in her back.

She knew she should be washing her hair, but she was too tired, and it felt wonderful to just sit in the hot water. When Kane returned half an hour later, carrying a steel pot that he placed carefully over the fire, she hadn't moved a muscle.

"Reese? Are you awake?"

"Mmm-hmm," she murmured.

"Are you ready to get out?"

"No." She shook her head. "I might just sleep here tonight."

He grinned and knelt next to the tub. "You like this then?"

She opened her eyes. "I love it. Thank you."

"You're welcome." He touched her head and then moved around behind her. "Dip your hair into the water and then sit up."

She did as he asked as Kane stripped out of his shirt and reached for the soap. He smeared a large portion of it onto his hands and washed her hair, rubbing and massaging

176

the soap into her scalp before carefully soaping her long tresses.

"Thank you, Kane. That feels really good," she murmured.

"You're welcome, Reese."

Using a cup, he rinsed her hair clean of the soap. She was surprised but didn't protest when he gently and efficiently washed the rest of her body. When he was finished, he helped her to her feet and dried her quickly with a soft piece of fabric before wrapping it around her body.

"Where did you get this?" She touched the soft fabric as he lifted her from the tub.

"There is a human village a few days' journey from here. We go there to trade meat and fur for clothing and other items from time to time," he replied.

"Oh."

He pointed to a bundle of clothing on the table. "Raina brought these while you were sleeping. She thought you could use some clean clothes. They belonged to her mother. She was tall like you."

Reese picked up the stack of folded cloths from the top. They were made of a soft, absorbent material and she rubbed them curiously.

"They are for your - "

"Yeah, I get it," she interrupted hastily.

"Raina says they will absorb the blood better than the fabric of your shirt," Kane said.

"Right." She supposed she should have been embarrassed but Kane's matter-of-fact tone and his obvious lack of discomfort in regard to her cycle had stripped away any embarrassment she might have felt.

Kane handed her a pair of underwear before lifting her into her arms.

"I can walk," she protested as he carried her out of the cabin and to the outhouse.

"It's fine." He set her at the door of the outhouse and she nodded thanks before disappearing inside.

He waited patiently and gave her a small smile when she stepped back outside. "Better?"

"Yes." She tightened the towel around her as Kane lifted her again and carried her back to the cabin. He set her next to the bed and pulled a thick bear pelt from the basket at the end of the bed and threw it over the thin blanket. He pulled the bedcovers back and guided Reese toward the bed.

She climbed in with a soft sigh and he shook his head when she started to lie down. "Don't go to sleep yet, Reese."

He poured some liquid into a mug from the pot over the fire, and grabbed a wide-toothed comb from the table before bringing the mug to her.

"Drink this."

"What is it?"

"Tappin root tea. Adina made it for you."

She sipped cautiously at the hot liquid as Kane pulled the fabric away from her body and used it to blot her hair. He combed her hair and untangled the snarls with a gentle touch as she sipped at the tea. It had a minty taste and she was surprised when the cramping in her belly eased almost immediately.

"Are you hungry?" Kane asked.

"Not really," she replied. "Tired, mostly."

The warmth of the bath, the hot tea and the gentle motion of the comb through her hair was relaxing her and she closed her eyes and yawned hugely. Kane pulled the cup from her hand and urged her on to her side. "Lie down, Reese."

"Sure," she agreed sleepily.

She curled into a ball as Kane rubbed her lower back. "Does your stomach feel better?"

She nodded. "Yes. That feels wonderful, Kane. Don't stop."

"I won't." He continued to rub her naked back as her breathing slowed and deepened. After nearly ten minutes he pressed a gentle kiss on the soft skin of her upper back. "Reese?"

There was no reply and he smiled with satisfaction. His mate was feeling better and she was happier. He continued to stroke her lower back as he placed a smattering of gentle kisses across her upper back. For the first time in a long time, he was content. Taking care of his mate and easing her pain made him feel good, he realized. He never thought that –

"Kane? What are you doing?"

He jerked and sat up, staring guiltily across the room. Radek had entered his cabin without knocking and the younger shifter was staring at him in confusion.

"Radek? I thought you were hunting?"

"I was," he said briefly. He crossed the room and Kane hurriedly pulled the pelt up, covering Reese's naked upper body as Radek sniffed at her.

"Why do you have a human in your bed?" Radek couldn't hide the distaste in his voice.

"She is one of Dagon's potential mates. The moon is full for her and he wants nothing to do with her until it is finished."

He stepped away from the bed, indicating for Radek to follow him. They sat at the table and Kane could feel the heat rising in his cheeks when Radek stared silently at him.

"What?"

"What?" Radek raised his eyebrows at him. "You have a

half-naked human in your bed. You were rubbing her back and – and kissing her. What the hell is going on with you, Kane?"

"Nothing. The human wasn't feeling well and I was simply trying to help her," Kane said shortly.

"She is covered in your scent."

"They cannot hold their heat. Theran, Hanif and I were forced to keep them warm with our body heat while we travelled."

"Them? How many did you bring back with you?"

"Three."

Radek made a soft noise of disgust. "It is bad enough that Dagon is going to mate with a human, you had to bring back three of them?"

"We thought it would be better if he had a choice."

"And which one did he choose?"

"He hasn't chosen any of them yet. They're worn out from the journey and Dagon is giving them time to recover before he chooses his mate."

"How many times have you fucked the human?" Radek asked abruptly.

Kane shook his head. "I haven't. I told you – she carries my scent because I - "

"Stop lying to me, Kane," Radek said. "You have never lied to me before."

"Fine. I fucked the human. She was taken by a tagen just before the rains started. I killed the tagen but we were trapped in its den until the rains stopped. I only fucked her because I was curious what it would be like to fuck a human."

"Since when? You hate the humans," Radek replied. "They killed your parents or have you forgotten that?"

"Of course I haven't. But Reese did not kill my parents," he snapped irritably.

"Reese? So now it has a name."

"Radek, it meant nothing," he said in a low voice. "I know I shouldn't have but the human knows she cannot tell anyone. No one will find out."

"Are you sure it meant nothing?" Radek asked. "It didn't seem like nothing to me when I walked in here."

Kane rolled his eyes. "I told you, the human wasn't feeling well. If she is to be Dagon's mate, she needs to regain her strength. Since I have been tasked with finding his human mate, I'll do what needs to be done. The humans are fragile and need extra care."

"Another reason we should not be bringing them into our pack. What do you think their children will be like? Our pack will be weakened by the half-breed babies they produce."

"Enough, Radek," Kane said harshly. "Our alpha has decided to bring humans into the pack and if you are smart, you will keep your thoughts about them to yourself."

He glanced again at Reese as Radek made a low growl. "Since you feel the need to give me advice, perhaps you'll take mine as well."

Kane gave him an impatient look and Radek growled again. "Do a better job at hiding your emotions. If you're not careful, the others will see your love for the human."

"I don't love her," Kane said immediately.

"Do you not?" Radek stood and walked toward the door. "Welcome home, cousin."

"She smells strange."

"She's a human. Of course she smells strange."

"No, I mean she smells strange even for a human."

"Oh be quiet, Mia. How would you know what a human even smells like?"

"I have been to the village with my parents, Raina. I know what humans smell like."

Reese opened her eyes and stared blearily at the two young girls standing at the end of the bed.

"Good morning, human!" Raina said brightly. "Are you feeling better?"

"A little. Can you hand me a shirt?" Reese asked. Mindful of Kane's warning to keep his bite mark hidden, she kept the blankets to her neck and wiggled into the shirt Raina handed her before sitting up.

She pushed the hair out of her face and smiled at the two girls. Truthfully, she still felt like crap and she wished she could just curl back up in bed but the two young shifters had climbed on to the bed and were staring at her.

"This is Mia. She's my best friend," Raina said.

"Hello, Mia."

"Hello," Mia said shyly. She was tall with sandy brown hair and freckles and she stared curiously at Reese as Raina slid off the bed and hurried to the fireplace.

She came back with a mug and handed it to Reese. "Here. Kane said I should give this to you when you wake."

"Where is Kane?" Reese asked as she sipped at the tappin root tea.

Raina shrugged. "I don't know. Out in the forest with Radek maybe. Are you hungry? Kane caught and cooked a rabbit for you before he left."

"He did?"

"Aye." She skipped to the table and returned with a plate piled high with meat. She slid it on to the bed in front of Reese. "Eat, human."

Reese picked up a piece of meat and chewed it gingerly.

It was good and her stomach growled. Mia and Raina grinned at each other before Mia leaned over and sniffed at the meat.

"It doesn't smell very good."

"Have you – do you ever eat your meat cooked?" Reese asked.

"No. Shifters don't like cooked meat. What's the point?" Mia said.

"I've always wanted to try it cooked," Raina said hopefully.

"Help yourself." Reese pushed the plate toward her and Raina picked up a piece of meat and popped it into her mouth. She chewed thoughtfully at it as Mia stared at her.

"How does it taste?"

Raina shrugged. "Odd. It's very dry. You should try it."

Mia hesitated before taking a small piece of the meat. She put it in her mouth and Reese grinned when she made a face and spit it out into her hand.

"Ugh, it's awful."

The two girls watched as she nibbled at the rabbit and drank more tea. When her cup was empty, Raina refilled it and handed it to her again.

"Thank you, Raina."

"You're welcome, human." Raina smiled at her. "You have very nice hair. Can I braid it?"

"Uh, sure." Reese shifted forward as Raina scrambled behind her and began to comb through her hair with her fingers.

"How old are you, human?" Raina asked curiously.

"I'm twenty-five. How old are you?"

"Mia and I are both fourteen. You're the same age as my brother, Radek."

"Kane is your cousin?"

"Yes. He practically grew up with us after the humans killed his parents. It's why he hates your kind."

"Where are your parents?" Reese asked. She had a bad feeling about the answer and it was confirmed when Raina sighed.

"They died two years ago."

"I'm sorry."

"Thanks." Raina gathered her hair and began to braid it as Mia sniffed the air.

"You smell strange, human."

"Do I?"

"Aye. Where are you from?"

"Not anywhere you've heard of," Reese said evasively.

"How did you end up at the auction?" Raina asked.

"Men captured me in the forest." Reese cleared her throat. "So do you spend most of your time in your human form or your wolf form?"

Mia shrugged. "It depends. Some shifters prefer to be in their wolf forms, like Radek and Kane, and others like their human form. Dagon usually stays in his human form which is odd for an alpha."

"No it isn't," Raina argued. "Radek says Dagon's father preferred his human form too."

"So why do Kane and Radek prefer their wolf form?" Reese asked.

"Probably because they hate humans so much," Raina replied.

"I understand why Kane hates humans but why does your brother?"

"He just does," Raina said evasively. She looked away, the smile dropping from her face, and Reese touched her arm before sliding out of the bed. She crossed the room and picked up a pair of pants from the pile on the table.

"Thank you for letting me use your mother's clothes." She smiled at Raina.

"You're welcome."

She pulled on the pants. They were a bit tight in the ass and a little big around the waist but they were comfortable enough. She grabbed one of the folded cloths before heading to the front door. "I'll be right back."

When she returned, Kane was standing in the kitchen with a large blond-haired man. Raina was standing beside him with the plate of meat and poking him in the stomach.

"Just try it, Radek. Come on. Try a little piece," she cajoled.

He shook his head. "No. Do not be a pest, Raina."

She pouted at him as Reese shut the door and gave Kane a nervous smile.

"Good morning."

"Good morning Ree – human." He spoke gruffly to her but there was an anxious look in his eyes. "Are you feeling better?"

"A little," she replied. Feeling oddly anxious herself, she crossed the room and stood in front of Radek. "Hello, I'm Reese."

Radek turned to face her. He looked her up and down and she took a nervous step back when his face reddened and he growled.

"Enough, Radek," Kane said sharply.

"Why is it wearing my mother's clothing?" Radek snarled.

"I gave them to her." Raina frowned at him. "Her clothing was dirty and I knew mama's clothes would fit her."

Radek growled again and glared at Reese. "Take them off. You have no right to wear her clothes."

"I'm sorry," Reese said. "I'll change right now."

"You're being an ass," Raina snapped at Radek. "The human is nice and mama would have lent her clothing if she was still alive."

"Be quiet, Raina!" Radek scowled at her. "The human isn't fit to lick our feet let alone wear our - "

"Get out, Radek," Kane said.

"Kane, it's okay. I understand and I - "

Kane shook his head at her as Radek gave him a look of betrayal. "You would choose the human over me, Kane?"

"I'm not choosing anyone," Kane replied. "But Reese is a guest in my home and I will not allow you to insult her. Apologize for your remarks or leave."

"What is wrong with you, cousin?" Radek glared at him. "Do you think because she spread her - "

"Enough, Radek!" Kane roared as a thick beard grew on his face. "Leave now before I make you leave."

Mia gave a nervous squeak and even Raina took a step back as Radek bared his teeth at Kane and his eyes glowed a bright green.

"I never thought I would see the day that you would defend a human," he snarled. He glared again at Reese and pushed past her angrily, nearly knocking her over. Kane made a hoarse howl of rage. Reese grabbed his arm and hung on grimly when he went after his cousin.

"Kane, no! Calm down!"

Radek slammed the door and Reese stroked Kane's arm as he growled.

"Girls, I think you should go now. You can come back and visit later, all right?" Reese tried to smile reassuringly at the two young shifters as Raina nodded and took Mia's hand.

"Good-bye, human." She yanked Mia out of the cabin, shutting the door behind her.

Reese continued to stroke Kane's arm. He was staring at

the floor of the cabin, his chest heaving and his hands clenching and unclenching.

"Please relax, shifter. It's no big deal."

"No big deal?" He glared at her. "He insulted you."

She shrugged. "It didn't bother me. Besides, I have a feeling that I need to get used to being insulted. Based on the way some of your pack mates were staring at us yesterday, I get the feeling you and Radek aren't the only ones who think humans in the pack are a bad idea."

She switched to rubbing his back, waiting patiently for him to calm down and doing her best to ignore the pain in her stomach. The cramps were back and all she really wanted to do was drink some more tea and lie down.

After nearly five minutes, Kane raised his head and stared at her. "You didn't eat."

"I did," she assured him. "I ate some of the meat you cooked. Thank you for that, by the way."

He searched her face carefully. "You are still pale, Reese."

"I still don't feel great," she replied. "If it's okay with you, I think I'll lie down again."

He stared anxiously at her. "Is it always like this? Female shifters do not seem to suffer the way you do when the moon is full for them."

She patted his arm. "I'm fine. This is nothing new – I just usually have a lot more drugs to dull the pain."

He continued to stare anxiously at her. He didn't like the way she looked – pale with fine lines of pain still around her mouth and eyes.

"You need more tea," he said abruptly.

She jerked when he scooped her up and carried her to the bed. He undressed her down to her panties and urged her to climb into the bed before bringing her more tea. "We are almost out. I'll ask Adina to make more."

"Thank you." She sipped at the tea. "Are Adina and Ghita okay? Have you seen either of them?"

"They're fine. Ghita has not left Theran's cabin but Adina met a few of my pack mates this morning."

"Were they nice to her?"

He nodded. "Aye. They're not monsters, Reese. I know that Radek did not make a good impression but many of my pack mates are willing to accept humans. They will treat you fairly, I promise."

She didn't reply and he sat on the side of the bed as she finished drinking her tea. "Lie down, Reese."

She slid under the covers with a soft sigh and closed her eyes. When Kane joined her in the bed, she blinked at him in surprise but didn't object when he pulled her up against his naked body. She relaxed against him, enjoying the warmth of his body, as he rubbed her lower back and nuzzled her throat affectionately.

She knew she should be telling him to stop. In a week or two there was the strong possibility that she would be mated to his alpha and she would never feel Kane's touch again. His refusal to take her as his own mate, his willingness to just hand her over to Dagon without a second thought, brought the sting of tears and a low burn of anger toward him. She blinked rapidly before shifting out of his arms and turning her back to him.

"Reese? What's wrong?"

"Nothing," she said hoarsely. "I'm just tired."

He curled his arm around her waist and moved her backward until she was pressed against his hard warmth again. She squirmed and tugged at his arm. "I'm not comfortable."

He shifted her slightly but refused to let her go. After a few moments, she stopped squirming.

"Just relax and go to sleep." He kissed her throat as his fingers stroked the scar on her shoulder obsessively. "Close your eyes. I will keep you safe."

His words sent a pang of sorrow through her. "Will you?"

"Aye." He kissed her throat again as his fingers stroked and caressed and circled the bite mark. "No harm will come to you, Reese."

CHAPTER 18

W hen she woke, Kane was gone. She slid out of the bed and helped herself to more tea. Her stomach and pelvis were throbbing, but she didn't feel as tired as she had before. When Kane still didn't appear after half an hour, she gathered her dirty clothes from the floor and dressed.

She sniffed Kane's shirt and grimaced. His shirt and her skirt were filthy and smelled terrible, but she didn't want to risk offending his cousin again. She re-braided her hair and then nervously stepped out of the cabin and into the cold sunlight. She picked her way through the trees toward the large clearing.

To her relief, Adina was sitting next to the campfire with four female shifters and she smiled cheerfully when Reese joined them.

"You look better." She wrinkled her nose when Reese sat down beside her. "But you smell terrible."

"Thanks." Reese scowled playfully at her. "And thank you for the tea. It's really helping."

"Did they not give you clean clothes?" Adina frowned.

She was wearing a long green skirt and a heavy sweater and she rubbed Reese's arm. "You're freezing already."

Reese smiled tentatively at the other women as she held her hands out to the fire. "Raina brought me some of her mother's clothing but then I met her brother and there was an issue."

She didn't want to say much more, unsure of what the female shifters staring curiously at her would think, but one of the females nodded.

"Aye, I imagine Radek would have been displeased to see you wearing his mother's clothing."

Reese gave the shifter another tentative smile. She was the oldest of the four with silver hair that hung almost to her knees. She had bright blue eyes and skin marred with wrinkles.

"Hello, I'm Reese." She hesitated and then held out her hand. The old shifter stared curiously at it for a moment before glancing at the others.

They shrugged and, blushing, Reese let her hand drop.

"I'm Anna," the shifter said. "And this is Verna, Kavine and Deena."

"Hello. It's nice to meet you," Reese replied.

The shifter named Verna sniffed in her direction. "You smell strange for a human."

Kavine covered her nose with her hand. "She smells rotten."

"Kavine!" Anna gave her a fierce look. "This human could be our alpha's mate. You will speak kindly about her or hold your tongue. Do you understand?"

"Aye, Anna," Kavine replied. She gave Reese a sour look. "Although why must Dagon believe that a human would make a better mate than a shifter? They look like a strong wind would knock them over."

Verna laughed. "Not the big one. She could stand against a gale force wind and not be injured."

She cocked her head curiously at Reese. "How much food do you eat, human? I bet you eat more than our men. You should know that we will not simply gather food for you to eat, even if you become our alpha's mate. You will be expected to help."

Reese bit back her scathing retort and smiled at Verna instead. "I know. I'm more than willing to help out wherever it's needed."

Anna glared at Verna before turning to Reese. "Pay them no mind, human. They're both spoiled little pups with nothing better to do than gossip."

Both Kavine and Verna started to protest and Anna silenced them with a harsh growl. "I said to mind your tongues!"

They lowered their gazes to the ground at their feet and Anna smiled kindly at Reese. "We will find you some warmer clothing."

"We have no clothing that will fit her, Anna. She is too fat." Kavine couldn't resist saying. "Neela's clothing would be the only clothing close to her size, and Radek will tear her apart before he allows her to wear his mother's clothing. She will have to continue to wear Kane's clothing."

She paused and leaned forward, studying Reese with bright curiosity. "Does Kane make you sleep on the floor?"

Reese blinked at her. "What?"

"Kane hates humans. I'm surprised he even allowed you through the door of his cabin."

"He had no choice," Verna reminded her. "Dagon ordered him to keep watch over her, remember?"

"I remember," Kavine replied. "Does he make you sleep on the floor like a dog?"

Reese didn't reply and Verna stared at her. "Well, does he? I could see him doing that. I'm surprised he even gave you his shirt. Although I suppose the last thing he wants to see is a naked human."

"He bathes her and feeds her and holds her close to him in his bed. He cares for her like one would care for a delicate flower. She is precious to him." A raspy and stilted voice, spoke.

Reese, her face paling, stared at the shifter named Deena. The female looked to be around her age and she had dark brown eyes and long, dirty black hair that was tangled with bits of dried leaves and twigs. Her face and arms were smeared with dirt and her clothing stained. Her eyes darted back and forth and she licked her lips repeatedly.

Verna and Kavine stared at her in shocked silence before bursting into peals of loud laughter. Verna with tears leaking down her face, held her stomach and shook her head.

"Oh, Deena. You are mad, truly."

"Verna!"

"I'm sorry, Anna. But even you must admit that is the maddest thing Deena has ever said. Kane caring for a human?"

Kavine, whose laughter had begun to taper off, was sent into another wild fit of giggles. "Remember the time he and Radek went to the human's farm? They nearly killed the humans who lived there until Maven showed up and stopped them."

"I remember." Verna wiped the tears from her eyes and stared at Deena. "Whatever possessed you to say such a thing, Deena?"

Deena didn't reply and Verna leaned over and touched Reese's arm. "You must ignore whatever Deena says. Her brains were addled a year ago by an angry bear shifter and since then she says the strangest things."

She paused and then stroked Reese's arm. "This human's skin is as soft as hers." She pointed to Adina. "How do you make your skin so soft, humans?"

Adina shrugged. "It just is."

"Here, feel mine." Verna squeezed her way between them and Reese and Adina both touched the shifter's arms. She was incredibly warm and Reese thought her skin was soft.

"Your skin feels soft to me," she said.

"Does it?" Verna glanced at her. "Yours feels much softer. I hope it does not convince our males to mate with you."

She hesitated. "No offense."

"None taken," Reese replied.

"They won't," Kavine said with finality. "Just because our alpha desires human women does not mean the others in our pack will lower themselves the way he has and take a human to their beds."

Anna slapped her viciously across the face and Kavine made a loud whine of pain and shock as she fell from the log she was sitting on.

"Speak that way of our alpha again and I'll take your tongue, foolish girl. This is your last warning," Anna snarled.

Kavine whined in submission. "I am sorry, Anna. I'm just," she stole a glance at Adina and Reese, "worried."

"You have nothing to worry about," Verna said dismissively. She was holding the end of Reese's braid and a lock of Adina's hair and rubbing her fingers through the strands. "Radek will never take one of the humans."

She smiled in a friendly manner at Reese. "Kavine is in love with Radek. She's been trying for months to get him to mate with her, but he refuses."

"Shut up, Verna!" Kavine snapped as she brushed the dirt from her pants and sat back down on the log.

"You have very pretty eyes," Verna said thoughtfully to Reese. "Their colour is so strange." She leaned closer and sniffed her. "But you do smell terrible."

"Is there somewhere I could wash my clothing?" Reese asked.

"Aye, you could wash them in the lake. Come, I'll show you the way." Verna took her hand and tugged her to her feet.

"WELL, HOW ARE MY POTENTIAL MATES TODAY?" DAGON SAT down in the chair and stared at the three shifters standing before him.

"Better, Dagon," Hanif said quickly. "Adina is feeling much better."

"Adina? Is that the blonde woman's name?" Dagon asked.

Hanif nodded and Dagon glanced at Kane and Theran. "And the other two? What are their names?"

"Ghita is the smaller one and Reese the bigger," Theran replied.

"Sit down, all of you." Dagon waved irritably and the three shifters joined him around the fireplace. "Tell me your thoughts on them."

Theran glanced quickly at the others. "All of them are very healthy, my alpha. Although Ghita may be a bit too timid for you."

"Then why did you pick her?"

"I did not realize how timid she was until later."

Dagon sighed. "I knew I should have sent Teagan and not you, Theran. You are quite useless."

Theran turned a dull red but said nothing as Dagon gave

him a cruel grin. Hanif cleared his throat. "Adina is not timid, my alpha, and she says that the women in her family are quite fertile."

"Are they? That is good. She is prepared to have my pups then?"

"Aye," Hanif answered.

"And what of yours, Kane? Is she a suitable mate for your alpha?"

Kane didn't reply and Dagon frowned irritably as Theran leaned forward. "She would be, Dagon. She has a fiery spirit and I know you like that."

Kane had to stop himself from glaring at the man. He understood what Theran was trying to do but he could barely control his urge to throttle the man into silence.

"I do. She's a bit on the large side though, isn't she?"

"It would probably make it easier for her to have your pups," Theran said.

"That is something to consider. Still," he glanced at Kane, "we will restrict her food until she is at a more pleasing weight. A few months of just plants and a bit of meat will help thin her down."

"Dagon, you cannot starve the human," Kane snapped.

Dagon gave him an assessing look. "Are you disobeying my command, Kane?"

"Of course not," he muttered.

"Good. Then you will tell our females to feed the human only once a day. In fact, do not give her any meat at all."

He paused. "Can the humans eat raw meat?"

"No, my alpha," Hanif replied. "Adina says it will make them sick. They must eat cooked meat."

Dagon sighed with annoyance. "Are we sure of this? Have you tried them on raw meat?"

"No, but the humans aren't like us, Dagon."

"I suppose they are not. I should have thought of that before I brought them into the pack. The smell of cooked meat turns my stomach. The one I choose will have to get used to eating raw meat or eat only plants."

"They can cook the meat outside, Dagon," Kane replied. "There is no need to force them to eat the way we do. You want your mate to be healthy enough to give you pups, do you not?"

"What has gotten into you, Kane? Since when do you care about humans?"

"I don't." Kane gave him a brittle smile.

Dagon stared into the fire for a moment. "I will spend time with each of them before I make my decision. Does the fat one still bleed?"

"Aye, and will continue to do so for a few days. The moon is only just full for her," Kane replied.

A look of disgust passed over Dagon's face. "Shifter or human, it does not matter – females are more trouble than they are worth. Always whining and crying, and always demanding your attention. It is enough to drive a wolf mad."

The three shifters didn't reply and Dagon stood up. "Once I have chosen my mate, any of the pack who wish to do so can try out the other two."

"Try them out?" Theran asked.

"Aye." Dagon nodded. "I will not expect my pack brothers to hold the female humans in the same regard as our pack females. If they want to try fucking either of the humans, they will be allowed to."

"You cannot be serious!" Kane shouted. "What has gotten into you, Dagon? Not even you would be so cruel as to allow innocent humans to be raped and abused by your pack."

Dagon's face turned red and he struck Kane across the face. Blood flowed from Kane's mouth and he clenched his hands into fists as he glared at the alpha. Dagon stared at his clenched hands, an amused smile playing on his lips.

"Will you challenge your alpha, Kane? Is that what this is about? You covet my right to rule?"

Kane, breathing like an angry bull, continued to stare at Dagon.

"Well, do you?"

After a long tense moment, Kane relaxed his body. "No, Dagon. I do not."

"Good." Dagon smiled thinly at him. "Now all of you get out of my sight."

The three shifters left the alpha's cabin. As they walked toward the clearing, Theran placed a tentative hand on Kane's arm. "Kane? What got into you back there?"

Kane glared at him. "So you think it's fine that Adina or Ghita or Reese will be raped by our pack? What has gotten into *you*?"

"You know as well as I do that no one in our pack will rape the human females." Theran gave him a surprised look. "Dagon will make his choice and if our pack brothers desire the other two, they will treat them as well as they treat our females. It does not matter what Dagon tells them they are allowed to do."

Kane didn't reply and Theran shrugged before calling across the clearing to Anna. The old shifter was sitting alone by the fire and she raised her hand in acknowledgment before walking toward them.

"What is it, Theran?"

"The bigger female, Reese is her name?"

"What about her?"

"Dagon wants you to restrict her food. She is to have only one meal a day, just plants and no meat. He believes her to be too fat."

A low growl was rising in Kane's chest and Anna gave him an odd look. "What is it, Kane?"

"Nothing," he snapped before storming away.

"What is wrong with Kane?" Anna asked.

"We have no idea," Theran replied. "He has been acting odd since the rains ended."

"He is just unhappy that there are humans in the pack now," Hanif said. "He had to spend the entire rains alone in a cave with Reese and she drives him crazy."

"Does she?" Anna said thoughtfully.

"She does. She never stops talking and keep this to yourself, but the human is as mad as Deena."

"She does not appear mad."

"She is," Hanif said cheerfully. "Completely mad."

"Be quiet, Hanif," Theran said nervously as he glanced behind him at Dagon's cabin.

"Where are the humans, anyway?" Hanif asked.

"They went to the lake so that the big one could wash her clothing," Anna replied. "Kavine and Verna took them."

"Do you like the humans?" Theran asked curiously.

"They seem nice. I have yet to meet the one you keep hidden in your cabin."

Theran smiled nervously. "She is very tired. She needs a bit more rest."

"Perhaps if you allowed her to sleep at night she would not be so tired, Theran."

He blushed. "I do not know what you mean, Anna."

"Do you forget that your cabin is next to mine?" Anna said dryly. "You should either close your windows or teach your human to lower her voice when you are fucking her."

Hanif laughed and clapped Theran on the back. "Come, Theran. Let us find the rest of the pack and join them in the hunt."

CHAPTER 19

"Kane is going to be angry that you took another of his shirts," Verna said.

She watched as Reese finished rinsing the soap from her skirt and wrung it out before hanging it over one of the lower branches of the large tree that grew beside the lake.

"Is she going to be okay?" Reese glanced upward. Deena had wandered after them and climbed the tree. She was sitting on one of the branches that grew out over the lake and staring down into the water.

"She's fine," Kavine said dismissively. "She's always doing stupid stuff."

She shaded her eyes against the sun and shouted at Deena. "Why don't you go into the lake and bathe, Deena? You're filthy!"

The shifter ignored her and Kavine rolled her eyes before sitting next to Adina on a large boulder. "Why Borek doesn't just take her out into the woods and end her misery, I'll never understand."

"Kavine!" Verna gave her a shocked look. "Why would you say such a thing?"

"She cannot be happy. Borek can't even get her to bathe. She hardly eats, and everything she says is nonsense," Kavine replied. "Borek is wasting his time with her. She'll never bear him pups now."

Reese, wearing just Kane's shirt and shivering in the cold breeze, frowned at Kavine. "That's a very cruel thing to say."

Kavine rolled her eyes. "Hold your tongue, human. You know nothing."

"Ignore her, human. She's just being nasty because Radek spoke dismissively to her this morning. Something put him in a foul mood," Verna said.

She studied Reese's lips. "Your lips are blue. Is that normal for human females?"

"I'm a little cold." Reese stomped her feet and waved her arms around.

"Well, you'll have to get used to it. We have no warm clothes to fit you."

"Do the male shifters not have warmer clothes?" Adina asked curiously. They had stopped at Kane's cabin on their way to the lake, and she and Reese had searched through Kane's limited amount of clothing but had found only thin pants and shirts.

Verna shook her head. "No. They have no need for warmer clothing. Female shifters stay quite warm but our mates are even warmer - even in their human forms. Besides, most of the men stay in their wolf forms."

"Do you prefer your human forms?" Reese asked.

"It depends. In the warmer months we spend more time in our human forms. In the colder months, our wolf forms."

She eyed Reese's shaking body. "If Dagon does not take you as his mate, you'd better hope one of the other males in our pack decides to. Now that the rains have come and gone, it's only going to get colder. You'll freeze to death without a male to keep you warm."

"She'll be fine," Kavine said. "She's got plenty of fat to keep her warm."

Reese ignored the shifter and straightened the wet shirt that was draped across the branch next to her skirt. If Dagon didn't choose her, perhaps Kane would.

He won't. Stop with your silly dreams and figure out what you're going to do if Dagon does choose you.

She sighed and picked up the soap that Verna had given her. Her feet and lower legs were black with dirt already and steeling herself against the cold, she waded into the water and scrubbed at her legs and feet.

If Dagon did choose her, she would try and escape into the forest during the night. She would wait until he let his guard down and then –

"Deena, stop that!" Verna cried shrilly.

Reese looked up as Deena jumped from the branch she was standing on and dropped like a stone into the lake.

"She can't swim!" Verna cried. Fur was growing on her face and she gave Kavine a panicked look.

The girl shrugged. "We cannot swim either."

"Here we go again," Reese muttered. She swam toward the spot where Deena had disappeared and dove under the water. The female shifter was sitting on the bottom of the lake, a string of bubbles rising from her nose and staring calmly at her. Reese swam to her, grabbed her arm and lifted her to the surface.

They broke through the water and Deena took a deep breath and lay limply against Reese as she struggled toward the shore. When her feet touched the bottom, she helped Deena to stand.

"Are you all right, Deena?"

The woman studied her carefully. Despite the coldness of the water she wasn't trembling and her skin was flush with warmth. She reached out and touched Reese's mouth.

"You are precious to him."

"Shh," Reese said nervously. She glanced at Adina and the two shifters standing anxiously on the shoreline. "I'm not, Deena. Kane doesn't like me, okay?"

Deena grinned at her. "Kane's pretty little flower. He wants to put a pup in his flower's belly." She pressed her hand against Reese's stomach and Reese shook her head.

"No, he doesn't. Just keep your voice down, okay?"

"Okay," Deena said.

Reese was still clutching the soap in her hand and Deena ran her finger through the rapidly disintegrating gel.

"Do you want to bathe, Deena?" Reese said. "I can help you wash your hair."

Deena shrugged and then surprised Reese by pulling her shirt over her head and dropping it into the lake.

"Oh, Deena." Reese stared horrified at the scars that criss-crossed the woman's abdomen and chest. "Did the bear shifter do this to you?"

"Bear," Deena said.

"I'm sorry, honey."

"Sorry, honey," Deena repeated. She scooped some of the soap from Reese's hand and rubbed it haphazardly against her scalp.

"Here, let me help you." Although her body was beginning to go numb from the cold water, she waded behind Deena and lathered her long dark hair as the shifter tilted her head and stared silently into the sky.

"KANE!"

"Borek? What is wrong?" Kane asked as the older shifter jogged toward him.

"Where is the big human?" Borek asked anxiously.

"In my cabin, I assume. Why?"

"Deena is missing! Verna said she fell into the lake earlier and the big human took her to our cabin, but she is not there. I want to speak to the human!"

They were almost at Kane's doorstep and Borek growled under his breath. "If the human has hurt her, if she has harmed my mate, I do not care what Dagon says. I will rip out her throat."

"Enough, Borek. Reese will not have hurt Deena," Kane growled back. He opened the door, growling again when Borek pushed past him.

"Deena! Deena, are you in here?" He shouted before stumbling to a stop.

"Deena?" He whispered.

Kane peered past him. Reese had pulled one of the chairs close to the fire and Deena was sitting on it. She was dressed in fresh clothing, her skin was pink and clean and her usual wild and dirty hair was washed and combed. Reese looked up with her fingers tangled in Deena's hair as Borek stared at them.

"Hi there. You must be Borek. I'm Reese." She smiled at him before continuing to braid Deena's hair.

"Deena?" Borek whispered again. He knelt in front of his mate and took her hand. "Are you all right, my love?"

"All right, my love," Deena said in a sing-song voice. Borek kissed the knuckles of her hand tenderly.

"What happened?"

When Deena didn't reply, Reese smiled at him. "She just took a bit of a dip in the lake while I was washing my clothes.

We decided we might as well bathe while we were in there. Isn't that right, Deena?"

"Deena smelled bad," the woman said solemnly.

Reese squeezed her shoulder. "That's okay, Deena. I didn't smell that great myself."

"Stinky flower." Deena laughed and Reese grinned at her.

"Well, we both smell better now." She finished braiding Deena's hair and tied the end with a small piece of leather. "There you go, honey, all done."

Borek stood and helped Deena to her feet. He stared at his mate before putting his arm around her and kissing her temple. "You look lovely."

"Pretty Deena?" Deena smiled shyly at him and put her arm around his waist.

"Very pretty," Borek said. He glanced at Reese. "Thank you."

"You're welcome."

"Come, my love, it is time to eat." He guided Deena toward the door. "Kane, are you coming?"

"Aye. We'll be out shortly."

"Kane's flower," Deena said.

"What, my love?" Borek frowned.

"Kane's pretty little flower. She is precious to him." She pointed to Reese.

Borek glanced first at Kane and then at Reese. A strange look came over his face and Kane hurried toward him. "Borek, she speaks nonsense. You know that."

"Aye," Borek said. He nodded to Kane and holding Deena's hand, led her from the cabin.

Reese gave Kane a nervous look. "I don't know why she keeps saying that. I told her it wasn't true and asked her not to say it."

"She speaks nonsense. No one in our pack listens to her," Kane replied.

Reese frowned. "I know she says odd things, but it isn't nonsense, Kane."

Without replying, Kane took her arm and led her toward the door. "Come, it is time to eat."

"Do you eat together all the time?" She asked curiously.

He nodded. "For the most part. We like to be together."

Reese supposed they did. The pack was important, even she could see that. If the way Kane and Theran and Hanif refused to disobey their alpha didn't indicate a pack mentality, nothing did.

"Reese? Hold your tongue, all right?" Kane said anxiously. "Dagon will be there and he won't go near you but he'll be watching and listening. Do not speak of your world."

"I won't."

"Do you promise me?" Kane's fingers were digging into her arm and she pulled it free with an irritated look.

"Yes, shifter. I promise. I am capable of keeping my mouth shut from time to time. I spent two days not speaking to you in the cave, or have you forgotten?"

"I have not forgotten," Kane growled at her before pulling her into his embrace. He squeezed her full ass and nipped at her earlobe before breathing hotly, "Do not plan on doing that again, Reese. I did not like it."

She pushed her way out of his embrace and straightened her skirt. "What's with your fearless leader and menstrual cycles, anyway?"

Kane shrugged. "He is squeamish about certain things."

Reese rolled her eyes. "Well, let's hope his squeamishness doesn't seep into the bedroom. He sounds like a prude, and I might not be that experienced but I'm not a pr - "

She squeaked in surprise when Kane snarled angrily and

yanked her back into his embrace. He wrapped his hand in her hair as he glared at her. "Do not speak of being in his bed again. Do you hear me, human?"

She scowled at him. "Jealous, shifter? Don't worry, if he picks me I'll keep the sex details to myself."

Kane howled angrily, his eyeteeth lengthening with a harsh pop, as he squeezed her more tightly.

Reese, what are you doing? Her inner voice moaned. *Stop goading him, for God's sake!*

He bent his head until his mouth was only inches from hers. "You are mine, human. Mine! Say it!"

"No." She shook her head. "I will not."

"Say it!" He growled.

She gave him a defiant look as there was a knock on the door of his cabin. It opened and Verna stuck her head in. "Kane, we are waiting for - "

She paused, her eyes widening and her hand squeezing the door nervously. She stared at Kane's hand wrapped in Reese's hair, the fangs that were protruding from his mouth and the way his large body was bent over hers.

"Do not kill her, Kane. Dagon will kill you if you do," she said quickly. She glanced behind her. "Calm down and let go of the human."

Kane released her so quickly that she stumbled. Verna, keeping a wary eye on the shifter, reached out and snagged Reese's arm. She pulled her toward the door. "Come, Reese. You can sit with me at dinner."

She pulled Reese out the door and Kane made a short howl of frustration before slamming his fist into the wall of the cabin. The skin on his knuckles tore on the rough wood and he grunted in pain before sucking the blood from his skin. He took a few deep breaths as he waited for the bleeding to stop. Verna seeing them was a good thing. She had thought he was close to killing Reese and she would quickly spread what she had seen to the rest of the pack. The girl was more talkative than his mate. His pack mates knew of his hatred for the humans and Verna's gossiping would ensure that no one suspected he felt differently about Reese. Well, no one but Radek, but his cousin would keep his secret.

REESE, HER HEAD SPINNING, SMILED AT THE WOLF SHIFTER standing in front of her. Kane's entire pack was milling about the clearing when Verna had dragged her from his cabin, and the woman had wasted no time introducing her to nearly everyone. She had already forgotten most of their names and she rubbed her aching belly as Verna hooked her arm around hers.

"Teagan, give her some space," the shifter said irritably.

The wolf shifter, he was short and built like a barrel with long black hair and dark brown eyes, was surreptitiously touching her hair. He blushed and gave Reese an apologetic look.

"I'm sorry, human. I just wanted to see what your hair felt like."

"I don't mind," Reese smiled cheerfully at him, "as long as I get to touch your hair in return."

He laughed and swept his hair forward. "Go ahead, human."

She touched his long hair and marvelled at the softness of it before grinning at him. "Your hair is softer than mine."

"I take very good care of it," he boasted.

From the corner of her eye, Reese could see Kane edging closer to them as Teagan gave her a curious look. "Do you have hair on your body, girl?"

"Oh, um…"

"I asked the blonde one." Teagan pointed in Adina's direction. The woman was standing on the other side of the clearing, surrounded by a few of the male shifters and about five female shifters. "She said she had a little. Is it different for you because of your dark hair?"

He eyed her stomach and reached out and grasped the bottom of Kane's shirt. She took a nervous step back and Teagan followed her. He was actually lifting her shirt when Kane appeared and growled angrily at him. He knocked Teagan's hand away and snapped his teeth. "Keep your hands off of her, Teagan."

Teagan gave him a startled look and bowed his head. "I am sorry, Kane. I did not mean any disrespect. I only wondered if her skin was as smooth under her clothing."

Kane glared at him as Verna said helpfully, "If our alpha does not choose her, perhaps Reese will mate with you, Teagan. Then you can find out."

Teagan gave Reese a hopeful look. "Will you, human? I find you pretty and would be happy to take you to my bed."

"I, uh,…" Reese stared at the shifter as beside her, Kane began to growl under his breath. "That's a very kind offer, Teagan, but I'm not sure that I - "

"My dick is large," Teagan said. He reached for the button on his pants and grabbed her hand. "Here, you can touch it and see for yourself."

"Teagan!" Kane snarled, his fangs glowing in the setting sun. "Touch her again and I'll take your head."

Teagan dropped Reese's hand and backed away. "Easy, Kane. I meant no disrespect."

"Aye, you keep saying that, but you are asking our alpha's potential mate to grab your dick." Kane snapped. He gripped the back of Reese's neck and tugged her back toward him. "Have you gone mad?"

Teagan didn't reply and Reese tried to ease away from Kane. He scowled and pulled her even closer. "Stay still, human."

He fixed his glare on Teagan again. "Apologize to her."

"I'm sorry, human."

"Her name is Reese," Kane snarled

"I – I'm sorry, Reese." Teagan was giving Kane an odd look and Reese stepped on Kane's foot. The shifter's grip eased and she pulled away from him and gave Teagan a small smile.

"Apology accepted, Teagan. If you'll excuse me, I'm going to say hello to Deena."

She walked toward Borek and Deena who were sitting alone near the campfire as Kane growled again at Teagan. "Do not touch her again, Teagan. Even if Dagon does not choose her, you are not to touch her. Do you hear me?"

"Aye, Kane." Teagan bowed his head again and Kane glared at Verna until, with a small whimper, she bowed her head as well.

"HELLO, DEENA." REESE SAT DOWN ON THE LOG NEXT TO THE shifter. The woman was staring at her hands and she glanced up as Reese touched her shoulder.

"Flower. Kane's pretty flower." The woman turned to her husband and stroked his cheek. "She is precious to him."

"I know, my love." Borek smiled at her. "As you are precious to me."

Reese, her stomach twisting nervously, shook her head. "Kane hates me."

Borek snorted laughter as Deena ran her fingers through the thick beard on his face. "Does he now?"

"Yes."

"Deena, does Kane hate the human?" Borek asked his wife.

Deena giggled before touching Reese's cheek. "Precious flower. He bathes her and holds her so tightly in his bed. He will never let her go."

Borek raised his eyebrows at Reese. "It does not sound like Kane hates you."

"Please," Reese gave him a desperate look, "you cannot say anything, Borek. Kane has been, uh, kind to me but he does it only because Dagon ordered him to. I would freeze to death if I didn't sleep in his bed."

"Borek, please." She begged again when he didn't reply. "I don't want to cause any trouble."

Borek touched Deena's hair before staring gravely at Reese. "I know you saved her from drowning."

He sighed heavily and stared at the ground between his feet. "I know what my pack mates say behind my back. I know what they say I should do to Deena and that they believe it is an act of mercy, but I love her."

He gave Reese a tortured look. "Have you ever loved someone so deeply that you would die for them, human?"

"I – no, I don't think so," she whispered.

He stared at his wife. "I wish every day that I had not allowed her to go into the forest alone that day. She was so strong though, so stubborn, and I could refuse her nothing. It is my fault."

"It isn't, Borek," Reese said. "Blaming yourself isn't going to help."

"What do you know of blame, human?" He said bitterly.

"My parents died. I was supposed to be with them but I

wasn't because I'd had a fight with my father a few days prior and I was still angry with him. My father died without knowing how much I loved him and that's my fault. I shouldn't have been so petty and childish."

Deena took her hand and she squeezed the shifter's fingers. "I spent months blaming myself. I actually believed that if we hadn't fought and I had been with them that day that they wouldn't have died. I finally realized that my father wouldn't want that. I loved him and I know he knew that, even if I was angry with him before he died."

She took a deep breath and smiled at Borek. "Deena loves you, that's easy to see. Despite what your pack mates believe I do not think she speaks nonsense."

"She doesn't," Borek said.

Reese hesitated. "Except for the stuff about me being Kane's precious flower. That's complete bullshit."

Borek stared at her and then burst into loud laughter. Deena clapped her hands and giggled as Reese grinned at both of them. After a few moments, Borek's laughter tapered off and he took Deena's hand and squeezed it affectionately.

"My love, look at me."

She turned to her husband obediently and he kissed her on the mouth. "Will you do something for me? Will you keep Kane's love for his flower a secret between us?"

Deena raised her finger to her lips. "Shh."

"Aye, that's right, my love," Borek said. "It's very important that you speak to no one but me of Kane and his precious flower. All right?"

"Aye, Borek," Deena said. She turned to Reese and pressed her finger against Reese's mouth. "Shh, flower."

"Yes, shh." Reese agreed solemnly before touching Borek's hand. "Thank you, Borek."

"Thank you for being so kind to my love," he said

hoarsely. "It has been many months since she has had a friend."

"You're welcome," Reese replied.

The smell of cooking meat drifted to them and Reese's stomach growled as Borek made a face and Deena put her hand over her nose.

"It smells good to you, does it?" He said curiously.

"Yes." Reese laughed. "You have no idea how good."

She was suddenly starving. She had eaten nothing but the bit of rabbit that Kane had cooked for her this morning and despite her menstrual cramps, she was looking forward to eating dinner.

Dagon stepped closer to the fire. He clapped his hands sharply and the rest of the pack grew quiet as he cleared his throat. "Come, my brothers and sisters. Let us welcome the new members of our pack with a hearty meal. We have prepared meat for you in the manner you are accustomed to, although," he grinned at Adina who gave him a tentative smile in return, "you will have to learn to appreciate the smell and sight of raw meat."

He pointed behind him where a table was set up. Platters covered in raw meat covered most of the table and a smaller section had bowls of greens.

He nodded to Anna. "Anna, feed our newest members first."

"Aye, Dagon."

The shifter pulled the rabbit from the spit over the fire and working quickly, pulled the meat from its bones. Reese's stomach growled again and she licked her lips as Anna handed plates of meat and greens to Adina and Ghita.

They took their plates with a nod of thanks to Anna and Dagon raised his eyebrows at them. "Will you not thank your alpha?"

"Thank you, my lord," Adina said politely.

Ghita, tears standing in her eyes and her hands shaking so badly she could barely hold the plate, swallowed nervously. "Th-thank you, my lord."

Dagon rolled his eyes in irritation as Anna walked to where Reese was sitting with Borek and Deena. She handed the plate over and Reese stared at in confusion. There was nothing but plants on the plate and she caught Anna's arm as the shifter began to walk away.

"Anna? Could I have some of the meat as well, please?" She asked.

Anna shook her head. "No, I'm sorry, human."

"Why not?"

Anna hesitated and Deena shrank back and made a small moan of fear when Dagon appeared in front of them.

"You are too fat, human. Only plants for you until you are more pleasing to my eye. Do you understand?" He took a short whiff of Reese and stepped back a few feet, his nose wrinkling.

"Well, do you?"

Reese, her face burning, stared down at the plate before looking across the clearing. Kane was standing with Raina, his body rigid and his hands clenched. He gave her a look that she had no trouble reading.

With extraordinary willpower, she swallowed down her scathing reply and smiled at the alpha. "I do, Dagon. Thank you for the plants. It is very generous of you and I'll enjoy them."

"Aye, I'm sure you will," Dagon replied before walking to the table of food.

CHAPTER 20

"Wake up, Reese."

Reese squinted at Kane before pulling the covers over her head. "Go away, shifter. I'm tired and hungry and in a really bad mood."

"I know. I have something for you."

"Unless it's food, I'm not interested."

She closed her eyes and held onto the blanket and sheet as Kane sighed. After dinner, the pack spent a few hours talking and laughing and sharing stories. Surprisingly, most of the shifters were rather friendly with them and even Ghita managed to relax a bit by evening's end.

Reese, starving and her stomach throbbing with cramps, smiled and nodded and tried to be friendly with Kane's pack members. But she couldn't hide her relief when the others finally started to return to their own cabins, and Kane took her arm in a rough grip and marched her back to his.

She immediately drank some tappin root tea, hoping it would both ease her cramps and fill her stomach as Kane paced anxiously in the small cabin. Finally, just when she was going to snap at him to sit down, he pulled open the door and growled at her to stay in his cabin before leaving.

She flipped him the bird, but he had already slammed the door shut. She considered leaving the cabin just to piss him off. But in the end, a headache starting from lack of food and feeling tired and defeated, she simply went to bed instead.

Now, she pulled away when Kane touched her hip through the blanket and ignored his grunt of disapproval.

"Like I said, unless you have food I'm not interested in anything you have for me," she said peevishly. "You could have warned me that your stupid alpha would starve me. I would have loaded my pockets with charkas before we got to your stupid house. How was your stupid meal, by the way? Did you enjoy it? You certainly looked like you were enjoying it."

"If you would stop your talking and take a deep breath, you would know I have brought you food, human," Kane snapped at her.

She pulled the covers down just enough to inhale and sat up when the delicious smell of cooked rabbit hit her nostrils. "You brought me food!"

"Keep your voice down, Reese!" Kane said with a scowl.

He stood and went to the fireplace. A rabbit was cooking over the fire and Reese slid off the bed and joined him.

"That smells so good." She moaned as her mouth watered.

He tore pieces of meat from its body. "Wait until it cools," he admonished as he handed her a plate piled high with the meat.

She sat down cross-legged on the floor and held the plate like it was gold. She eyed the meat as Kane stretched out on his back beside her and stared at the ceiling.

"What time is it?" She asked.

"Late."

"Where have you been?"

"I went to Borek's and Deena's for a while and then I went hunting."

"Why did you do this? Won't you get in trouble?" She picked up a piece of meat and blew on it before eating it quickly. "Oh my God, that's so good."

He smiled happily at her. "You are enjoying it?"

"Hell, yes." She stuffed more of the rabbit into her mouth and closed her eyes. "It's the best thing I've ever tasted."

Kane sat up and pressed his large body against hers. "You're the best thing I've ever tasted."

She blushed and slapped his thigh. "I'm not sleeping with you while I have my period, Kane. Let's make that clear."

"I know." He kissed her cheek and lay back down on the floor, one big hand rubbing her lower back lazily. "How is your stomach? Do you want more tea?"

"No, thank you. Don't avoid the question. Why are you doing this? If Dagon finds out, he'll be angry with you."

"I do not care." He shrugged.

"What happened to obeying your alpha's every command?"

"I will not obey a command that puts my ma - "

He stopped and gave her an oddly guilty look. "I will not follow Dagon's rules when it means another must suffer."

"How nice of you," she said dryly. They sat in silence while she finished eating. When she was done, he took the plate from her and gave her an anxious look.

"Do you feel better, Reese?"

"Yes. Thank you." She shivered and he stood and tugged her to her feet.

"Come. I will warm you in my bed."

"How much colder is it going to get?" She asked.

"Why?"

"Because there aren't any warmer clothes to fit me, and I'm trying to decide if I need to go into the forest and kill a bear or something for its pelt."

"Do not go into the forest alone. Do you hear me?" He shook her lightly. "It is very dangerous. I will keep you warm."

"That's not exactly a solution. I won't be in your cabin forever. I need something warmer to wear." She frowned at him. "I can't stay indoors all winter and I - "

She gasped as eyes glowed at her from the window. Kane immediately thrust her behind him and blocked her with his large body before growling threateningly. After only a few seconds, he relaxed. "It is only Deena."

"Well that explains how she knew about the bathing and the feeding and the holding me in your bed," Reese replied.

Deena disappeared from the window and she frowned at Kane. "Why is she out there so late?"

Kane shrugged. "I do not know. Her brains are addled, Reese. There is no explanation for what she says or does. Why Borek does not take her into the forest and - "

"Don't say that!" Reese slapped him sharply on the back. "I know this will be hard to understand for someone who doesn't want a mate and is content to fuck whoever will spread her legs for him, but think about it for just a minute. If you were in love, if you did have a mate, would you be able to just take her out in the forest and kill her because she's suddenly different?"

His face paled so abruptly that she thought he was ill. Despite her anger with him, concern flooded through her and she touched his face. "Kane? Do you feel sick?"

He shook his head and took her arm. "No, I am fine. You are right. It was a thoughtless thing to say."

He led her to the bed, but she balked at climbing into it. "Deena shouldn't be out there by herself. You said the forest was dangerous."

"She'll be fine. She is still a shifter."

She frowned at him and with an irritated sigh he left the cabin. He returned only a few minutes later. Reese was still standing by the bed and he urged her to lie down as he stripped off his clothes.

She refused. "Did you take her back to Borek?"

"Borek was already leading her back to their cabin."

"Good." A look of relief crossed her face and he smiled at her. He loved that his mate was so concerned about the members of his pack already.

"Climb into bed."

"I don't think that's a good idea." She tugged nervously at the hem of his shirt as a thunderous look crossed his face. "I'm going to sleep on the floor by the fire. I'll use the bear pelt to keep warm."

"Get into my bed, Reese." He scowled at her.

"Just hear me out. What if one of your other pack mates peek in the window or just come wandering in like Verna did earlier this evening? If they see us in the bed together, we'll both be in trouble with Dagon."

"My bed, now. I won't ask again," he snapped.

"You didn't *ask* in the first place!" She retorted.

He growled angrily and she gave a squeal of surprise when he pulled his shirt over her head, leaving her in just her underwear. He lifted her up and dumped her on the bed. He covered her body with his own and pressed her into the bed, trapping her wrists with one large hand when she tried to smack his broad chest.

"You will stay in my bed until I give you permission to leave it," he said. "Do you understand?"

He waited for her fiery response and grunted in surprise when she relaxed under him and gave him a sweetly submissive smile. "Of course, shifter."

He released her wrists and leaned down to lick his claiming mark. "That's my good girl," he murmured before tracing the scar on her shoulder with a light stroke of his tongue.

She shivered beneath him and he grinned in satisfaction. He liked the stubbornness and independent nature of his mate, but the sudden submissiveness was not entirely displeasing to him.

He grunted in surprise when she punched him hard in the stomach. He rolled off of her and she pushed him onto his back and quickly straddled him. Although he could have stopped her, he didn't protest when she yanked down his arms and pinned them to the bed with her knees.

She grinned happily at him. "Not so tough after all, huh, shifter?"

He gave her a mock glare. "Were you trying to break my ribs?"

"Oh please." She rolled her eyes. "My hand probably hurts more than your stomach. It's as hard as granite." She stroked his abdomen muscles as he stared at her large, firm breasts. Her nipples had hardened in the cool air of his cabin and she made a soft sound when she felt his cock rise against her.

"Be good, shifter."

"I am being good," he said innocently. "It is not my fault you feel the need to walk around my cabin half-naked."

She whacked him on the stomach and he grinned at her. The grin dropped from his face and was replaced by a hard look of lust when she cupped her breasts and tugged on her nipples. He watched, his cock growing harder and his need for her overwhelming him as she pulled and stroked her nipples until they were hard, tight buds and swollen from her touch.

She paused and he growled under his breath. "Keep doing that, Reese."

She smiled sweetly at him before stretching. He licked his lips and made another soft growl. "Do not stop."

"I'm tired, shifter," she said teasingly as she slid off of him and lay with her back to him.

He curled his body around hers. His cock was throbbing and pulsing with need, but he had to grin at his mate's bravery. Of course, she didn't realize the way he would torment and tease her mercilessly for this once the moon was no longer full for her.

The smile dropped from his face. When she was finished her cycle, if Dagon chose her, he would have no choice but to take Reese and leave. His wolf made a whine of dismay and panic at the thought of leaving his pack and Kane could think of no words to comfort it.

"Kane?"

"Aye?"

"Has Dagon said anything about…"

She trailed off, her body tensing, and he cupped her breast in a soothing manner and kissed her bare back.

"I believe he will choose Adina. Ghita is too timid for him and he does not have the patience to wait for you to grow thinner."

He expected her to relax at his words but she remained stubbornly tense. He reached up and stroked his claiming mark, touching the raised skin with his fingertips as he nuzzled her neck. "What is wrong? Are you not happy that he will most likely not choose you?"

"I'm worried about Adina," she said. "What if he decides to kill her like he killed his other mates?"

"We don't know that he - "

"You're not stupid, shifter. Don't pretend to be," she interrupted.

He buried his face in the soft skin of her throat. "I do not know what you want me to say, Reese."

"Tell me about the farmhouse," she said abruptly.

He frowned at the sudden change in conversation. "What?"

"Tell me about the farmhouse," she repeated. "I want to know what you and Radek did."

He didn't want to speak of it but unable to deny his mate's request, he said, "I was young and foolish. It does not excuse my behaviour but it perhaps will help you to under-stand why I did it."

When she didn't reply he sighed and tugged her closer to his warm body. "I was fifteen and got it into my head that I needed to take revenge for my parents. Radek was more than happy to join me. There was a humans' farm not far from here, only a few hours travel, and so we snuck out one evening and headed toward it."

"Was it the farm where your parents were accused of killing their cows?"

He shook his head. "No. But it didn't matter to me that the human I would take my revenge against was an innocent. My parents were innocent and the humans showed them no mercy."

"An eye for an eye," she whispered.

"What?"

"Nothing. Go on."

"When we got there, the humans were in their beds. Radek and I began to terrorize the animals in an attempt to lure the humans out. It worked. The human and his mate left the safety of their house when they heard the frightened cries of their livestock."

He fell quiet. Reese turned in his arms and stared up at him. "Did you hurt them?"

He shook his head. "No. Raina had overheard us talking of our plan the night we left, and she had gone to her parents. She was only a young pup but even she knew how dangerous and foolish we were being. Radek's parents went to Maven and he came after us."

"So he stopped you before you could do anything."

"Aye. The humans had barely left their house when Maven arrived. He shifted to his human form and told them to go back into their home and not leave it until morning. Then he shifted back to his wolf form and went after Radek and me."

"How did he convince you to return without killing them?" She asked.

A small smile crossed his face. "He used his teeth and his claws until we were covered in blood and begging him for mercy."

She frowned at him. "I thought Maven was a good alpha."

"He was."

"Doesn't sound like it to me." She scowled. "How does hurting foolish teenagers do anything? What if he had seriously injured you?"

Kane brushed her hair back. "We deserved it, Reese. We would have killed those humans without hesitating. Maven knew he needed to use more than words to make us understand how foolish we were. If Radek and I had killed the humans it would have put our entire pack in grave danger."

She didn't reply and he kissed her on the mouth. "Get some sleep. It is late."

CHAPTER 21

"You're big for a human."

Reese turned to stare at the shifter standing in the doorway of the cabin. She pasted a smile on her face. It was mid-morning and she was hungry and irritated. She and Kane had joined the pack for breakfast, and she hadn't been surprised to discover that Dagon had ordered her to be given only one meal a day. She had sat in silence as the others ate their breakfast and forced herself to be polite and cheerful to the pack members who had approached her. Like the evening before, many of them were anxious to touch her hair and her skin and she hoped the novelty of humans would wear off soon.

Dagon had spent some time sitting with Adina and he had appeared kind enough to her. When breakfast was done, Dagon had returned to his cabin. Reese had wanted to question Adina about what they spoke of but the weather was cold. After staring at her blue lips and the way she shivered, Kane had insisted she return to his cabin before she had a chance to speak to her.

Kane hadn't stayed in the cabin with her and she had

hoped he would return with food but it was nearly two hours and he hadn't returned. She was about to leave the cabin despite the way the wind was blowing, and find Adina when the old shifter had walked in.

"I get that a lot," she said briefly.

"Aye, I imagine you do."

He joined her at the fire, easing his body into the chair across from hers and fanning his face before studying her thin shirt and skirt. "I am surprised that Kane keeps it so warm in his cabin for you. He hates humans and it's odd that he would care if you froze to death or not."

"I'm certain he has no wish to anger your alpha."

"Perhaps not." The shifter reached into his pocket and pulled out a handful of charkas. He peeled one and as the smell of the rich meaty insides drifted to her, Reese tried not to drool. Her stomach growled and a brief frown crossed the shifter's face before he tossed the charka to her.

She caught it and studied him closely, trying to decide if he would tell Dagon if she ate it.

As if he had read her mind, he said, "Go on and eat it, girl. I won't tell my alpha."

She continued to hesitate and he gave her a look of irritation so similar to Kane's that she knew he must be related to him. "You have my word."

"Thank you." She ate the charka quickly and nodded her thanks when he handed the rest of the charkas to her. She finished them off and threw the peels into the fire before returning to her chair.

"I'm sorry, I've forgotten your name."

"We haven't met yet," he replied. "My name is Asher."

"I'm Reese. It's nice to meet you."

"Aye, you as well."

They sat in silence for a while before she gave him a tentative look. "You're related to Kane?"

"I am. How did you know?"

She shrugged. "You have similar manners."

He laughed. "I am his uncle. His father was my youngest brother."

"Kane said his father's siblings raised him."

"Aye, we did. Although Maven did his fair share of it." Asher cocked his head at her. "What else did Kane share with you?"

"Nothing," she said nervously. "He doesn't talk very much to me."

He continued to stare at her and with her nervousness growing, she said, "I just wondered why he hated humans so much. He told me what happened to his parents."

Asher raised his eyebrows at her. "What did he tell you?"

"Uh, nothing specific, just that his parents were hunted and killed by humans."

"That is more than he usually shares." Asher was giving her a scrutinizing look and when he leaned forward and inhaled, she leaned away.

"You're covered in his scent, human."

"He's just trying to prevent me from freezing to death before your alpha makes his choice."

"Indeed. Tell me about yourself, human."

"I'd rather not."

Asher laughed. "Theran and Hanif say you like to talk. They say it's why my nephew acts so strange now. They believe you drove him nearly mad with your talking when he was trapped with you during the rains. Yet now your tongue grows quiet?"

Reese shrugged. "Perhaps my time in the cave with your nephew has taught me to hold my tongue around shifters."

"Was Kane cruel to you?"

She shook her head. "No."

"Good. I am the last of his elders and it would have fallen to me to discipline him if he was cruel to a defenseless female. I am way too old for that sort of thing."

"What do you care? I imagine you hate humans as much as Kane and Radek do."

"My advanced age gives me clarity that Kane has yet to discover," Asher replied. "Although I believe that is changing."

"Why does Radek hate humans?" Reese asked suddenly.

Asher stared into the fire. "Many years ago, our pack lived at the edge of the forest, closer to the humans. We did not have much to do with them. We occasionally traded with them, but we mainly kept to ourselves and they did the same. And then - when Radek was young he was captured by the humans."

"Why did they take him?" Reese asked.

"For their own amusement. They beat him and collared him and forced him to perform tricks for their own children like he was a dog. We are afraid of water. Did you know that?"

Reese nodded. "Yes. Kane almost drowned when we were traveling here."

"The humans repeatedly held him in the lake, nearly drowning him. They starved him and hurt him just to see how long it would take for him to heal."

"Oh my God." Reese's stomach churned. "How old was he?"

"Only five or six, if I remember correctly."

"Jesus."

"It took us nearly a week to track his scent down. His parents were going crazy, as you can imagine. When we

230

finally discovered him chained to a wall in one of the human's barns, Maven, Radek's father and Kane's father, killed the humans that lived there and returned Radek to the pack. He has hated the humans ever since."

"That's terrible. Poor Radek."

"A year later, other humans killed Kane's parents. Maven moved the pack deeper into the woods and here we have remained. Despite the dangers lurking in the forest, the humans were more of a threat to us. Do you understand?"

"Yes. Why would Dagon bring humans into the pack, knowing what they did to Kane and Radek?"

Asher sighed again. "A number of reasons. Our numbers dwindle, while the human numbers grow. Dagon is right in believing that sooner or later we will be forced to coexist with them. As well, rumours have spread of his cruelty to his mates and females from other packs have refused to even consider becoming his mate."

He hesitated before looking at her. "Truthfully, I believe his strongest reason was simply to torture Kane and Radek. He always envied the bond they had with his father, especially Kane's. I find it rather amusing to see his plan to torture Kane with humans in the pack backfire so spectacularly."

Reese cleared her throat nervously and stared into the fire as Asher grinned at her. "Has my nephew mated with you?"

"Why would he?"

"I see the way he looks at you. He desires you for himself."

"No he doesn't," she said briefly.

Asher sighed irritably and leaned forward. "Perhaps if I share a secret, you will be more willing to spill yours. What do you say?"

She just shrugged and Asher rolled his eyes. "I despise our alpha, human. I believe him to be weak and cowardly at heart. Maven would have been better off to have drowned him at birth. But he loved the boy and in return, was killed for it."

"Did he kill his other mates?" She asked.

He nodded. "Aye, I believe he did. The others do not speak of it. They pretend that the stories he weaves are true, but I am too old and too tired to pretend. I believe our pack needs to be led by another. Dagon is too unstable, too cruel, to be a leader. Do you know who our pack needs, human?"

"Kane," she whispered.

"Aye, it does. He is a natural leader, is he not?"

She nodded and he smiled at her. "Even you, a mere human, can see that he is meant to lead. I have spent many nights urging him to challenge Dagon for alpha position, but he refuses."

The thought of Kane challenging the bigger, stronger, Dagon sent icy tendrils of fear down her back and she gave Asher a sharp look. "Perhaps it is because he is smart enough not to challenge a man who would kill his own father."

Asher cocked his head at her. "Your feelings for my nephew are readily apparent, human. You should hide your emotions better. If Dagon does choose you, he will not be pleased that you are in love with another."

"I have no feelings for Kane other than gratitude for not killing me as he is so obviously tempted to do," she said shortly.

He laughed. "He may be able to hide his affection for you from the others, but I am his blood. I see the truth."

"You speak foolishly, old man," she replied.

He laughed again. "You are brave for a human. I can see why Kane desires you."

She didn't reply and he gave her an oddly gentle look. "Do not fear, human. Your secret is safe with me."

"I have no secrets."

"Do you not? You try so hard to convince me that you and Kane have not mated. Why is that?"

"Because Dagon will kill him!" She suddenly snapped. "I would think you would understand that."

"The rumour is that Dagon will take the blonde one as his mate. Will you still deny Kane's feelings for you when he takes you as his mate?"

She gave him a scathing look. "Did I mention that you speak like a fool? I feel like I did but maybe that's just my imagination."

"My nephew will claim you as his mate. Make no doubt of that, human. I can see it in his face, in the way that he looks at you and how he reacts when other shifters touch you. You will find yourself mated to him the moment that Dagon takes the blonde one."

"No, I won't!" She suddenly hissed at him. "Do you want to know why your nephew fucked me, Asher? Because I was a goddamn experiment for him! He wanted to know what it would be like to fuck a human and I was lucky enough to be the human he chose. He has no feelings for me other than that weird possessive bullshit you shifters seem to thrive on. His behaviour is nothing more than keeping other shifters from playing with his new toy until he hands me over to his alpha. He told me himself that he would not disobey Dagon's orders and that he has no desire to be mated to *anyone*, let alone a human. He hates us and you know what? He should. Humans murdered his parents and if anyone has the right to hate us, it's him!"

She took a deep breath and glared at the old shifter. "If Dagon does choose Adina, Kane might keep me for a few weeks longer. If I get really lucky he'll keep me for the winter before he tires of me, and maybe I won't fucking freeze to death. If he doesn't, then I guess I'll be whoring myself out to someone else in the pack in exchange for warmth and food. If, that is, your fucking asshole of an alpha ever lets me eat something more than fucking plants!"

The door opened and Kane walked into the cabin. He closed the door behind him and checked the window as he opened the bag tied around his waist. "Reese, I have brought you some charkas. You must eat them before - "

"No need, nephew," Asher said cheerfully.

Kane whipped around, his hand holding the bag closed. "What are you doing in my cabin, Uncle?"

"Talking to your human." The old shifter winked at Reese and smoothed his long silver hair back from his face. "And feeding her."

Kane frowned. "You should not disobey our alpha's orders, Uncle."

"It was only a few charkas, Kane. Besides, why are you allowed to disobey Dagon, but I am not?"

"I don't know what you're talking about," Kane said innocently.

Asher's laughter was loud and infectious. Despite her anger, Reese could feel a grin breaking out on her face and even Kane's face relaxed.

"I will leave you to your bag of secret charkas. It was nice to meet you, human."

Reese made a soft noise of surprise when Asher pulled her into his embrace and hugged her. She was about to awkwardly pat his back when Kane, growling loudly, pulled her away from Asher. He put his arm around her waist and cupped her hip possessively before growling at his uncle again.

"Do not touch her again, Uncle."

Asher studied him closely. "And if I do?"

"I will take your head," Kane snarled.

"Kane!" Reese gave him a look of horror and pushed her way free of his embrace. "What is wrong with you? He's your uncle – you shouldn't speak to him that way."

Asher with a small smile playing on his lips, shook his head. "It is fine, human."

"It isn't." Reese reached to touch his arm. "He didn't mean it. He just - "

Kane pulled her back into his arms before she could touch Asher and she gave him a look of frustration mixed with anger. "What is going on with you?"

"Hold your tongue, Reese!"

"Make me, shifter!"

Asher laughed again. "Your mate's temper is a fiery one, nephew. I cannot tell you how much I will enjoy watching the two of you spar."

"She is not my mate, Uncle," Kane said cautiously. "The human means nothing to me. In fact, the sooner I can rid myself of her presence, the better."

"You and me both, asshole!" Reese booted him in the shin and Kane winced and released her. She gave Asher an 'I told you so' look before stomping from the cabin and slamming the door behind her.

REESE STORMED INTO THE FOREST BEHIND KANE'S CABIN. She had gone about thirty feet before she remembered the shifter's warning and stopped. She glanced cautiously around the woods. She was alone and she sat down beneath a tree and tucked her knees up. She wrapped her arms around her legs and rested her forehead on the top of her knees as the cold wind seeped through her thin clothing.

Her heart was racing and the charkas she had eaten were sitting like a stone in her belly. Kane drove her crazy and she would be much happier when she was no longer forced to share his cabin.

Really? So the thought of never feeling Kane's touch again, never seeing him smile at you or whisper in your ear that you belong to him doesn't bother you?

She sighed in frustration and banged her head against her knees. Having any sort of feelings for Kane was utter madness. Even if Dagon didn't choose her, Kane had just made it perfectly clear that he couldn't wait to get rid of her.

Then why does he tell you he will keep you safe? Why does he react so strongly when another shifter touches you? Why does he insist that you belong to him?

"I don't know! Maybe he has a split personality!" She spoke out loud and jumped when a bird was frightened by the sound and flew off from the tree above her with a shrill cry.

There was a rustling in the bushes behind her and she jumped to her feet. She backed away in the direction of the cabin, praying like hell it was nothing more than a rabbit. When the wolf appeared with its dark brown fur shining in the sun, she made a soft noise under her breath and held her hands out. Unsure if it was a shifter or not, she continued to slowly back away.

"Good puppy. Nice puppy. I'm just going to leave now. Be a good puppy and - "

"Mia! Wait for me!"

She breathed a sigh of relief when Raina emerged from the bushes. She stared in surprise at Reese. "What are you doing in the woods, human?"

"Just getting a breath of fresh air."

"Oh. You probably shouldn't be out here, it's dangerous."

"What are you doing out here?" Reese asked pointedly.

Raina laughed. "I'm a shifter, I can take care of myself."

"I'm sure you can but I think it's best if all three of us head back now," she said.

Mia barked and Raina rolled her eyes. "You're being ridiculous, Mia. He's way too old for you."

Mia snarled at her and stalked a few feet away. She stared moodily into the trees as Raina sighed.

"What's going on?" Reese asked curiously.

"Mia is in love with my brother. She's upset because he was cross with her earlier and then she saw Kavine sitting on his lap and stroking his hair.

Mia growled under her breath and Raina rolled her eyes again before shouting to her, "He doesn't like Kavine either, you dummy! He thinks she's stupid and annoying."

She turned back to Reese and lowered her voice conspiratorially, "Why either of them even like him, I'll never know. He's bossy. He's messy. He barks in his sleep and he never lets me do anything fun. And he's not the least bit handsome."

Reese grinned. "He's your brother – he's supposed to be bossy."

"I'm old enough to take care of myself. Besides, he's been in a bad mood ever since Kane kicked him out for speaking so rudely to you. Kane still won't speak to him and it's upsetting Radek."

"I'll speak to Kane. He shouldn't be ignoring your brother."

"He shouldn't have been so rude to you. Mama would want you to wear her clothing. She liked humans."

She suddenly frowned. "At least she used to."

"How many humans did she know?"

"None." Raina grinned at her. "But she found them fascinating. Uncle Asher told me once that sometimes papa would take her to the village just so she could watch the humans. One time a female human spoke to her and told mama she liked her dress. Mama was so excited. Uncle Asher said she didn't stop talking about it for days. But then the humans hurt Radek and mama didn't like them anymore."

Her eyes widened and she gave Reese a look of panic. "Please do not tell Radek I told you that."

"I won't," Reese said quickly.

Raina cleared her throat. "I wish mama could have met you. She would have liked you even with her anger over what they did to Radek. I know it."

"I wish I could have met her too." Reese touched the young shifter's hair and Raina stared up at her. Her eyes were swimming with tears and Reese hugged her. She stiffened before leaning against her and wrapping her arms around Reese's waist. Reese stroked her back and Raina sniffed repeatedly.

"I miss mama."

"I'm sorry, honey." She kissed the top of the shifter's head and Raina wiped the tears from her face before turning to Mia.

"Come on, Mia. Stop sulking over my stupid brother and come back. I told you – he's way too old and gross for you!"

With a loud whimper, Mia bounded through the trees.

"Not again," Raina muttered.

Reese grabbed her arm when she started to follow the wolf. "Honey, I don't think you should go into the woods alone."

"It's fine, human. I do this all the time."

She smiled reassuringly at Reese and Reese shook her head. "Kane says it's dangerous in the forest. I think - "

"It's dangerous for you because you're just a weak human," Raina said earnestly. "I'll be fine."

She started forward and blinked in surprise when Reese joined her. "What are you doing, human?"

"I'm coming with you." Reese took her hand and Raina stared at their hands before smiling at her.

"All right. I will keep you safe."

"Right." Feeling nervous and unsettled, she followed the young shifter into the woods.

When they had disappeared, Deena stepped out from a large pine tree. She sniffed the air, a frown crossing her face.

"Babies and Kane's precious flower in the woods."

CHAPTER 22

"I've made my decision."

Kane's stomach dropped and he stopped pacing in front of the fire in Dagon's cabin and stared expectantly at his alpha.

"So quickly, my alpha?" Theran asked. "I thought you were going to wait until the big one had stopped her cycle."

Dagon shrugged. "I grow tired of waiting. I want the blonde one."

Relief flooded through Kane and he glanced quickly at Theran. The smaller shifter had an obvious look of happiness on his face and Kane elbowed him discreetly. If Dagon knew that Theran had feelings for Ghita, it wouldn't be unlike him to change his mind and choose Ghita just to be cruel.

He stared at his alpha and wondered not for the first time, how a good shifter like Maven could have a son like Dagon. The man had always been odd. As a child, he was cruel to his playmates and smaller creatures he happened upon in the woods but no one in the pack had ever dreamed he would be capable of killing his own father.

He winced and closed his eyes as the image of Dagon

tearing out Maven's throat flooded through him. The entire pack had been in shock and their period of mourning for Maven had gone longer than any mourning period before. Finally, Dagon had forced them to end their daily mourning rituals and the shifters had reluctantly complied.

He wondered if Dagon knew of the whispers. If he knew that many of his pack were simply considering leaving in the night. He was the biggest and the most powerful of them and no one was foolish enough to challenge him for leadership, but the atmosphere of fear that Dagon cultivated was tearing the pack apart.

"Kane!"

He realized Dagon was glaring at him and he gave him a polite smile. "Aye, Dagon?"

"I said I imagine you'll be happy to have the big human out of your cabin."

"Aye," Kane replied briefly. He had no intention of letting Reese go anywhere. Once Dagon announced his decision to claim Adina, he would take Reese as his mate.

"I'll announce my decision tonight after dinner," Dagon said. "Hanif, you will make sure the blonde one is bathed and ready for me. I will take her as my mate tonight."

"Aye, Dagon," Hanif said quickly.

Kane glanced at the door of the cabin. He was anxious to find Reese. Theran had come to his cabin only moments after she stormed out, and insisted he come directly to Dagon's cabin. He was certain that Reese had gone to Adina or perhaps to Deena's and Borek's but not knowing exactly where his mate was, was making his wolf anxious and jumpy.

"What has you so anxious, Kane?" Dagon asked.

"Are we finished, Dagon? I have business elsewhere," Kane said harshly. He realized he was no longer capable of hiding his disdain for his alpha and was surprised to feel a thread of relief go through him at the thought.

"Watch your tongue, Kane," Dagon snapped. "I am your alpha or have you forgotten?"

"How could I? You feel the need to remind all of us on a daily basis."

Dagon's eyes widened and his body began to swell. "You dare speak to me in such a manner?"

"Kane did not mean it, my alpha. He is just tired," Hanif said nervously. "We all know how he hates the humans. It is difficult for him to have them in our pack and he needs time to adjust."

Dagon snorted. "That had better be the only reason he speaks so disrespectfully. You would be wise to remember that I am not my father, Kane."

"You are right about that, Dagon," Kane said. "You are not your father."

Before Dagon could reply there was a knock on the cabin door and Radek and Borek entered the cabin.

"Dagon," Radek said urgently, "Mia and Raina have gone into the woods."

"So?" Dagon frowned at him.

"Teagan and the others returned early this morning from hunting and said they spotted a mantorian not far from here."

Dagon scowled. "We will go after the young ones."

"The human is with them as well," Borek said suddenly.

Kane grabbed him by his shirt. "Which human, Borek?"

"Reese."

"How do you know this?" Kane struggled to hide the fear in his voice.

"Deena saw them leave. She came to me and told me."

Dagon's body relaxed. "Deena's brains are addled. The young ones are probably not even in the forest."

Borek made a soft growl. "Deena is not lying, Dagon. If she says she saw them go into the forest, then she did."

"We have searched all the cabins," Radek said. "We cannot find any of them and all three of their scents lead into the trees behind Kane's cabin. Please, Dagon. She is my sister."

Dagon nodded and Radek breathed a sigh of relief as the alpha strode toward the cabin. "Radek and Borek will come with me. Where is Mia's father?"

"He is waiting for us at the edge of the forest. If he has not already left on his own," Radek replied.

Dagon scowled as Kane left the cabin with them. "Where do you think you're going, Kane?"

"I'm coming with you."

"We don't need your assistance."

"If there is a mantorian out there, then you will," he snapped.

Dagon stopped and stared at him. Instead of bowing his head in submission, Kane returned his gaze. Nothing would stop him from going after his mate, not even his alpha. The others made soft whines of anxiety as the two shifters glared unblinkingly at each other.

"Kane is right," Radek said quickly. "We should take as many as possible."

Dagon snorted and looked away from Kane. "Do you not believe your alpha will keep you safe, Radek?"

"Of course not. It's just - "

"Kane will accompany us. The five of us will be plenty. No doubt we will find the human and the young ones wandering safely in the forest without a mantorian in sight," Dagon interrupted.

The four of them, followed by Theran and Hanif, walked to the edge of the forest. Mia's father, Befloc, had already shifted to his wolf form and he barked at them with impatience.

"Aye, Befloc," Dagon said irritably. The four of them quickly stripped off their clothes and shifted to their wolf forms before loping silently into the forest.

"I DON'T EVEN KNOW WHY SHE LIKES RADEK," RAINA grumbled as she helped Reese climb over a fallen log. "Did I mention he's bossy?"

"You did." Reese laughed. "But I think older brothers are supposed to be bossy."

"Do you have any siblings?"

"No."

"Why not?"

"My parents only wanted one child."

"How strange. Shifters like to have as many children as possible. My papa and mama were sad that they only had Radek and me. Papa said that mama lost four pups between when Radek was born and when I was born. Isn't that sad, human?"

"Very sad," Reese said.

"Do you want children?"

"Yes."

"Lots?" Raina asked curiously.

"Well, I always thought at least two."

"Two isn't very many."

"I suppose it isn't."

"Mia has seven older sisters. Her papa, Befloc, really wanted a boy but he ended up with eight girls." Raina giggled. "Most of them have mated with shifters from other packs and left but Mia says the three that are still here drive him crazy."

She squinted into the distance where they could see Mia sitting next to a tree. "Last year it was Kane she had a crush on. She followed him around like a little puppy for moons and moons."

Reese grinned. "What did Kane do?"

"He was very patient with her," Raina replied. "But eventually he sat her down and told her she was too young for him and that he only thought of her as a friend."

She shook her head. "Next thing you know, she has a crush on Radek. I will never be as boy crazy as Mia."

Reese laughed and squeezed her hand. "Perhaps you haven't met the right boy yet, Raina."

"Perhaps." Raina shrugged.

"Is there any in the pack that you find handsome?" She asked curiously as they moved closer to Mia.

Raina shook her head. "No. I have never found a boy to be anything more than annoying. Do you find that strange, human? I am nearly fifteen. My mama was mated to my papa and pregnant with Radek at my age."

"It's not strange," Reese said. "Fifteen is too young to be married and having babies. You have plenty of time to find a boy that you like."

Raina gave her a funny sidelong glance. "Or a girl?"

"Is there a girl that you like?" Reese asked.

Raina shrugged. "No one in particular. But I do find girls to be very pretty and I enjoy their company so much more than boys."

She gave Reese an anxious look and lowered her voice. "Please don't tell anyone. I haven't even told Mia. Mama said it was okay that I liked girls but I do not wish for Radek to know. He will be angry with me."

"I won't tell anyone, I promise," Reese said quickly. "But why do you think Radek will be angry with you? Your mama was right – it's okay that you like girls."

"Radek wants me to be normal."

"You are normal, Raina."

"Do you really think so?" Raina gave her a pleased look and Reese squeezed her hand again.

"Yes, I do."

"Good. I like you, human."

"I like you too, Raina. Do you think you could call me Reese?"

The shifter nodded. "Aye, I will try."

They approached Mia and she let go of Reese's hand and crouched next to her. She petted the wolf's fur. "I'm sorry that my brother was rude to you, Mia. I will make him apologize. He's just cranky because he hates humans."

She glanced up at Reese and mouthed the word 'sorry'. Reese winked at her before wrapping her arms around her torso. The wind was blowing heavily and she was starting to feel nearly frozen to the bone.

"Come on, Mia. We need to get back. Our alpha will be angry with us if we let the human freeze to death. I will make us some tea and we can talk about how awful my brother is."

Mia whined and Raina smiled at her. "I know. Are you ready to - "

She stopped and Reese frowned at her when she stood up abruptly and turned around. She inhaled, and a trickle of fear went down Reese's back when she realized the young shifter was starting to swell.

"Mia?" Raina whispered. "Do you smell that?"

Mia lifted her head and sniffed the air before starting to whine again. Raina clapped her hand over the wolf's mouth and gave her a frightened look. "Be quiet!"

"Raina? What's wrong?" Reese scanned the woods as she moved closer to the two young shifters.

"We need to go, human." Raina was trembling badly. "You must run quickly. Do you hear me?"

"What do you smell?"

"A mantorian," Raina nearly sobbed. "We have to go. We have to run and we have to hide before…"

She trailed off as the thick bushes to their left shivered wildly.

"Too late," she moaned and the hair on the back of Reese's neck tried to stand up at the pure terror in Raina's voice.

The bushes parted and a creature emerged from the shadows. A startled scream peeled from Reese's throat before she could stop it. The creature had the body of a man but all resemblance to a human ended there. It was over eight feet tall, pure white in colour, and giant white wings covered in tiny feathers sprouted from its back. Her frightened mind guessed its wing span to be at least ten feet. Her gaze drifted to its face and another whine of horror escaped her throat. It was the face nightmares were made of. The skin on its face was covered in the same tiny feathers that adorned its wings, and its eyes were huge, pulsing orbs of red that glowed brightly. Where its mouth should have been was a gaping hole lined with hundreds of small razor-sharp teeth, and two large feelers sprouted from the top of its skull. They rubbed together making a horrible buzzing noise that Reese could feel in her bones. The sound made her want to throw up and pass out at the same time and she took a stumbling step backward.

"Human, run!" Raina suddenly shouted as Mia, her tail between her legs, darted past her. Raina shifted to her wolf form, her clothes shredding around her, and with a frightened bark took off after Mia.

"It's the goddamn mothman," Reese said in a breathless little voice as she took another step back.

Run, you fool! Her mind screamed as the creature tilted its head and stared at her.

That was a brilliant fucking idea. Reese turned and ran after the two wolf shifters. Behind her she could feel more than hear the sound of the creature rising into the air. Its wings flapped and it made that inhuman buzzing sound again. Just ahead of her Raina barked, and Reese screamed at her to run faster as the beating of the wings grew closer.

She screamed when the creature's hands tipped with black claws, closed around her body. She was lifted into the air and she beat at the creature as it stared curiously at her. Its tongue flicked out, long and black and coated in a slime-like goo, and touched her cheek delicately.

She shrieked in disgust and punched it in the chest. The buzzing grew louder and her shirt ripped with a soft purr when the creature threw her to the ground and flew past her.

"No! Get away from them!" She screamed as it swooped down on the frightened wolf shifters. She struggled to her feet and ran toward the creature as Raina howled in fear. It had landed in front of the two young shifters and both of them had flattened to the ground. Their bodies shook with terror as it reached for them.

"Get away from them!" Reese screamed again before throwing herself on to the back of the creature. She shouted in disgust and horror when the creature's wings flapped against her face. They were hideously warm and she spat out a mouthful of feathers as she hooked her arm around the mothman's thick neck and squeezed as hard as she could.

The creature reached behind, grabbed her around her throat and tore her from his back with ease. He held her by her neck in front of him, her feet dangling and her body swaying as she beat frantically at his hands. Her face was turning purple as the creature opened its mouth and hissed at her.

Reese, her oxygen cut off, fought bitterly for her life. Black roses bloomed in her vision as her struggles weakened and her hands fell to her side. There was a loud howl of anger and her eyes widened when she saw Kane in his wolf form come bounding out from behind a tree. The creature hissed at Kane, its feelers moving frantically back and forth as more shifters appeared.

It turned his glowing gaze to Reese's face for a few seconds longer before it threw her into a tree and turned to face the shifters. She hit the tree with a muffled thud and fell to the ground, screaming shrilly when her left leg bounced off a large boulder and blinding pain shot through it.

KANE HOWLED IN ANGER AND FEAR WHEN HE SAW HIS MATE dangling in the mantorian's grip. She stared at him with wide and frightened eyes before the mantorian threw her into a tree. She screamed in agony and his wolf snarled angrily at the sound.

The mantorian was rising into the air, unwilling to face five full-grown shifters. Kane leaped upward and wrapped his powerful jaws around its foot. The mantorian squealed, its wings beating frantically at the air as it lifted Kane upward. Radek, growling ferociously, took a running jump and snagged the mantorian by its left leg. The two shifters dragged it downward and the creature squealed and writhed when Befloc and Borek fell on it and began to tear its stomach open with their sharp teeth.

Kane squirmed past the flapping wings of the mantorian and plunged his fangs into its throat. Its blood, black and horribly bitter, filled his mouth and he snarled and tore the soft flesh wide open before releasing his grip. As blood spurted out of the mantorian's neck in a black torrent, he raised his face to the sky and howled deafeningly.

RADEK IN HIS WOLF FORM, BOUNDED TO HIS SISTER AND nudged her with his head. She whimpered and licked at his face before running to where Reese was collapsed at the base of the tree. Raina shifted and crouched naked next to her as behind her, Kane sunk his teeth into the mantorian's neck.

"Radek! She's hurt!"

Radek shifted to his human form and studied Reese's leg. It was lying at an awkward angle and when he touched it, she made a harsh cry of pain and glared at him. "Get away from me, shifter!"

"Radek?" Raina's voice could barely be heard over Kane's triumphant howl.

"Radek!" Raina grabbed his arm in a tight grip when he didn't reply.

"What's wrong? Are you hurt?" He gave her an anxious look.

She shook her head before pointing to where Reese's shirt was torn. "Her shoulder, Radek."

Radek stared at the claiming mark on her shoulder before cursing and yanking up the fabric of her shirt to cover it. "Do not speak of this to anyone, Raina. Do you hear me?" He muttered as Dagon approached.

She nodded and bowed her head in submission when Dagon stopped in front of them. "Does the human live?"

"Aye, Dagon. I believe her leg is broken though."

"You think?" Reese snapped.

"Can you walk on it, human?" Dagon asked.

"Oh sure, no problem," she sneered at him. "I'll get right on that!"

Dagon blinked at her fury and took a step back. He made a harsh noise of surprise when Kane shoved him out of the way with a loud snarl. He knelt next to Reese and cupped her face.

"Are you all right, Reese?"

"Do I look okay, shifter?" She scowled.

A small smile crossed his face and he stroked her cheek with his thumb. "I'm going to lift you. It will hurt your leg. Are you ready?"

"Give me a minute," she muttered. She took several deep breaths, steeling herself against the pain, before nodding. "All right."

He lifted her into his arms, trying to support her broken leg as best as he could but she shrieked in pain. Her entire body stiffened before she slumped against his chest.

"Is she dead?" Raina cried.

"No. She's fainted from the pain. It's better for her," Kane said grimly.

Cradling Reese, he strode through the trees toward home.

CHAPTER 23

Reese stared up at the ceiling of Kane's cabin. The cabin was filled to the brim with shifters and she wished they would leave. Anna and Asher both leaned over her and stared at her pale face. She ignored them grimly as Asher patted her arm.

"You're even braver than I thought, human."

"Did you really attack a mantorian, human?" Anna asked.

Reese didn't reply. The pain in her leg was relentless and it was taking all of her concentration not to throw up.

"Leave the human alone." Radek tugged on Anna's arm and she and Asher moved reluctantly away as Radek stared down at her.

She closed her eyes and didn't open them again until Adina spoke to her. "Reese, open your eyes, my love."

She blinked wearily at the blonde woman. "It hurts so much, Adina."

"I know," she said. "Drink this. It will help with the pain. Can you sit up?"

"I don't think so," she muttered.

Before she could try, Radek pulled her gently into a

sitting position and Adina handed her a cup of steaming liquid.

"Drink, Reese," she urged.

She sipped at the foul-tasting liquid as her leg throbbed and burned and her stomach rolled with nausea.

"My leg is broken."

"Aye, it is," Adina said. "I need to set it, Reese. It's going to hurt badly, even with the tea."

"Maybe you could drive over to the drugstore and get me some morphine. What do you say?" A weird warmth was starting in her stomach and she thought the pain in her leg wasn't quite as bad.

"What does she mean?" Radek asked curiously.

"Nothing," Adina replied quickly. "The tea is making her a bit foolish, that's all."

"Foolish," Reese sang. She finished the liquid in three large gulps and smiled at Adina. "I feel better."

"Good." Adina stroked her hair. "In a few minutes, I'll set your leg."

"Have you done this before?"

She nodded. "Aye, don't worry."

"Where's Kane?" She asked suddenly. The cabin was full of people but she couldn't see the familiar bulk of Kane anywhere and she suddenly, desperately, wanted him.

"He's getting a few things for me. He'll return shortly."

"Do you promise?" She clutched at Adina's hand.

"Aye. I'll be right back, okay?"

Reese nodded and Adina slipped away as Radek continued to study her.

"What?" She scowled at the shifter.

"Why did you save my sister's life, human?"

"Go away, Radek. I don't want to talk with you right now," she muttered.

"Tell me," he insisted. "Why did you attack a creature you had no chance of defeating to save a girl you barely know?"

"Because I like your sister!" Reese snapped at him.

He stared silently at her and she closed her eyes. "Please leave me alone."

"WILL THESE WORK? THEY WERE THE STRAIGHTEST I COULD find," Kane asked Adina anxiously. They were standing by the main fire outside and she looked over the branches he had gathered. Like she instructed, he had peeled away the bark and she tested each of them.

"Aye, they will work to keep her leg straight once I have set the bone. Do you have rope?"

"Aye, Raina has gone to fetch it."

"Good." She hesitated and then patted the large shifter on his arm. "She will be all right, Kane. She's young and strong and the break is a clean one."

He nodded and she hesitated before glancing at Dagon's home. He was standing in the doorway watching them silently and she gave him a tentative smile. He nodded impassively before disappearing into his cabin and she breathed a sigh of relief.

"Are you ready, Kane? I will need you to hold her down while I set her leg."

His face paled and she patted his arm again. "I can have Hanif and Theran help me."

"No," he said hoarsely. "I will not leave her alone in her suffering. Did you give her the tea?"

"Aye and it is helping but it will not be enough to ease her pain when I fix her leg. You must be prepared that she will scream."

He nodded and pulled a short branch from his pocket. He had stripped it clean as well and he gave Adina a sick look. "I thought she could bite down on this."

"It is a good idea," she said. "Come, the sooner we do this, the better."

"OPEN YOUR EYES, REESE."

Her eyes popped open and she smiled with relief at the large shifter. "Where have you been?"

"I was gathering some supplies for Adina to help fix your leg."

"That's nice of you." She reached out to touch his face and, acutely aware of the shifters in the room, he caught her hand and placed it on the bed.

She sighed before staring hazily at the roomful of shifters. "Please make them leave. I don't want them here."

He nodded and stood up to face the others. "Leave. You do not need to be here."

There was some grumbling and he snarled viciously at them. The shifters bowed their heads and scurried from the room as Adina held Radek and Borek back.

"Thank you," she sighed as he sat back down beside her.

"You're welcome, my love." He leaned down and kissed her on the mouth. "It will be all right. I promise you."

She nodded and groaned when Adina eased her skirt up to her thighs. "Are you ready, Reese?"

She nodded again and made a short sound of fear when Borek placed his hands on her right thigh and Radek rested his hands on her right arm and shoulder. Kane snarled at them and Adina said quickly, "We will need their help to hold her steady, Kane. It's better if she doesn't move."

He nodded and cupped Reese's cheek when she tried to raise her head to look at her leg. "No. Look at me, Reese, only at me."

She latched on to his hand with a panicked grip and he stroked her face. "Be brave, my love."

She stared up at him with wide eyes. She wanted to be brave but oh she was afraid. It was going to hurt, hurt badly, and she had never been more afraid in her life. Her heart was thudding like a freight train in her chest and there was a weird buzzing in her ears. She was breathing in short, harsh pants and there was suddenly not enough oxygen in the room.

"Reese?" Kane's voice was filled with alarm and Adina leaned over her.

"You breathe too quickly, Reese. You must slow it down. Do you hear me?"

She continued to pant as her eyes rolled with fear, and then Kane was there. His warm hand cupped her face again and his forehead rested against hers.

"Like this, my love," he whispered, his warm breath washing over her. "Do what I do."

He took a deep breath in through his nose and she tried to mimic him, letting her breath out through her mouth as he exhaled. She continued to mimic him with long flat inhales through her nose and harsh exhales through her mouth until the buzzing was gone and the light-headedness had passed.

"Good," he whispered before kissing her on the mouth.

She stared at the piece of wood Kane was holding. "Bite down on this."

She opened her mouth and gripped the smooth wood with her teeth as Kane kissed her forehead. She was still holding his hand and he kissed her knuckles before lowering her arm to the bed. He held her hand in a tight grip and slipped his other hand under her torn shirt to press against her shoulder. He stroked the scar with the tips of his fingers before pressing her into the bed. "We're ready, Adina."

He smiled reassuringly at Reese. "Look only at me, my love."

Reese stared into his dark eyes as Adina gripped her leg. Her hands were warm but she trembled violently at her touch and moaned when pain shot through her leg.

"Steady, Reese," Kane murmured.

Adina pulled on her leg. Reese, sweat rolling down her face and her jaw clamping down on the stick between her teeth, cried out. The pain was enormous, like nothing she had ever felt or even imagined. As it filled her world with bright, unending agony, she tried to hold back the scream building in her throat.

It was impossible. As Adina pulled again and new agony flared in her leg, she shrieked piercingly and tried to buck free of the men holding her down.

"Hold her!" Adina said sharply.

The three of them with pale and grim faces, pressed their considerable weight on to the screaming, trembling woman. Kane stared down at his mate. Her face was completely bloodless and he could see the deep bite marks on the wood she held in her mouth.

"It is all right, my love." He tried to speak soothingly but his wolf was howling in misery over his mate's pain and it was hard to think past its relentless call.

"Almost there," Adina said. She pulled again and Reese gave one final shriek of pain, her entire body arching upward before her eyes rolled up in her head and she collapsed on the bed.

Kane, feeling sick to his stomach, pulled the piece of

wood from her mouth and smoothed her hair away from her face. His hand was shaking badly and he nodded when Borek gripped his shoulder. "She will be fine, Kane."

Adina was laying the large smooth sticks against Reese's leg and she looked briefly at them. "I will need someone to help me with this."

"I will help," Kane said hoarsely.

Borek shook his head and glanced at Radek. "Take Kane outside for some fresh air. I will stay and help the human."

"I will not leave my mate!" Kane said angrily.

Borek stared in surprise at Radek who gave him a tiny shake of his head.

Kane glared at Adina. "If she wakes and I'm not here - "

"She's not going to wake," Adina replied. "If she does, we will find you."

"Come with me, Kane," Radek said. He urged the large shifter outside. There was no one there but Asher and Raina, and Radek gave him a curious look.

"I made them leave when she started screaming," Asher said.

Kane shoved his hand through his hair and strode into the trees. He leaned against a large pine tree, his head down and his hands clenched into fists.

"Is the human – Reese – is she all right?" Raina asked.

"Aye, she is." Radek hugged her. "Are you?"

"Aye. She saved my life, Radek."

"I know." He hugged her again. "What about Mia?"

"She'll be fine," Raina replied. She headed to Kane and wrapped her arms around his waist, resting her head against his back and hugging him. He patted her arm and stared at the ground without speaking.

"He loves the human," Asher said.

"Aye, he does," Radek replied. "If Dagon chooses her as his mate…"

"Kane will challenge him for alpha."

"Will he?" Radek asked.

"Aye. He should be our alpha. Maven loved his son but I know he hoped that Kane would take over the pack. I hope that Dagon does choose the big human."

"Have you gone mad, Uncle?" Radek said angrily. "Kane does not wish to lead. Even if he decides to challenge Dagon, what makes you think he will win? You know how powerful Dagon is."

"Kane is stronger and smarter than him. Just because he does not believe he is, does not make it untrue."

"She has a claiming mark on her shoulder," Radek said in a low voice. "Kane has bitten her and claimed her as his own."

"I am not surprised," Asher replied. "If Dagon does choose her, Kane will be left with no choice but to challenge him for alpha."

"He will leave the pack," Radek said. "I know Kane – he has no desire to be the alpha. If Dagon chooses Reese, he will leave with her in the night."

Asher scoffed. "Kane is not a coward."

"I didn't say he was!" Radek snapped. "What is wrong with you, Asher? I know you hate Dagon but there is no one amongst us who can defeat him. Not even Kane."

"You're wrong," Asher said. Before Radek could protest, he clapped the younger shifter on the back. "Go to your friend, Radek. His mate is wounded and in pain and he could use your support."

"He has not spoken to me since I treated his mate so rudely."

Asher grinned at him. "Then it is time you apologized."

"I never thought we would have humans in our pack. Or that Kane would fall in love with one."

"The humans' numbers grow with each passing day while ours dwindles," Asher replied. "We need to find a way to coexist with them. As useless as Dagon is, he had the right idea in bringing humans into the pack. Although," he frowned, "it would be handy if they healed as well as shifters do and enjoyed raw meat. The smell of cooked meat really does turn my stomach."

He clapped Radek on the back and left. Radek walked toward Raina and Kane and touched Raina's back.

"Go back to the cabin, Raina."

"No." She frowned at him. "Kane needs me."

"I will stay with him. You need to get some rest. Go on, now. I wish to speak to Kane privately."

She glared at him and Kane patted her arm. "Your brother is right, Raina."

"Can I see Reese?"

"She is resting. You can visit her when she wakes."

She kissed Kane's back and rolled her eyes when Radek ruffled her hair before leaving. Radek waited until she was in their cabin before speaking.

"I am sorry for the way I treated your human, Kane."

"It is not me you should be apologizing to. And her name is Reese, not human."

"I will apologize to Reese."

When Kane didn't reply, he said, "I am sorry, Kane. Truly. It's just – we have spent nearly our entire lives hating the humans. It is difficult for me to forget that hatred."

"Aye, I know. You, more than any of us, have your reasons for hating them," Kane said. "I was horrible to her when I first met her, Radek. I insulted her and told her I did not care if she died. I was attracted to her from the moment I laid eyes on her but it did not stop me from nearly letting her freeze to death."

He gave Radek a haunted look. "In return for my cruelty, she saved my life. I was drowning and without hesitating, she dove into the lake and saved me. Later when the tagen took her and I went after them, she saved my life again. She took on a tagen to save me, Radek. A tagen! I had no idea that there were humans like her."

"She does seem…kind."

Kane snorted laughter. "She saved my life, and she saved Deena from drowning and your sister from a mantorian and all you can say is that she seems kind?"

Radek gave him a crooked grin. "I have never had a way with words, Kane."

"She is not from our world," Kane said suddenly.

"What do you mean?"

"She is from another world. She was brought to ours by a glowing orb, she says. She speaks of strange metal carriages and warmth and light without fire."

Radek gave him a hesitant look. "She sounds mad, Kane."

"Aye, I know. But she is not. I believe her. I didn't at first, thought she was as mad as you think her to be, but her scent is so strange, Radek. When she speaks of her world, I see the truth of what she's saying."

"She does have a strange scent," Radek agreed. "But what she says is impossible."

"Is it? There are many things in our world that cannot be explained."

"Aye, but another world outside of this one? If what she says is true, why was she brought to ours?"

"I do not know," Kane replied. "But whatever magic brought her here, I will forever be grateful for it."

He gave Radek a searching look before saying hoarsely, "I love her."

"Aye, I know you do." Radek squeezed his shoulder. "Kane, you need to - "

The door to Kane's cabin opened and Borek stuck his head out. "She is awake and asking for you, Kane."

Kane hurried to the cabin and disappeared inside as Radek followed more slowly. He stood with Borek in the cold sunshine and rubbed wearily at his forehead. Borek shut the door and leaned against it.

"Kane's precious flower."

"What?" Radek frowned at him.

"Deena refers to the human as Kane's precious flower, and I am beginning to see the truth in it."

"The human means nothing to Kane," Radek said shortly.

Borek laughed. "Does she not? I was there, Radek, when he called her his mate."

"A slip of the tongue, nothing more."

"And the claiming mark on her shoulder?"

Radek gave him a startled look and Borek nodded solemnly. "I saw it when she was struggling on the bed. Kane has claimed her as his own."

Radek grabbed Borek and pulled him forward until they were nose to nose. "You will speak to no one of what you saw unless you want Deena to find herself without a mate. Do you hear me, Borek?"

"Enough, Radek!" Borek pushed him away with a scowl. "The human saved my mate's life. Do you really believe I will run and tattle to our alpha like a child?"

"I do not know what you will do. You are loyal to our alpha," Radek replied.

"Am I?" Borek said suddenly. "Do you know that after Deena healed from the bear shifter's attack and it became apparent that she was not the same, our alpha told me it would be best if I killed her and put her out of her misery? He said she weakened our pack."

He snarled angrily. "He honestly expected that I would do as he said. That I would take the woman I loved into the woods and put her down like a dog that can no longer serve its master. Our alpha is not fit to rule us. He is more mad than my mate."

He gave Radek a solemn look. "I must get back to Deena. I will speak to no one of what I heard and saw today, Radek. You have my word."

"REESE, ARE YOU SURE YOU CANNOT EAT JUST A LITTLE?" Kane said anxiously. "You need to regain your strength."

Reese shook her head. Darkness had fallen and Adina had just left. She had spent most of the day drifting in and out of consciousness which she suspected had something to do with the foul-tasting tea Adina had kept forcing her to drink. The tea dulled the pain in her leg, but it also made her sleepy and weak. Still, she was grateful for it.

"I'm too tired, Kane. I just want to sleep."

"Do you need to use the bathroom?"

She shook her head again. "No, Adina helped me earlier." She was totally humiliated when Adina had brought a shallow dish to the bed. She had even changed the soft cloth in her underwear for a fresh one and had shrugged off Reese's apology.

"Do not worry, Reese," she said. "I am more than happy to help. Tomorrow when you are feeling better, I will wash your hair and help you bathe. Get some rest tonight."

Now, as Kane climbed carefully into the bed beside her, she closed her eyes and melted into his warm embrace.

"What you did was very foolish, Reese," he whispered into her hair.

"It would have killed Raina and Mia," she murmured.

"It nearly killed you." His stomach clenched at the memory of his mate dangling in the mantorian's grip. He touched her throat. It was swollen and bruises were rising on her pale skin.

"If I hadn't gotten there in time - "

He stopped, his hand tightening around her waist and she rubbed his arm. "You did. I'm fine, shifter."

He grunted. "A broken leg is not fine, Reese."

She smiled sleepily at him. "It's better than being dead. I'm so tired, Kane."

"I know, my love. Go to sleep." He kissed her and she closed her eyes. She was asleep in a matter of moments and he stared at her, memorizing every line of her sweet face, before resting his forehead against hers.

"I love you," he whispered.

She didn't stir and he placed his head next to hers and closed his eyes.

CHAPTER 24

"How is Reese?" Radek asked.

It was three days later, and Kane had finally joined the others for the evening meal. "She is healing. She's been having nightmares about the mantorian."

"Aye, Raina as well. It was a close call for them."

"Too close," Kane replied.

He glanced around at the others before frowning. "Why is Adina not sitting with Dagon?"

"Why would she be?" Radek asked.

"Has he not chosen her as his mate?"

Radek shook his head. "Not yet."

"The day that they were attacked, Dagon told us he was choosing Adina. He was going to make the announcement that night."

"He did not. Perhaps with everything that happened, he has decided to wait."

"Perhaps."

As if he had heard them, Dagon appeared in front of them. He sat down next to Kane and clapped him on the back. "How is the human?"

"She is healing."

"Good. Is the moon still full for her?"

Kane gave him a cautious look. "No."

"Good, good." Dagon stared at the others in the pack. "She is rather brave for a human."

Kane didn't reply and Dagon cleared his throat. "I have instructed Anna to give the human some meat this evening. As a thank you for saving Raina and Mia. She will like that, will she not?"

"Aye," Kane said. He had gone out every night and hunted for Reese. She had worried that he would be caught but he had refused to let his mate starve.

"When will you make your announcement that you are taking Adina as your mate?" He asked abruptly.

"All in good time, Kane," Dagon said smoothly. "I thought it would be best to wait until the excitement had died down."

He stood and nodded to the two of them before walking away. Kane watched him leave, a narrow look of suspicion on his face, as Radek touched his shoulder.

"You see? He will make the announcement soon and then you are free to claim Reese as your mate."

"Aye," Kane said. He stood. "I'm going to check on Reese. Goodnight, Radek."

"You should be eating dinner with the others, Raina." Reese said as the young shifter sat beside her on the bed.

Raina shrugged. "I'm not that hungry."

She stared at Reese's leg for a moment before saying solemnly, "Thank you for saving my life, Reese."

"I didn't. Kane saved all of us," Reese said.

"Aye. Kane would do anything to save his mate."

"I'm not his mate," Reese replied.

Raina blinked at her. "Aye, you are, human – I mean, Reese. You bear his mark, do you not?"

"What do you mean?" She frowned at Raina.

Raina leaned forward and brushed her shirt aside before touching the scar from Kane's bite. "His mark. Was it not Kane who bit you?"

"Yes," Reese whispered. "But it was an accident, Raina."

Raina laughed. "A shifter does not accidentally claim his mate, Reese."

She gave Reese a curious look. "How could you not know? Did Kane not talk to you before he bit you?"

Reese shook her head. "No. He told me after that it was an accident and that he hadn't meant to do it."

"He's lying," Raina said cheerfully as she slid off the bed. "No other shifter will go near you when they see the mark. You belong to him now, Reese. He loves you."

"Raina! You cannot say anything to anyone! Promise me!" Reese said.

"I won't," Raina replied. "If Dagon finds out that Kane claimed you for his own, he will be so angry."

"Shit," Reese muttered under her breath.

"Don't worry, Reese," Raina said. "If Dagon does choose you for his mate, then Kane will fight him and he will become our new alpha."

Reese's face paled. "I don't want him fighting Dagon. He's too big and too strong."

"Kane is stronger," Raina said simply. "Uncle Asher always says he should be our alpha."

Reese stared up at the ceiling. Her head was reeling, her stomach was rolling with an odd combination of fear and happiness, and Raina's declaration that Kane loved her was ringing in her brain.

Kane loved her. He had claimed her as his mate and he loved her.

"Reese?" Raina's face appeared above her. "Are you all right?"

"Yes. Would you mind leaving, Raina? I'm very tired." She smiled at the shifter.

"Aye. Do you want me to bring you some food?"

"No. Kane will bring me some."

Raina hesitated before placing a kiss on Reese's cheek. "Bye, Reese."

As the shifter left the cabin, Reese held her hand up and stared at it. It was trembling badly and she lowered it to the bed. Her cheeks were warm and a fierce type of joy was flooding through her body in a hot, sweet rush. Kane loved her.

You love him.

She did. She loved him more than she thought was possible. The relief at finally admitting her feelings poured through her, and she wiped away the tears that were beginning to run down her cheeks. She loved him and he loved her.

REESE RESTED HER HEAD AGAINST KANE'S BROAD CHEST AND listened to the steady beat of his heart. Her leg ached dully but for the first time in nearly five days, she didn't need to drink tea to dull the pain enough to help her sleep. She wasn't the least bit sleepy, but she was ridiculously happy, and she smiled as Kane rubbed her back.

Kane rubbed Reese's warm skin. She had fallen asleep nearly

ten minutes ago and he buried his face in her soft hair and breathed in her scent. He was feeling restless and jumpy. Dagon's refusal to name Adina as his mate was worrying him. What if he had changed his mind? What if he chose Reese instead?

We will kill him, his wolf whispered persuasively.

He pushed the thought away. Dagon would choose Adina – he had to – and Reese would belong to him forever. He kissed her smooth forehead and, as he did every night now, whispered, "I love you."

He jerked in surprise when her low voice came floating out of the darkness. "I love you too."

He sat up, his heart thudding in his chest, and stared at her in the soft light of the fire. "Reese, I – I thought you were sleeping."

"No," she replied.

"I – did you mean it when you said you love me?"

"Yes," she said. "I love you, Kane."

"You are mine," he said. "Mine forever."

"Yes – yours forever." She touched his face delicately, tracing the stubble on his jawline. He turned and kissed the palm of her hand.

"Reese, the mark on your shoulder, it is - "

"I know. You've claimed me as your mate."

He gaped at her. "How do you know this?"

"Raina was here earlier while you were having dinner with the others. She told me what the mark meant. She was surprised that I didn't already know."

There was no anger in her voice but shame filled him and he looked away from her steady gaze. "I'm sorry, Reese. I should not have lied to you about it."

"Why did you?" She asked.

"Because I should not have claimed you without your

permission and because I – I was confused by what I had done."

"But you aren't confused anymore?"

He shook his head and kissed her palm again. "No. I love you. You are my mate, Reese, and I will love you for the rest of my life."

Her mouth began to tremble and tears slipped down her cheeks. "I love you too, Kane."

"You are not just saying that?" He said anxiously. "Did Raina tell you that no shifter will touch you when they see my mark?"

"Yes," Reese replied. "But I'm not saying it because I have no choice. I could find a human who wouldn't know what the mark means."

He began to growl. "You belong to me, Reese. You are not to - "

She laughed and patted his face. "God, I love you, Kane. You're stubborn and bullheaded and a raging Neanderthal but you're also kind and gentle and sweet. I am ridiculously in love with you."

He kissed her on the mouth and she immediately parted her lips and coaxed his tongue into her mouth. She sucked on it, moaning when his big hand cupped her naked breast and kneaded it. His thumb circled her hardened nipple and she ran her fingers through his hair restlessly. He kissed down her neck and she reached under the covers and gripped his cock.

He moaned and she smiled at him as she stroked him. "I've missed you."

"I've missed you too," he panted as his hips moved with the motion of her hand.

"Touch me, honey," she pleaded.

He slipped his hand between her legs and rubbed at her

clit. She parted her legs and he froze when she made a cry of pain and her face paled.

"I'm okay." She gave him a look of disappointment when he moved his hand away from her.

"No, my love, you are not," he said. "We cannot do this – not while you still heal."

"We can go slowly." Disappointment laced her words. "Please, Kane. It's been so long."

He shook his head. "No, it is not worth the risk of hurting your leg, Reese."

"It is to me," she muttered before pouting at him.

He laughed and kissed the tip of her nose. "Once you are healed fully I will fuck you, Reese."

"So romantic." She rolled her eyes.

"I am very good at sweet talking." He laughed again.

He cupped her breast and kissed the top of her head. "Go to sleep, my love."

She snuggled against him and lay quietly for a while. As her happiness faded and worry set in, he rubbed her back.

"What is wrong, my love?"

"Nothing."

"Do not lie to me, Reese. Your body is tensing and your scent has changed," he replied.

She sighed. "If Dagon chooses me - "

"He will not," Kane interrupted. "He told us that he was claiming Adina as his mate."

"Adina?" Reese stared up at him. "She didn't say anything to me."

"He hasn't announced it yet."

"Why not?"

"He was going to make the announcement the day you were attacked by the mantorians."

"That was nearly a week ago," she pointed out.

"Aye, he decided to wait."

"Why?"

"I'm not sure." He rubbed her back again. "Go to sleep, Reese."

"What if he's changed his mind?" She spoke the words that he had refused to articulate to himself.

"He hasn't."

"But what if he has? What if he hasn't said anything because he's decided not to choose Adina?" She asked worriedly.

"If he chooses you, I will challenge him for the alpha position."

"No!"

Her cry of dismay startled him and he jerked in the bed. She groaned when it jostled her leg and he cupped her face. "My love, I'm sorry. Are you all right?"

"Yes." She gave him a frightened look. "Kane, I don't want you challenging Dagon."

"I will have no choice, Reese."

"Yes, you do! We could leave, Kane. We could just leave in the night."

"You would have me leave my pack? Have me run away like a frightened pup?" He said.

"It is better than watching you die!" She said angrily. "Dagon is too big and strong, Kane. He killed his own father and his mates for God's sake!"

"I can defeat him."

"And if you can't?" She was starting to cry. "You will be dead and I'll be Dagon's mate. I'll kill myself before I let that happen."

"Don't say that!" His voice was rough with fear.

"I can't live without you," she said. "I can't, Kane."

He held her and stroked her hair as she buried her face in

his throat. "Promise me you won't challenge him, Kane." Her voice was muffled.

"Reese - "

"Promise me!" She said fiercely. "We will leave together and make a new pack. I'm sorry, I know you'll miss your pack mates, but I would rather you miss them then watch as they bury you in a shallow grave."

"I am not as weak as you believe me to be, Reese." There was an edge of anger in his voice. "Is it so hard for you to believe that I can be alpha?"

"Of course not!" She said immediately. "You'd be an amazing alpha, Kane. But your life isn't worth the risk to me. I would rather have you alive and in my arms."

She kissed him. "I love you, Kane."

"I love you too," he sighed. "Do not worry, my love. Dagon will choose Adina. And I will speak to my pack mates and tell them that we cannot allow Dagon to hurt Adina like he hurt his other mates. All right?"

"All right," she said in defeat.

He held her close and rubbed her back as Reese stared into the darkness. He hadn't promised not to challenge Dagon and she trembled violently in his arms as an image of Dagon taking Kane's head flashed through her.

CHAPTER 25

"Do you want to go back to the bed, Reese?" Kane asked.

It was two days later and for the first time since she had broken her leg, Adina had allowed her to leave the bed. She was sitting in the armchair in front of the fire, her injured leg propped up on a chair in front of her and she was wrapped snugly in the bear pelt from Kane's bed.

She shook her head. "God, no."

"Are you sure? If your leg is hurting you should go back to bed."

"I'm fine, shifter." She smiled. "It feels so good to be sitting in an actual chair. Let me enjoy it, okay?"

"Aye, I can do that." He grinned at her.

There was a knock on the cabin door and Asher opened it and stuck his head in. "Hello, Kane. Hello, human."

"Uncle, how are you?"

"I cannot complain."

Asher crouched in front of Reese and examined her lower leg. It was covered from ankle to knee in a thick layer of rope to keep the branches firmly against it and he touched her knee briefly.

"How does it feel, human?"

"Better."

"Good." He stood and gave Kane a grave look. "Dagon sent me to bring you and the human outside. He is making his announcement."

Reese's face paled and she gave Kane a frightened look. He smiled reassuringly at her before picking her up from the chair. She winced a little and he kissed her.

"I'm sorry, my love."

"Kane, promise me," she muttered as Asher led them to the door.

"Everything will be fine, Reese." He carried her outside and she blinked at the bright sunlight. It was cold and although Radek had brought a pile of his mother's clothing to her yesterday, she was thankful for the pelt still wrapped around her.

"There you are!" Dagon said jovially. "Bring the human to me, Kane."

His entire body tense, Kane walked past his pack to where Dagon was waiting with Adina and Ghita. Adina's face was pale and she held Ghita's hand as the smaller woman cried silently.

Theran, his face a hard mask and his hands rolled into fists, was standing stiffly to the left of them and he nodded to Ghita when she stole a quick glance at him.

Dagon patted the chair next to Adina. "Here, I have even been kind enough to have a chair for her."

Kane set Reese down. She held on to him a few seconds longer before forcing herself to release him. Dagon watched them with bright interest as Kane tucked the pelt closer around her before straightening.

He stayed where he was, and Dagon frowned at him. "Join the pack, Kane. I do not need you hovering like a nursemaid."

Kane stared at him for a moment before turning and walking slowly away. He joined Radek and Raina and didn't seem to notice when Raina took his hand and squeezed it.

"Brothers and sisters," Dagon clapped his hands together, "I know many of you questioned my decision to bring humans into our pack, but I trust you understand that I do what is best for us. While two of the humans will make a suitable mate, there is no doubt in my mind that the third is useless."

He stood behind Ghita and patted her head like a dog before shoving her in the back. "Go on, girl. Get out of my sight."

She pitched forward to her knees with a startled yelp and Theran growled before stepping toward her. He lifted her to her feet and guided her to the others. He placed a possessive arm around her shoulders as Dagon laughed.

"I do not believe it will be long before Theran claims himself a mate."

He turned his attention back to the crowd of shifters. "I made my decision to take the blonde human as my mate."

Reese reached out and gripped Adina's hand as the woman's body stiffened and her face paled even further.

The shifters began to shout congratulations at them, and Dagon held his hand up. "But that was before I witnessed the big human's bravery. She attacked a mantorian to save the lives of our young. Does that not bear the marking of an alpha's mate, my brothers?"

The shifters nodded as Kane, growling under his breath, stepped forward. Before he could speak, Dagon smiled. "I choose the big one to be my mate."

Reese's stomach dropped and she released Adina's hand as numbness washed over her. The shifters cheered and surged forward. They shook Dagon's hand and crowded around her, kissing her cheeks and touching and patting her arms and shoulders. She tried to search past their bodies for Kane but they blocked him completely from her view and she felt a moment of pure panic when Dagon placed one heavy hand on her shoulder and growled.

"Do not overwhelm my new mate. Remember, she is injured." He smiled down at her. "I will go easy on you tonight. Do not fear, human."

"What?" She whispered through numb lips.

"I will claim you as my mate this very evening," Dagon said cheerfully. "I know you are injured but I will do my best not to hurt you."

"No, I – I need one more day," she said quickly. "Please, Dagon. I just need one more day to -"

He laughed and patted her on the head. "I'm afraid not, human. Now that I have made my decision, my cock is eager to find a home in your warm body."

She recoiled at the thought and a look of dark anger flickered across his face. "Do not even think to deny me, human. You belong to me now and I will take what is mine."

He glared irritably at the other shifters. "Stand back, you fools."

As they shuffled backward, he gripped Adina's arm. "You will go to my cabin and help my new mate bathe and ready herself for me. Do you understand?"

Adina nodded slowly and Dagon released her arm before turning back to Reese. "Come, I will help you to your new home."

Before he could pick her up, Kane's voice rang out. "The woman belongs to me."

Dagon froze and Reese watched as a knowing smile crossed his face. He straightened and turned to look at Kane.

"Get away from her, Dagon," Kane growled.

"Watch your tongue when you speak to your alpha," Dagon said sharply.

"You are not my alpha. Maven was my alpha," Kane snarled.

Dagon's face flushed and he growled at Kane. "I will give you one more chance to walk away, Kane."

"The woman is my mate. Not yours."

"Do you think I am stupid, Kane? Do you think I did not know that you have been fucking my potential mate? I'll admit I was surprised that you would fuck a human after what they have taken from you, but I assumed it was nothing more than a curiosity for you. I ignored your disobedience because of the affection my father had for you. But the woman belongs to me now and you will stay away from my mate or I will tear out your throat."

"She bears my mark," Kane said calmly.

Dagon jerked in surprise and Kane grinned bitterly at him. "Show him, Reese."

"Kane, I - "

"Show him!" He snarled.

She pushed her sleeve down until the cold air washed over Kane's bite.

Dagon howled angrily at the sight of it and there were gasps and mutters of surprise from the other shifters.

"You fool!" Dagon spat at Kane. "You have spoiled her for me and now you will watch as I take your mate's life."

"I challenge you," Kane said.

Dagon stiffened and gave him an incredulous look. "What did you say?"

"I challenge you."

"You will not win, Kane. You would die for this human? Is she worth your life?"

"Aye, she is," Kane replied.

Dagon studied him for a moment longer before nodding. "Very well. I accept your challenge."

He turned and moved to the center of the clearing as Kane knelt in front of Reese.

"Kane - "

"It will be all right, my love." He took her hands and rested his forehead against hers. "Do not cry."

"Please don't do this. Please," she begged as she put her arms around his shoulders and clung to him. "I don't want you to do this, Kane. I can't - "

He pressed his mouth to hers. Her lips were cold and he could taste her fear as she clutched the back of his shirt in a tight grip.

"I will defeat him, my love," he whispered against her mouth. He tried to untangle himself from her grip and she held on grimly.

"NO!" She shouted. "Don't do this, Kane!"

She kicked at him with her good leg when he pried her hands open and kissed the palms of them.

"I love you, Reese."

"Don't do this!" She shouted again as she punched and kicked at him. As Kane stepped back she staggered to her feet and tried to limp after him. Radek appeared beside her and he wrapped his arms around her and held her in a tight grip. Pain coursing through her leg, she shrieked at him and tried to head butt him. He dodged it easily and when her broken leg smacked against his, she cried out and slumped against him in defeat.

Kane had moved to the middle of the clearing and was

staring calmly at Dagon. She called his name desperately and he turned to stare at her.

"I love you!" She cried. "I love you!"

"I love you too."

She watched in agonized silence as Dagon stripped off his clothes and shifted to his wolf form. He was huge. His dark brown fur gleamed in the sunlight and his muscles rippled as he stalked toward Kane.

Kane eyed him silently as the shifters made soft whimpers of nervousness. Borek and Deena joined Radek, and Deena stroked Reese's hair silently as Borek glanced at Radek. "Why does he not shift?"

"I don't know," Radek said worriedly.

Kane stripped off his shirt and dropped it the ground as he and Dagon circled each other. Dagon seemed to be waiting for him to shift and when he didn't, he barked at the smaller shifter.

Kane shook his head and gave him a bitter smile. "I have no need to shift. I will defeat you easily, even in my human form."

Dagon howled with rage and Reese screamed when the giant wolf bounded across the clearing and leaped at Kane.

Kane, his face serene, caught the wolf in midair. He sunk his hands into the thick fur around his neck as Dagon snapped at him. Dagon's fangs narrowly missed his face and with a harsh roar and his biceps bulging, he flipped the wolf over his head. Dagon landed with a heavy thud on the ground and Kane fell on him. He straddled the wolf as Dagon twisted and snarled and scrabbled to get free. Kane grabbed the struggling wolf's head in his massive hands and twisted Dagon's head viciously to the left. The wolf's neck broke with a sharp crack and it slumped to the ground, its long tongue hanging from its mouth and its eyes staring lifelessly into the sky.

"What just happened?" Radek said in a weak little voice entirely different from his normal one.

The shifters stared in stunned silence at the dead body of their alpha as Kane climbed to his feet. Breathing heavily, he raised his head to the sky and howled deafeningly. One by one the wolves fell to their knees before their new alpha and answered his call.

THE WOMAN'S SOFT CRIES OF PLEASURE FILLED THE LARGE cabin and her mate smiled before licking a slow path across her inner thigh.

"Shifter!" She lifted her head and glared at him impatiently.

"Aye, my love?" He gave her an innocent look.

"If you don't put your tongue in my pussy right now, I'll give you nothing but plants to eat for a month!"

He kissed the dark curls at the top of her core. "If you do that, I'll be too weak to fuck you or eat your sweet pussy."

She wrapped her fingers in his hair and tugged sharply. "Fine. The next time you ask me to suck your cock, I'll refuse."

He laughed. "I doubt that, my love. You enjoy sucking my cock too much to deny me."

She pulled his hair so hard that he winced before she whacked him in the ass with her foot. "Last warning, shifter."

He winked at her before dipping his head and sliding his tongue across her wet and swollen clit. She moaned and clamped her thighs around his head as her pelvis arched and her fingers tightened in his hair. He sucked on her clit, sliding his thick fingers in and out of her tight center, until she made a sharp cry and her body shook violently.

He licked away her sweet-tasting cream before sliding up her body and positioning himself between her thighs. His cock probed at her entrance and she reached down and took him in her hand, stroking him before guiding him into her.

He sunk into her with a harsh moan and she wrapped her legs around his hips and kissed him. She could taste herself on his lips and it sent a dark arrow of desire through her as he thrust in and out of her. As her mate's moans grew louder and the steady rhythm of his body grew more erratic, she stroked his face.

"I love you, Kane."

"I love you too, Reese."

KANE RUBBED REESE'S LEG. "IS YOUR LEG ALL RIGHT, MY love?"

"It's fine, Kane. It's been almost two months." She stretched in the bed and he cupped her breast before placing a light kiss on her nipple.

She grinned at him. "I'm gonna need a bit more recovery time, big guy."

He laughed and relaxed against the pillows beside her. After a moment she flipped onto her stomach and propped her hands under her chin.

"You're worried about him."

"Aye, a little."

"It's only been a couple months since you became alpha, Kane. He needs time to adjust to that as well as the fact that you're mated to a human. He hates humans and he has a good reason for it."

"Has he been rude to you?" Kane asked anxiously.

"Of course he hasn't. He doesn't speak much to me, but I

understand why. Radek is trying his best and that's all we can ask for."

Kane stared at the ceiling. "He spends too much time away from the pack. Even now, he is gone again. It has been nearly a week since he left."

"I'm sorry, I know you miss him."

"I do. And so does Raina."

Reese rubbed his chest. "Raina will be fine. She has Mia to keep her company."

"Aye, and you," Kane replied. "Every time I walk into my cabin, she and Mia are in here giggling about something."

She poked him in the chest. "She enjoys being here and I enjoy her company."

"Aye, I know, my love. And I love that you are so sweet to my pack mates but sometimes I want to be alone with my mate in the middle of the day."

He squeezed her ass and gave her a dirty little grin. She rolled her eyes. "We have plenty of alone time in the evenings for sex. I can barely walk as it is, Kane. If we add afternoon sex, you'll have to carry me around."

He laughed and she kissed his chest before relaxing against him. After half an hour, he stirred beneath her and she sat up and pouted at him. "It's dark and raining."

"Aye, I know. But it's the best time for hunting. Food is growing scarce as it gets colder and we must make sure we have enough to last us through the winter."

"Will it snow soon?" She asked as he climbed out of bed and stretched.

"Aye, I think so."

"Adina and I are going to pick plants tomorrow and see if we can get the last of the charkas before they drop." She sat up and tucked the covers around her naked body.

He gave her an anxious look. "Do not go alone, Reese. If

I am not back by the morning, you are not to go into the forest until I return."

"I know." She smiled at him. "Stop worrying, Kane. Borek and Deena are going to go with us."

"Good." He leaned over and kissed her. "Get some sleep. I will see you in the morning."

"Be careful." She returned his kiss, letting her tongue trace his upper lip as she dropped the blanket and pressed her naked breasts against his chest. He groaned before pulling away from her.

"You do that on purpose, human."

"What?" She said sweetly.

"I am going hunting. When I return, you will pay for that."

"I look forward to it," she said tartly.

He laughed and shook his head before opening the door to the cabin. "Sleep well, my love."

———

THE PACK OF WOLVES MOVED SILENTLY THROUGH THE DARK forest. Their alpha trotted at the front. His fur rippled in the cold wind as he inhaled repeatedly. The thunderstorm had finally stopped and moisture dripped steadily from the trees as he searched for the scent of the deer. He growled under his breath when another strange and unfamiliar scent drifted to him on the wind.

He followed the scent with his pack following dutifully behind him. When they heard the voices, he froze and made a warning growl to the pack. They stopped and waited patiently as he cocked his head and sniffed the air. He moved forward cautiously, his large paws not making a sound on the damp ground until he could see the humans through the trees. He chuffed and nudged Theran and Hanif with his head before staring at the other pack members. One by one they slipped silently into the trees until they were hidden.

He moved forward, followed by Theran and Hanif, and gave a low growl.

The group swung around, their eyes widening at the sight of the wolves. A dark-haired woman wearing a collar around her neck and a tiny skirt and top whispered, "Does anyone have a weapon?"

Kane blinked at her. The woman had the same scent as Reese and his heart thudded heavily in his chest as one of the men held up a dagger. "I have this."

"We don't need weapons," a short woman replied. "We have Val."

Kane chuffed in surprise when the creature with the long hair hissed at him and revealed sharp fangs.

"Val, wait." The dark-haired woman grabbed his arm. "Just wait and - "

Kane shifted to his human form. Behind him, Theran and Hanif did the same and he studied the group silently.

"Shifters," a blond man breathed. "Perhaps we are still on our world, after all."

Hanif frowned at Kane. "What manner of creature has teeth like that, Kane? And why do they smell so," he wrinkled his nose, "dreadful."

"I do not know, Hanif," Kane replied.

The blond man sighed. "Fuck. Not our world. Stupid fucking ball of light sending us who the fuck knows where."

Kane stiffened and frowned at the man. "What did you say, creature?"

"Creature? I have a name," the man hissed.

Kane growled and the man hissed again as the dark-haired woman held her hands up.

"Okay, um, before we get off on the wrong foot, let's just everyone take a deep breath. My name's Abby. These are my friends, and we're not from around here. So we're just going to head on out and um, it was really great to meet you. Take care, okay?"

Kane growled again and took a step toward her. The creature named Val pushed the woman behind him and bared his fangs. "Take one more step toward her and I'll have your head."

"I would like to see you try," Kane said. "I don't know what you are but you do not frighten me."

Val glared at him. "You would be wise to be frightened of me, shifter."

"Val, stop!" Abigail squeezed his arm and gave Kane a friendly smile. "We're friendly, honestly. And if you would just step aside, we'll be on our way."

"You are on my lands," Kane said. "Tell me, and do not lie about this, if what the creature said about the ball of light is true."

Abigail hesitated and then nodded. "Yes, it's true."

Theran squeezed Kane's arm before sniffing in Abigail's direction. "She smells like Reese."

"Aye, Theran. I am aware of that," Kane said.

He studied them for a moment before coming to a quick decision. "You will come with us."

"I don't think so," Val said sharply.

"You have no choice," Kane said simply.

"There are only three of you and six of us," Val replied. "You do not stand a chance."

Kane laughed. "You are a brave one. Foolish, but brave."

He lifted his head and barked. Abby gripped Val's arm when a chorus of barking responded and the trees around them were lit with dozens of glowing eyes.

"Our pack is large," Kane said with a hint of pride in his voice. "You are returning to our home and you will neither fight nor try to escape. Do you understand?"

Val opened his mouth to argue and Abigail gripped his arm and gave him a warning look before smiling at Kane. "Of course. Thank you for the hospitality."

Kane grunted in reply and shifted to his wolf form before turning and loping into the trees. His pack surrounded the strangers and he glanced briefly at the dark-haired woman again. He would take her to his mate and find out if his suspicions that she was from the same world as Reese were true. The cold air ruffled his fur and he whined low in his throat and headed home to his mate.

END

Want to read more about Kane and Reese?
Check out "Rescued by the Wolf" Book 4 in the Other World Series.
It tells the story of Sara and Radek, but there is plenty of Kane and Reese, as well.

Keep reading for an excerpt from Rescued by the Wolf

RESCUED BY THE WOLF EXCERPT

(OTHER WORLD SERIES BOOK 4)

Sara groaned and touched her head without opening her eyes. She felt sick to her stomach and she wasn't surprised by the wetness on her fingertips. She opened her eyes and squinted at her fingers. They were red with blood and she groaned again before sitting up cautiously.

The world spun crazily for a moment and she dropped her head and waited to see if she was going to throw up or pass out. After a moment, the dizziness passed, and she lifted her head again. She studied her surroundings. She was in a forest with thick trees that rose high into the night sky, and she staggered to her feet.

"Abby?" She called. "Abby, are you there?"

There was no reply and she pinched back her moan of dismay and cleared her throat.

"Abigail? Can you hear me? Abigail!" She shouted this time and cringed when something in the dark answered with a loud and raucous cry.

"Okay, it's all right," she murmured to herself as she wrapped her arms around her thin body. The night air was cold, and she was soaking wet and already beginning to shiver uncontrollably. "Don't panic. They probably aren't far."

You don't know that. You don't even know where you are. For all you know, Darius and his men could be closing in on you right now. You need to get moving before they find you.

She squinted at the trees. They didn't look particularly familiar to her but until Darius had raided their village, she had never really been outside of it before. Besides, the last thing she remembered was stepping into the light with the man Abby had called Michael. She didn't have a clue how she could be in the arena one moment and then in the middle of the forest the next, but what was important was finding Abby and the others before Darius found her.

Gathering her courage, she moved away from the tree she was leaning against and stared up at the sky. She could just see the moon filtering through the trees, and she sighed. At least it had stopped raining, she was grateful for -

There was a soft rustling behind her, and she swung around, her heart beating fiercely and the coppery taste of fear flooding her mouth.

"Wh-who's there?" She whispered.

There was no response and she took a step backward as her heart began to slow to its normal pace. It was nothing. Just the wind perhaps.

What wind?

Never mind that, she really needed to –

The rustling happened again, and she gave a soft shriek of surprise when a large bird emerged from behind a tree. It was huge, well over nine feet tall, and its plumage was a rich, dark, green. Its head was a lighter shade of green and its red eyes stared curiously at her.

She blew her breath out in a relieved little rush as the bird shook itself and spread its short wings. It didn't look like it could fly at all with such short wings, but its legs were long and powerful looking and ended in thick, sharp talons. It tapped one talon against the ground as it cocked its head and studied her silently.

"Go on, bird. Shoo!" She waved her arms weakly at it and it took a step backward, shaking its body in a disgruntled manner. Feathers floated to the ground and she clapped her hands over her ears when the bird opened its beak wide and let loose with an eardrum shattering cry.

"Stop!" She shrieked. "Stop it!"

The bird continued and, feeling like her ears were bleeding, Sara groped on the ground for something to throw. Her fingers swept past a large stone and she gripped it firmly and threw it at the bird. The stone hit the bird dead center in the chest, and it gave a startled squawk and closed its beak.

"Get lost!" She shouted at it.

Her eyes widened when the bird lowered its head and scratched at the ground again with one large talon. It looked like it was getting ready to charge and she backed away as it made a high-pitched humming noise.

"Get out of here," she whispered.

The bird scratched twice more and then, with a quickness that surprised her, charged. She screamed and sprinted through the trees. She could hear the bird closing in on her. She dodged around the trees and thick bushes, looking desperately for a hiding spot as she forced herself to run faster.

She risked one terrified glance over her shoulder and

screamed again in sudden terror. The bird was nearly upon her, and its large and ridiculously sharp beak was opening and snapping with deadly force.

Her foot hit an exposed root and she went sprawling, landing on her belly with a hard thud. The breath was knocked out of her and she stared mutely at the bird standing over her. It made another screeching cry and then it was pecking at her, its beak tearing through the soft flesh of her side.

She gasped in air and shrieked. She beat at its feathery body with her fists before trying to crawl away. The bird clamped one talon around her calf and dragged her back as easily as a mouse, before pecking viciously at her once more.

She curled into a ball and covered her head with her arms as the bird pecked at her exposed back. Each peck of its beak was like a hot needle in her flesh and she screamed again, the sound muffled by her arms.

She was going to die. She was going to be pecked to death by some weird giant bird and no one would ever know that she –

There was a loud growling and the bird suddenly made its own terrified squeal before it was ripped away from her. It hung on grimly to her leg with its talons, and she screamed in pain when its sharp nails dug into her skin and tore it open.

There was more growling and snarling and she lowered her arms and sat up, staring in numb shock at the giant, black wolf that was ripping and tearing into the bird's belly. The bird squirmed and twisted but the wolf held it down easily. It tore a large chunk of intestine from the bird's stomach and the bird made one final scream of pain before collapsing.

The wolf leaped from the bird's body, raised its snout to the sky and howled deafeningly. Sara moaned and scooted backward on her butt as the wolf lowered its head and stared at her.

"No, please, no," she whispered, holding her hands out pleadingly in front of her as the wolf stalked toward her on stiff legs.

She closed her eyes in defeat as the wolf bent its head and sniffed at her face. If she was lucky the wolf would end her life more quickly than the bird would have. She jerked in fear when the wolf chuffed loudly and his warm breath washed over her face.

There was a moment of silence and she opened her eyes warily. The wolf had moved away from her and her eyes widened in surprise when it abruptly shifted into a man. He was the biggest man she'd ever seen, his shoulders broad and his arms thick and powerful. His hair was short and a slightly darker shade of blond than hers, and his eyes were dark brown.

His skin was tanned and the muscles in his abdomen rippled as he walked toward her. He looked like he had been chiseled out of granite and he was, she thought dimly, the most beautiful man she'd ever laid eyes on.

He was also completely naked.

She blushed furiously as her gaze dropped to his penis. She had never seen one before and her eyes widened at the size of it. How on earth would that ever fit into a woman? She wasn't naïve, she knew how sex worked, but there was no way something that size could fit into –

He crouched in front of her and she raised her eyes to his face. He was frowning and she gave a soft whimper of fear when he leaned forward and inhaled again. A brief look of distaste crossed his face. "You are human."

"Y-yes," she said. "My name is Sara. What's yours?"

"How did you travel so deep into the woods, human?" He asked.

For some odd reason his low voice sent shivers down her spine.

"I – I was with some friends and we got separated," she said.

He continued to stare at her, and she gave him a weak smile. "Thank you for saving me from that bird. Wh-what was that?"

He frowned again. "How do you not know what a floran is? Have you been living under a rock?"

"A floran?" She gave him a puzzled look. "I've never seen one before."

He grunted in annoyance before standing and walking away. She staggered to her feet and yelped loudly as pain coursed down her leg. She could see the blood flowing from the deep scratches left by the bird's talons and her entire back felt like it was on fire.

"Hey, don't leave!" She called. "Please!"

He sighed and turned back around. "Go and find your friends, human."

"I don't know where they are, and I don't even know what part of the forest I'm in. Could you – do you think you could help me find them?"

He hesitated, and she gave him a pleading look as she balanced carefully on one leg. "Please? I'm sorry. I hate to ask you for help but I'm -"

"No." He interrupted. "I have helped you enough."

When he refused to help the human, the shifter expected her to beg, perhaps to start crying and wailing like so many humans were prone to doing. But she only nodded and gave him an oddly gut-wrenching look of resignation. "All right. Thank you for your help."

He frowned when she turned and limped deeper into the woods. She should have been heading for the edge of the forest, not deeper into it. A floran would be the least of her worries if she continued on.

"Human!" He shouted.

She flinched and gave him a tentative smile. "Yes?"

"Do not go that way. Go in that direction." He pointed behind him and she nodded before limping toward him.

"Right, okay. Thank you."

He frowned again as she moved slowly past him. Her face was unbelievably pale, even for a human, and he could see the blood flowing steadily from her leg. She was dressed in an astonishingly tiny skirt and odd-looking shirt that barely covered her small breasts. Her skin was covered in goose bumps, and he winced when she passed by him and he saw the multiple puncture wounds from the floran's beak on her back. All of them were bleeding freely and he couldn't imagine how much pain she was in. The way she was bleeding she was lucky she hadn't passed out.

As if she heard his thoughts, she stopped and swayed alarmingly before reaching for a tree with one shaking hand. She gripped the bark and dropped her head forward, taking a few deep breaths before coughing lightly.

"You're okay, Sara," she whispered to herself. "You're okay, just - "

She swayed again and, as she crumpled to the ground, he ran forward and caught her before she could hit the hard floor of the forest.

She stared up at him with hazy eyes. "What's your name?" She whispered.

"Radek," he grunted.

"Radek," she breathed before her eyes rolled up in her head and she fainted.

He studied her pale face before cursing and lifting her into his arms. With a soft grunt, he carried her deeper into the forest.

ABOUT THE AUTHOR

Ramona Gray is a Canadian romance author. She currently lives in Alberta with her awesome husband and her super cute dog. She's addicted to home improvement shows, good coffee, and reading and writing about the steamier moments in life.

For more information about Ramona, check out her website at

www.ramonagray.ca

facebook.com/RamonaGrayBooks

twitter.com/RamonaGrayBooks

instagram.com/ramonagrayauthor

amazon.com/Ramona-Gray/e/B00OD26SAM

bookbub.com/profile/ramona-gray

The Welder

The Electrician

The Landscaper

The Firefighter

The Cop

The Paramedic

Working Men Series Bundles

Working Men Series Books One to Three

Working Men Series Books Four to Six

Working Men Series Books Seven to Nine

Other World Series

The Vampire's Kiss (Book One)

The Vampire's Love (Book Two)

The Shifter's Mate (Book Three)

Rescued By The Wolf (Book Four)

Claiming Quinn (Book Five)

Choosing Rose (Book Six)

Elena Unbound (Book Seven)

Other World Series Box Sets

Other World Series Books One to Three

Other World Series Books Four to Six